GLOW OF THE FIREFLIES

Also by Lindsey Duga

Kiss of the Royal

LINDSEY DUGA

Entangled Publishing, LLC
2614 South Timberline Road
Suite 105, PMB 159
Fort Collins, CO 80525
rights@entangledpublishing.com

Entangled Teen is an imprint of Entangled Publishing, LLC.

Visit our website at www.entangledpublishing.com.

Edited by Lydia Sharp and Judi Lauren
Cover design by LJ Anderson, Mayhem Cover Creations
Cover images by
Joseph Kirsch, Adobestock
TheFarAwayKingdom, Adobestock
dalomo84, Depositphotos
grandfailure, Adobestock
Interior design by Toni Kerr

ISBN 978-1-64063-731-3
Ebook ISBN 978-1-64063-735-1

Manufactured in the United States of America

First Edition October 2019

10 9 8 7 6 5 4 3 2 1

To Grandma.
And to Grandpa—I'll miss you always.

There are places in the world
that are special.

Where you may wonder
is this Heaven?

Or is this Earth?

It's in those places, where the lines between
what's real
and what's not are blurred,

Where the boundary
between the physical and
astral plane becomes so thin...

That spirits dwell.

Chapter One

With every pull and kick of my breaststroke, trails of bubbles exploded around me, disrupting my otherwise perfect view of the opposite end of the pool. The crystal clear water meant that it was *particularly* chemically enhanced today.

But they always did that for meets. Nothing new or unexpected, just irritating for a girl with sensitive skin and already dry hair.

I came into the wall hard. My hand slapped against the touchpad and my fingers curled around the edge, stopping my forward momentum before I rammed my knees into the pool tiles. Throwing my head back, I came out of the water like a mermaid princess—cue magic sparkles—and took a deep, shuddering breath. Almost immediately, my pathetic lungs rebelled, as muted cheers seeped through my swim cap.

I threw my elbows onto the side of the pool, gasping and trying to get my wheezing under control.

How embarrassing. How *not* mermaid princess of me.

"Here, Brye—here," Izzie said, and I didn't have to ask what she meant.

Without even looking up, I accepted the inhaler from

her, stuck it between my lips, and pressed down. I inhaled deeply and slowly to allow the medicine to reach my lungs.

In seconds, my breath was normal again. I stretched my neck back, dipping the top of my swim cap into the water, and felt the fresh, cool air tickle down my throat.

Asthma attack aside, I'd won my race. I heard the other racers come into the wall with large splashes a whole ten seconds behind me. Then the buzzer went off, signaling that it was time for the next swimmers to step onto their blocks... and that I needed to get out of the pool.

Izzie's brown arm came into view, and I accepted her help, pulling myself out of the pool and then maneuvering through the throngs of other swimmers awaiting their races.

The sun beat down, reflecting off the surface of the pristine water and the white concrete, but the heat wasn't completely unbearable yet. Summer league meets started early and went by quickly—fewer people and fewer races.

We came to the side of the pool with our gear on the benches, and Izzie tossed me a towel. "Well, you crushed your time but at a cost... Are you okay?"

I looked up from wiping my face to find her watching me with concerned eyes. Her goggles hung around her neck while her coiled hair remained tucked under a bright aquamarine swim cap with *Joyner Jellyfish* scrawled across it in an outdated eighties logo.

I gave a thumbs-up to my best friend and tucked my inhaler back into my bag. "Yeah, I'm good." I was used to these attacks. I'd had asthma for as long as I could remember. Granted, that wasn't as far back as most sixteen-year-olds.

Izzie's lips twisted to the side in an *I don't believe a word you just said* kind of way.

But she knew my limits. Or rather, she knew how stubborn I was, and she knew I wasn't sitting out the next relay just because of a little asthma, so she didn't argue. Not that she had time to give me her usual lecture, because Coach Brennan signaled from behind the lane blocks to line up.

The one bad thing about summer league was that there was hardly any rest between races. My muscles still screamed from my last race, but I told them to shut it and, instead, took a long pull from my water bottle before joining the rest of my teammates at the blocks.

The whistle went off, and Izzie jumped into the pool and got into backstroke start position. She pulled herself up on the block, hunching her shoulders and tensing the muscles in her arms and legs, ready to spring into the water and race toward victory.

Isabelle Jennison was the only person I knew who was not only good at backstroke, but also loved it. Personally, it was my least favorite stroke. I didn't like how I had to trust my ability to count the exact number of strokes to the end of the wall just to be able to time my flip-turn perfectly.

But Izzie was perfect in her timing. Perfect in her turn. Perfect in her faith that she wasn't going to run into the lane ropes or bang her head into the wall.

At the sound of the buzzer, Izzie sprang backward, propelling herself down into the water then dolphin-kicking her way to the surface. Immediately, she drew back her arm into a long stroke, rotating her shoulder and gliding her hand through the water as her other arm broke the surface. Her arms were like a windmill, and she was already ten yards ahead of her opponents.

As Izzie did her flip-turn and headed back toward the block, Jamie readied herself for the dive, her hands following Izzie's progress down the pool. At the exact moment when Izzie touched the wall, Jamie's feet left the block, diving in a beautiful streamlined position and gliding into her breaststroke. I stepped up on the block to take her place and watched as her opponent gained on her.

The antsy feeling that we were going to lose crept up my already exhausted legs. Inching my feet to the edge of the block, I curled my toes around the painted wood as Jamie crossed the halfway mark too slow—achingly slow.

My stroke was the butterfly, and I was good at it. State record time both years, so far. Monica, the freestyle swimmer behind me, was similar to Jamie in that she had great form but not much speed. There was no way she'd be able to catch us up. We'd lose for sure. I hated relay races for that reason. Relying on someone else to win made me anxious and restless. In my individual races, I controlled my time and my placement. If I lost, it was on me.

And now it came down to me to pull us ahead. To win.

Gritting my teeth, I bent low, pulled back, and waited.

Usually I didn't bend down until the final seconds out of sheer habit. When I was younger, I worried that if I bent down far enough, the back design of my swimsuit would reveal the four long scars stretching across my lower back. But after years of being self-conscious about the marks, I'd finally accepted them as a part of my identity.

As Jamie was coming in, I exploded off the block, hitting the water with a light splash and dolphin-kicking up into a strong butterfly. My arms came around in a wide arc, launching my upper body out of the water, and I gulped a breath before tightening my core and diving back in.

My stroke was fast, and my form was precise, pulling us ahead by an entire lap. Monica barely had to do any work to finish out the race, and by the time we helped her out of the pool, we were all high-fiving each other for our easy win.

After the last race, the swimmers had the opportunity

to use the pool for a cool down, and I always took it. A few lazy laps helped calm my pulse and relax my muscles. On my final lap, I took off my goggles. The chlorine stung my eyes, but it was worth it in these last few seconds of practice to see the underwater world without the filtering of a lens. Forgoing the stroke entirely, I dolphin-kicked toward the bottom, submerging myself into its dark depths..

When the pool was mostly empty, I liked to play pretend. While many little girls would start swimming because of their love of mermaids, I believed in different magical water creatures. I could never put a name to them because they were without shape or form. Instead, they were merely clouds in the water—more of a presence or energy that filled me with calm and a sense of longing.

I never told anyone about them because I knew they lived inside my mind and not inside a rec center pool. If anything, they were something like an old memory—an unfamiliar concept. Sometimes they would be darker or lighter, varying shades of blue and aquamarine, sparkling from the filtered sunlight.

So I allowed myself to pretend, in these peaceful underwater moments, that I could see them, even though they were nothing more than the lingering remnants of a childhood imagination that I couldn't much remember.

I tilted my head back, my face breaking through the placid surface with one last, strong kick.

Izzie stood over me, arms folded, a towel already wrapped around her waist. "Coach said our relay was disqualified. We lost."

She didn't even wait for me to ask why, but with a sinking feeling, I already knew.

"Your false start. You left the block too early again."

"Go ahead, say it," I said, closing the door to Izzie's Honda CRV then stuffing my swim bag at my feet. I kept my towel around my shoulders, using it to squeeze the ends of my light-brown hair.

Izzie pushed up her reflective aviator sunglasses and checked her rearview mirror before shifting into reverse. It wasn't until she had pulled out of the same parking spot she parked in every Monday, Wednesday, Friday, and Saturday that she finally responded. "I'm happy to give you the same lecture over and over again, Brye. But at some point, I just have to accept that I can't change you."

"Here we go," I muttered before taking a swig from my water bottle and then shoving it into the cup holder.

"Briony, you know I love you. You're practically my soul sister, but you suck at being on a team. In *any* capacity." She took a moment to sigh dramatically. "You didn't need to start so soon. You could've pulled us ahead, and Monica could've wrapped up the race. She's not *that* slow. You need to trust your teammates. This is just like when we tried to play doubles in tennis and you wouldn't let me get in a single swing—you had to go for the ball *every time*."

"I know, I know." I raised my hands in surrender. I was lucky swimming was a mostly solo sport, because Izzie was right. I was terrible at passing the ball to teammates or formulating any kind of strategy where I had to rely on others to do their part.

Group projects in school were the same. I preferred to do most of the work myself, not trusting my peers to do their share, sure they'd make us fail.

Dad would say it was because I was independent.

Mom wouldn't say anything. Because she wasn't here to say it.

"You forgot your lotion, didn't you? Do you want to use mine?"

Izzie's question pulled me out of my head. My skin was red and chapped, large red welts decorating my hands and arms.

The chlorine had been *especially* bad today.

Covering them with the towel on my lap, I shook my head. "No, I'm fine. Yours is scented. It'll make it worse. Besides, I can wait."

"Doesn't look like it," she muttered.

"Iz, I'm fine." I nodded toward the stoplight. "It's green."

As Izzie made a left turn instead of a right, I raised an eyebrow at her. "Where are we going?"

"You DQ'ed us. We're going to get ice cream."

I cracked a smile. "DQ doesn't mean Dairy Queen."

"Well, it should. Get me a cookie-dough Blizzard and your disqualification is forgiven."

I snorted, shooting my dad a quick text that I'd be getting home a little late. "Deal."

Two Blizzards and a medium fry later, Izzie and I were still in the parking lot of Dairy Queen, discussing plans to see the latest summer superhero movie, when my phone started buzzing.

Dad's face came on the screen and I couldn't help a feeling of impending doom. Dad was a decent texter. He only called if it was bad news or something really important.

Preparing myself, I pressed the accept button. "Hey, Dad."

"Hey, sweetie, how was the meet?"

I thought about my disqualification and the hefty amount of guilt that made my chest turn cold—though that could've been the ice cream. "It was hot, and now we're at Dairy Queen," I said, deflecting.

"I see…well, are you and Izzie about done?"

"Um, pretty much, why?"

"Just come home and we'll talk."

Closing my eyes, I leaned my head back in my seat, feeling my stomach drop. "Dad, you know I hate it when you do this. Just rip off the Band-Aid and tell me the bad news."

He was quiet for a minute. "Your grandmother broke her leg."

I blinked, not having expected that reply at all. "Well, that…sucks."

Out of the corner of my eye, I saw Izzie raise a quizzical brow, but I ignored her and waited patiently for Dad to continue, because that *couldn't* be the only reason he was calling.

My only living grandmother might as well be a complete stranger to me. She lived an hour and a half away in a valley deep in the Smoky Mountains, trapped in her own little reclusive world. Dad and I never tried to contact or visit her, even though it had once been our home as well. When I was ten, we'd left and moved to Knoxville and never looked back.

For a few reasons.

"Yes, it does suck," Dad agreed, his sigh making a crackling noise through the receiver. "One of Willa's—your grandmother's—friends called me. Mrs. Farrafield. They play bridge together. Anyway, Mrs. Farrafield said Willa needs a caretaker…"

Slowly, my jaw loosened, my mouth falling open in realization.

Oh, no.

Dad went on. “Normally, I’d take some time off work and you could stay with Izzie while I help her out, but I’ve got a major business trip and…”

I dropped my face into my hand, reading the subtext in his words. *There goes my summer.*

“Sweetheart…this is your only living grandparent.”

Yeah, my grandparent who I don’t remember and haven’t talked to in six years.

I lifted my gaze, as if some brilliant excuse was written on the roof of Izzie’s CRV. “How long would I have to go?” I asked finally.

“We can talk about it. But a month, likely.”

I heard the “or more” he didn’t say.

“Okay, Dad. I’ll be home soon.”

After a quick *I love you* and *bye*, I hung up, and Izzie started rapid-firing questions.

“What’s wrong? What happened? Where do you have to go?”

“My grandmother broke her leg. I have to go take care of her for a month.” My voice had slipped into a robotic tone. “Maybe more.”

Izzie gasped and then took up the anger that I should be feeling. “What? That’s like your whole summer! What about summer league?”

I shrugged, trying to cover the fact that my hands were shaking by shoving them under my thighs. Giving up my summer was one thing, but going back to that valley was something else entirely. Just the idea of it made me jumpy.

“Wait, your grandmother…so she’s your mom’s…”

I nodded, my stare fixed blankly ahead. “Yep.”

Izzie didn't say anything after that. She just started the car, probably regretting bringing up my mom—the woman who abandoned me and my dad after the fire that left me with scars and amnesia.

Chapter Two

The minute I walked through the door, I was hit by the smell of lemongrass chicken. It was my favorite dish, but a lot of work, so we didn't have it often. Really, Dad only made it for two things: my birthday and when he felt bad about something.

Making me give up my summer to take care of a woman who hadn't wanted to see me for six years definitely qualified as a lemongrass chicken occasion.

Before heading back to the kitchen, I raced upstairs to put my swim bag away and slather my skin with all-natural Vitamin E lotion. There were even more large red patches now. They were itchy and inflamed, as if my skin was furious with me for allowing so much chlorine into my system.

I'd always had sensitive skin—for as long as my shortened memory allowed—and over the years of trial and error with perplexed doctors, I'd found I could only use certain all-natural brands. My body reacted badly to anything else.

Dad didn't like seeing the rashes. One time, after a particularly bad reaction in eighth grade, he had threatened to take me off swim team entirely. I'd panicked then. I'd finally made some friends through swimming, and the sport calmed me in a way that few things had back then.

And the flames from my past couldn't get me underwater…

Since then, I had developed the habit of applying lotion as soon as possible afterward, only sometimes I accidentally forgot to pack it.

Heading downstairs, after my red welts calmed down to a subtle pink, I entered the kitchen and threw myself into a chair at the old wooden table.

Dad glanced over his shoulder as he stood at the stove. "Hey, honey. I hope you didn't spoil your appetite with ice cream and Oreos," he said with a chuckle.

I had, but that's why leftovers were a thing. I liked to think I was practicing for college. Rather than answering, I focused on why I was getting this fantastic dinner in the first place. "Are you sure she's going to *want* me there?" I asked, tracing the warped pattern in the wood with my index finger.

Dad turned back to the chicken sizzling in the lemongrass butter sauce and flipped it over in the pan, causing a cloud of steam to rise from the stovetop. "She's your grandmother, Brye."

"So? That doesn't mean anything. Think about Mom."

I knew my words were harsh before they'd even tumbled out of my mouth.

Dad winced, his arm jerking slightly, sloshing the sauce and causing another billow of steam. He turned down the burner and moved to the counter littered with vegetables that still needed to be sliced.

Wordlessly, I stood from the table and walked over to my dad, wrapping an arm around him and resting my head on his shoulder.

"Sorry, Daddy. I'm just…"

He patted my arm gently. "I get it, Brye. I'm asking you

to give up your summer, and summer league. If I were you, I'd be upset, too. But she's old and needs our help. And whether or not she wants you there, she's your grandmother. Don't forget...her daughter left her, too."

After losing the first ten years of my life, I hoped to never forget anything ever again.

As we prepared dinner together, both of us unusually quiet, I tried, for the millionth time, to remember more about Firefly Valley. But just like the other nine hundred ninety-nine thousand, nine hundred ninety-nine times, I couldn't.

Firefly Valley, where my grandmother lived—and where I was born—wasn't only where my mother had left us. It was also where our first house had burned down...with me still in it.

The fire that left me with no memories, a future without a mother, and a cluster of scars on my lower back still haunted my nightmares. Flickering flames, searing heat, thick gray smoke, and a voice calling my name over and over again...

It was partly why I loved the water so much. Why I got into the pool regardless of the way the chlorine bit at my sensitive skin. Because it gave me comfort to know that fire couldn't reach me there.

I never told Dad about the bad dreams because he'd get that look on his face, full of pain and regret.

It wasn't his fault, though.

In fact, no one knew whose fault it was. The firefighters had said it was a freak accident, unable to even pinpoint the origin of the fire after a week-long investigation.

Going back to the place of so much grief and so many mysteries—like how the fire started, why my mother had left only a few months after the incident, why the scars on my back didn't look like they were made by burns—had me riddled with anxiety.

And yet…I was also insatiably curious. My childhood was practically nonexistent because of the fire. Who had I been before my life got a hard reboot?

Of course, if I told my father any of that, he'd worry even more. I didn't want that. He'd been through enough.

We both had.

So I would get through this summer with a sunny caretaker attitude reminiscent of Mary-Freaking-Poppins.

"Hey, I've got an idea," Dad said, breaking our silence. "Why don't you see if Izzie wants to go with you?"

I paused in cutting my chicken. "Do you think Willa would be okay with that?"

"The way I see it, she'd be getting two caretakers for free. I'm sure it'll be fine. And don't call her Willa. That's disrespectful," he said, then took a sip of his iced tea.

I didn't know what else to call her. And I had my doubts everything would be fine, but if he was giving me the okay to bring Izzie, there was no way I would pass that up.

"Um, hell yeah, I wanna go!" Izzie shouted.

Wincing, I jerked my phone away from my ear then brought it back to my cheek with a relieved laugh. "Iz, are you sure? Think of what you'd be giving up. That's a whole summer without social media or a Starbucks within walking distance."

"If I stay here, I'll be giving up a summer without *you*, and that is simply unacceptable."

Izzie's tone was joking, but I knew that on the rare occasions when she said touchy-feely stuff like that, she meant it.

"What about summer league?"

"It's not like it's the school team. They'll be fine. Besides, summer league is for keeping in shape, and we already have rockin' bods, so no worries there. Oh! We can go hiking in the mountains!"

I turned over on the bed, kicking my legs up in the air, and laughed. I loved my friend's optimism, and she also seemed to understand, without me even having to tell her, that this was a "delicate family situation." It was a phrase I'd often heard her mother use.

Mrs. Jennison said it every time I'd wake up in the middle of the night during a slumber party and cry for my dad to come pick me up, when most people felt I was "too old for that type of behavior." Or when I'd refused to go on a Girl Scout camping trip when I was twelve because I was scared of sitting around a fire.

"So..." There was a long pause on the other line, then I heard Izzie snap her laptop closed, a telltale indication she was about to get serious. "How are you feeling about going back there?"

While most of my friends, the few close ones that I had, steered away from my weird, trauma-filled past, Izzie always rammed into the topic like a car wreck. She also didn't let things go.

I both loved and hated this about her.

I played with the fringe of the throw blanket on my bed and stared up at the ceiling, choosing my words carefully. "I'm nervous," I admitted. "Apart from the fact that I'm not going to know how to even *talk* to this woman, I'm worried I'm going to get there and not feel something."

"What do you mean?" Izzie asked.

Losing ten years of your life will mess with you. It felt like a giant hole was inside me. Someone had carved out a piece of Briony Redwrell and left it to burn in that awful fire. At first, I tried to be okay. For Dad. He was messed up, too. But then, half a year after moving to Knoxville, I did something wholly unexplainable. I wasn't sure *why* I did what I did. Just, one day I was telling myself I was okay, then the next I'd wandered into the woods of the nearest park. The entire neighborhood went on an epic search to find me. They found me curled up under the biggest tree in the park, dirt all over my clothes, and surrounded by a bunch of shredded wildflowers.

After seeing what my meltdown had done to Dad, I learned how to look to the past without feeling anything. Essentially, I drew up a wall between the time before Knoxville and the time after. I took all those empty, missing pieces of my life, this gigantic void inside me that told me I was only *half* of who I was, and locked them up in a box and threw away the key.

In cutting off that part of me, eventually, I became okay. Happy, even.

I made friendship bracelets with Izzie. I took swimming classes. Learned how to bake. Read a lot of books—and I mean *a lot*.

On the outside, I was a normal teenage girl. I was like a remodeled house from an earlier era, with hip new wallpaper covering the tattered walls.

A guidance counselor had once told me: *losing your memories means you start fresh. You don't have anything to haunt you. Except for maybe the loss of what you once had.*

That had always stuck with me.

I twirled a wavy strand of light-brown hair that had escaped from my ponytail around my finger and thought about what Izzie was asking me.

"I *mean*," I said finally, "what I really want to find there is something I can connect to." My voice was a little tight, and I wasn't sure my words made any sense, but Izzie was the only person in the world I could admit this to. "My amnesia stole my childhood. If I go there and feel nothing, then…"

There'll be this big hole inside me forever.

I realized I didn't want that. Maybe this was the opportunity I needed. Maybe this was what people meant by "closure."

I could do this. I'd had to live with amnesia, with mystery and loss, but now I could actually heal these wounds by going back to this place. Whether or not I found what I'd been missing for so long, I could finally face my past head-on and say *you can't hurt me anymore.*

Once and for all.

"You'll still be you," Izzie said, so quietly I barely heard her.

I smiled at the ceiling fan slowly turning hypnotically above me.

Izzie was my only friend who knew everything. She knew that Mom had left in the middle of the night after a shouting match with my father. She knew that Dad had been so hurt that he didn't go after her. She knew how hard it was for me to not feel bitter toward my mother.

More than anything, she knew *me*, and I was glad for it.

"You're right, but I think…I think I'm ready to find out who I was. Before."

She was quiet so long I thought the call had dropped. Finally she said, "I'll see you tomorrow at nine—and I'm driving, so don't you dare leave without me."

Forty minutes into the drive, Izzie and I had switched to my Spotify. We had lost all radio signals and grew tired of the Blue Ridge Mountains' number one hit: Static Pop. It was on all the stations, with some slight variation—Static Country, Static Oldies, Static Rock...

I stared out the window, watching the mountain scenery. The trees gave way to sloping hillsides and meadows lined with...yet more trees. While repetitive, the Tennessee countryside was beautiful. Summer wildflowers covered the meadow below, and the forest was alive with shadows and spots of sunlight peeking through the leaves. Beyond the trees and meadows, the Smoky Mountains stretched before us. It seemed as though no matter how far we drove, we never got any closer. We just stayed at their base, chasing after them.

Izzie, bless her, had tried to start a conversation several times, but I couldn't focus long enough to continue a single one. In fact, before I'd had time to quell the ball of anxiety rolling around in my stomach, Izzie was turning down the long driveway to my grandmother's house.

It was like something out of a fairy tale. I was Little Red Riding Hood visiting her sick grandmother deep in the woods. The house had two stories and a brick chimney on the side, overgrown with ivy. Really, the whole place was a bit rundown. But that only added to its charm. The siding might have once been blue, because the painted wood was a light kind of periwinkle, probably faded by time and baked by sunlight. Flowers grew everywhere—on the little pathway up to the porch, winding their way up into the short white fence that separated the garden from the rest of the wilderness—even though the garden was a bit wild itself.

For just a brief moment, I recalled sitting on that very

porch, Dad's car packed with the few things that had survived the fire, and trying to block out the voices from within. The confused, angry voices that talked about a woman who just up and left her family.

Izzie nudged me, giving me a questioning look, as if to say *it's not too late to turn back.* But it *was* too late. Six years too late. For so long, this valley and my unknown toxic past had hung over me.

Well, no more. I was ready to face it.

"Thanks for coming with, Iz," I said, still staring at the quaint cottage. "You're the best."

"Of course I am. It's why I've got the finest jewelry in the world." She held up her wrist, showing off the friendship bracelet of blue and orange thread I'd made for her over two years ago.

"That thing is so old. Let me make you a new one."

"Are you kidding? I've planned entire wardrobes around this bracelet. Getting a new one would throw off my fashion statement."

With a laugh, I opened the car door. The sound of nature was surprisingly loud—the buzzing of insects, the rustling of leaves from the birds, and the trickling water from a nearby brook. And the smell—it was sweet from the flowers and fresh from the leaves and mint plants. The combined scents brought on an overwhelming feeling of nostalgia.

Exactly *how* I felt nostalgia was a mystery, since I'd forgotten roughly ninety percent of my time in these mountains, but I recognized the feeling.

As soon as my feet touched the ground, the world seemed to tilt beneath me. It was just for a moment. A split second, even, but enough for me to feel it.

Then my world shifted back, and in that same instant, I felt like I'd just lost something. The pain came so sharp and sudden I sucked in a breath—and then found I was gasping for another reason. I was…crying.

Touching my eyelashes, my fingertips came away wet. *Why?*

As quickly as it had come on, though, the feeling was gone, like it'd never been there in the first place.

"Brye? Hey, you okay?" Iz asked, leaning over the hood of the CRV, tilting her sunglasses into her hair and squinting at me.

"I'm okay," I said hurriedly, trying to cover up the catch in my throat. "It must be all this pollen in the air making my eyes water."

Thinking the strange feeling might have come from my asthma, I took a moment to regulate my breathing. Only, I found it easier than usual. Actually, *much* easier, as if my asthma had vanished entirely. The air that flowed in and out of my lungs was crisp and fresh, and it almost tasted sweet.

The two of us followed the little stone path through the wild garden. I recognized flowers I'd never seen before but knew the names of, like cherry-red zinnias, violet-globe amaranths, golden-petaled black-eyed Susans, and then herbs like basil and coriander. From flowers to trees, I somehow knew every plant's name. I'd always been like that. After the thirtieth weird look from a kid in my biology class, I caught on that this ability wasn't exactly normal. Had Willa taught me, and I somehow retained their names past the amnesia?

After climbing the porch steps, I opened the screen door and winced as it screeched on its hinges. I knocked and waited. Then, beyond a lace curtain over the door's oval window, a silhouette came into view, and my heart skipped painfully.

Izzie gave my arm a reassuring squeeze as the door

opened, and I came face-to-face with both a stranger and my grandmother.

Willa Kaftan, while, old and wrinkled, was beautiful. Natural beauty like hers couldn't be destroyed by age. It was as if her white, white hair was the result of something more magical than just time. She wore an old T-shirt for a band that was popular in the sixties, a flowery skirt, and an apron stained by countless meal preparations over the years. She was balancing on crutches, her foot wrapped in a hot-pink cast.

I wondered if the color was because of her doctor's sense of humor or Willa's own preference for Barbie pink circa the new millennium.

For a moment, my words stalled in my mouth, remembering Dad's comment. What should I call her? She was a stranger to me in almost every way, and yet…

I had known her before. Something inside me told me I did.

The name was out before I'd even thought it. But it felt right somehow.

"Hi, Gran."

Chapter Three

"Briony," Gran whispered. Her soft brown eyes were wide behind tortoiseshell frames, and as the seconds passed, while I stood awkwardly, they grew glassy. She raised a trembling hand to her mouth with a gasp that sounded like a suppressed sob.

Then her eyes grew sharp. "I told Jim that I didn't need any…" She trailed off as she noticed the girl standing behind me. "And who's this?"

"My friend, Isabelle Jennison."

"Call me Izzie. Nice to meet you," she said cheerfully, maneuvering her way around me to hug my grandmother. The look of surprise on Gran's face was pretty priceless as Izzie pulled back and took her by the shoulders. "Whatever you need, Mrs. Kaftan, we got you. We're your girls."

Gran simply stood there, mouth opening and closing but nothing coming out. She looked from me to Izzie and, shoulders sagging, stepped back to allow us into her home. "Well, come in, then."

The house was warm and welcoming with the exception of a few shadowy corners tucked away from the windows. Dust motes floated in the vast patches of sunlight. Tiny figurines of fairies and elves sat on wooden shelves.

Bookcases overflowed with both paperbacks and hardbacks. Pictures covered the walls, and quilts hung on the back of worn furniture.

As I scanned the room, bits of old memories came rushing to the surface—they were so fast and fleeting that I closed my eyes in an attempt to hold on to them.

For years, I'd tried to remember my past. I'd been curious, but also *desperate* to find out what had created this void inside of me. But not once had I been able to remember anything significant.

My gaze honed in on a little fairy with a purple wing and a dress and gold curls on the mantel. I'd dropped it once and broken one of its wings. I'd actually cried over it, while warm, wrinkled hands had clasped mine. *"It's only a figurine, sugar pea, not a real one."*

The words came to me so sweet and soft, and the love in them hit me like a dropkick to the stomach.

Then the memory was gone, slipping away like a bar of wet soap.

While I'd been trapped in the past, Izzie had already ventured deeper into the cottage, chatting happily with Gran about things like *oh, Briony and I have been friends since she moved to Knoxville, I wanted to come,* and *where will I be sleeping?*

As Izzie vanished into a side bedroom off the hall, Gran hobbled back to me on her crutches, talking in a low whisper. "Briony, I...appreciate you and your father's concern. But I really don't need any help, and...well, given your history here, it's better if you go back home."

But that was exactly *why* I was here. My history. That, and to assist an injured senior citizen. Just around her living room was evidence of the help she needed—clusters of books and newspapers and old dishes, prescription bottles and empty water glasses. I could imagine a pile of laundry in her room that she'd been putting off, or a sink full of dirty dishes.

This was an old woman with a broken leg, who was struggling, and yet, she seemed to be more concerned with pushing me away, not wanting my *history* here to make me uncomfortable.

Maybe she really did care about me, but it was buried by layers upon layers of loneliness, bitterness, and a little regret. Perhaps she'd never come to see me in Knoxville because she thought her presence would only incite trauma.

Seeing Gran look at me, her eyes glassy and full of pain, I wondered if she saw my mom in my place. Did I remind her of Heather? Of my mom? Was not seeing me as much self-preservation of herself as it was protection of me?

I had barely known Mom when she'd left, yet I could still see her escaping out the front door in the middle of the night with only a bag slung over her shoulder. I could even picture her outfit when she left—a sunflower blouse and jeans of a light wash—down to the simple jewelry she wore. I'd still been awake after listening to my parents fight for hours, hearing things like, *"You need to trust me,"* and *"This family won't survive the fire,"* and, *"Jim, why won't you believe me?"* Her leaving, as I watched from the steps, hidden in shadow, was burned into my mind forever.

How painful was it for Gran, then, who'd given birth to her?

Carefully, I set down my duffle bag and faced my grandmother. Awkwardness widened like a chasm between us. If I waited much longer, I'd never be able to jump over it.

"Listen, Gran," I said softly, gently. "Iz and I are here to *help*. Cooking, cleaning, fixing you a cup of tea. Whatever you need. And thank you for worrying about me, but I'm fine."

Yep, totally fine. Not damaged at all.

Gran's silver brows pulled together as she looked at me like she still didn't believe me.

Then Izzie came out into the hall and paused, her gaze jumping from me to Gran. "Everything all right?" she asked cheerfully.

Gran looked at Izzie then back at me, and just as she opened her mouth, the phone rang.

The three of us stood frozen as it echoed through the small cottage. At the second ring, Izzie bounded down the darkened hall into what I assumed to be the kitchen, calling, "I'll get it for you, Mrs. Kaftan!"

Gran stood there, probably shell-shocked that a total stranger was in her house, had given her a hug, and was now answering her phone. Izzie was like that, though—she had a big personality to go with a big heart.

Not a minute later, Izzie hollered through the house, "Brye, it's your dad!"

"Oh, okay." I hurried down the hall past Gran, into a room with linoleum floors, a large round wooden table, an old gas stove, and appliances from the fifties. The scent of cinnamon and other spices filled my nose as I entered. Everything about it was quaint and adorable and perfect. I was certain this was the kitchen of every fairy-tale character ever made. Wind chimes and other baubles hung next to the curtained windows, and silver cutlery was displayed in a little wooden case hanging on the wall.

Izzie handed me a big, brown antique phone with a curling cord connected to the wall. One of those that you could cradle easily between your ear and your shoulder.

"It's not your dad," she whispered, her eyes big, trying to communicate something to me that I wasn't getting.

"Who is it?" I whispered back.

"Just talk," she said, shoving the phone against my chest.

I put the phone to my ear. "Hello?"

Izzie made a gesture to show she was going back to Gran. I nodded to her as a voice from the phone said, "Mrs. Kaftan? Are you there?"

"Um, this is her granddaughter. How can I help you?"

"Well, as I was telling the other girl," said the voice, a little more irritably, "I'm calling to confirm the demolition of the Redwrell place off Hummingbird Road."

Oh no… My old house. Did he say demolition?

My skin chilled over, while that gap inside my chest expanded, contracted, and expanded again, painfully.

"I need to talk to Mrs. Kaftan."

"She can't come to the phone right now," I said in a hollow voice.

"Well, whether or not she can come to the phone is not my problem. She has pushed this demolition back for months. Changed her mind five times. It's happening tomorrow whether she approves or not. I've gotten official orders from the county. You tell her that." The line disconnected, and I was left staring at an empty kitchen and listening to the dial tone.

Slowly, I put the phone back in its cradle, and my gaze passed the sink, skipping over the mountain of dirty dishes I had predicted, to look out the window at Gran's overgrown garden. My eyes were drawn to tiny things that felt familiar: big strawberry patches, the trellis on the outside wall with honeysuckle vines, hummingbird feeders hanging from the awning…

There was something about that garden. A memory that was itching to be brought to the surface but was buried deep. Still, I kept staring. Trying, trying to remember…

This whole place was like that. A little painful, but also familiar. If my grandmother's house made me feel this way, then what would my own house make me feel like?

I'd hoped that coming here would give me closure. Answer a thousand unanswered questions. Finally bring light to a past I'd always been too scared to bring out of the dark. But could I move on from my past if my house—the only clue to the fire that haunted my dreams—was bulldozed to the ground?

Truthfully, I'd never expected to confront it so soon. Maybe halfway through the summer I'd gather enough courage and go, but it looked like I no longer had that option.

It was now or never, and I was done living with regret or wondering about things that I'd never find out. I had to go see it, and I had to go now.

Heading out of the kitchen, I flew down the hallway and found Izzie and Gran sitting in the living room.

"Iz, keys, please?" I asked, breathless.

Without question, Izzie dug into her purse and tossed me the keys to her CRV. She knew I would want to go from the beginning. It was why she'd made sure that I'd taken that call.

"Wait—Briony? Where are you going?" Gran called as I hurried out to the porch and the screen door banged behind me. Hopefully Izzie would feed her some small white lie till I got back.

I felt bad, leaving so rudely, but they were going to tear it down and I couldn't let them without seeing it at least once.

The minute I'd left this valley, broken-hearted, motherless, and *empty*, I'd closed a door on my past. On this life I'd once had which had been *literally* burned away.

I'd been okay with it. Or, at least, I'd tried to be. Sure, I'd felt like a giant canyon had opened in my chest, and I couldn't trust a boyfriend not to cheat on me, or rely on anyone to finish a relay race or complete a group project...

But I'd been *okay.*

Except now I wasn't.

Now I had to see this through.

Pulling my phone out of my other pocket, I selected the maps app and typed in *Hummingbird Road, Firefly Valley.* I didn't have an address number, but thankfully, the road was only a mile long, so I could drive up and down and check the houses. Surely a burned-down house would be easy to find.

Pursing my lips, I waited impatiently as the shoddy Internet connection pulled up directions. It took so long that I grabbed a screenshot of them in case I lost the signal while I was driving.

The narrow road through the mountains was full of twists and turns, but I was careful, and Izzie's car moved like a dream. I drove almost ten miles below the speed limit and made turns at a snail's pace. My driving instructor would've been proud.

Finally, I got to a crest on a hill, and it looked so familiar that I had to be close. The meadows on the other side held purple, yellow, white, and light-pink flowers. Tall trees stood on the slopes, and off in the distance was a hint of green-blue. Maybe the edge of a lake?

Easing off the gas pedal, I coasted down the hill and followed the road until it curved around a bend in the trees, then I rammed on the brake. Hard.

The seat belt pressed against my chest, slicing a line between my breasts and cutting against my throat—but that wasn't the reason I felt like choking.

The house was still standing as if held up purely by magic. It was charred almost completely black. Half the roof was caved in, and bricks, burned wood, and other rubble peppered the surrounding overgrown lawn. The house was bigger than Gran's, and judging from the paint, it had once been mint-green. Windows had pieces of glass jutting out from the edges, broken and warped from extreme temperatures.

It had been mostly destroyed by the fire, but…it was somehow even more beautiful than when it had first been built. Because over the burned wood and remnants of plaster, flora had grown. On top of the wood was a thick covering of moss, and up from the moss, more flowers and weeds had sprouted over the house, giving it a living green carpet. Vines curled over the chimney and layers of honeysuckle fell on top of one another. As I stepped out of the car, their scent filled me to the brim, and all I wanted was to pluck a blossom and place the end of the flower between my lips to taste the sweet nectar.

I thought I'd never had honeysuckle before, but apparently I'd been wrong. I'd had them many, many times.

For a few minutes, I just stood under the trees, half in the shadow of my old house, and stared. Not at the dilapidated structure before me, but the Blue Ridges that loomed behind.

The Smokies looked like a painting off in the distance. Rich oil colors and pastels blending into shades of nature. A light periwinkle against a backdrop of bright blue, the mountains were like a jagged line on a heart monitor—up and down, up, up, and then down again. The breeze tickled my skin as the sun warmed it, nourishing it better than any all-natural lotion or oil I'd ever tried.

There was something about this valley. Something special. I'd felt it at Gran's, but it was more obvious here, or maybe I was just more mindful of it.

The sound of my feet over the gravel, then the grass and underbrush, came to my ears distant and muffled. In fact, I was hardly aware that I was moving at all. My legs took me from Izzie's car, up the rotted porch steps, and through the wooden frame where there once stood a door, and I looked inside my old house for the first time since losing my memory of it.

Like at Gran's, the ground rolled beneath me as a strong feeling of vertigo forced me against the charred door frame.

I blinked, and I envisioned my mother walking toward me through the large, high-ceilinged room with its burned wood floors and flowers growing between the floorboards.

She was as I remembered her—from the few weeks I knew her between the fire and the time she'd left. Long, thick dark-brown hair and beautiful green eyes. While I had wavy light-brown hair and pale gray eyes without a spark of the color my mom had. Dad had once told me that we both looked like foxes—the way our noses were straight and the shape of our eyes seemed to slant upward, sly like a vixen's.

Imaginary Mom bent down and threw her arms out, her face bright and beautiful and happy, and she wrapped me in her arms—five-year-old me, not sixteen-year-old me. I pressed my small hands against her cheeks and squished them together, puckering her lips. She planted a kiss on my forehead, making my chest glow with warmth and happiness.

Then the world tilted once more and the hands holding mine grew smaller. They were strong, though. Twisting in my grip, the hands threaded our fingers together and I looked up from our entwined grasp to see a young boy. His features were blurry, like a photo taken out-of-focus, but his eyes were bright and sharp, glowing like two fireflies against tanned skin.

His hands tightened around mine, so tight that his palms grew uncomfortably hot. I gasped, trying to let go, but he held on, and the walls of my house erupted in flames.

Chapter Four

Hot wind blew at my cheeks, smoke blocked the scream from my throat, embers fell on my skin, and they burned and burned. The house was on fire. The floors, the walls, the roof, the couch where Dad and I would watch *Friends* reruns and take naps, the bookshelf holding Mom's favorite paperback thrillers. Flames licked my arms and flickered against my shoulders and traveled up the grandfather clock that Mom had loved, consuming it.

Finally, the boy let go of my hands, but by then it was too late. I couldn't run…couldn't escape the wall of fire.

My chest constricted and breathing became impossible. It was the smoke. It had gotten into my lungs and it was sucking out the oxygen. I gasped over and over, trying to get air.

In the back of my head, I should've known that this wasn't how people died of smoke. They became heavy… sleepy. Not more awake, not panicking. Not shallow, gasping breaths. I also should've known that this was a memory—one I'd never had before. I'd never known Mom loved paperback thrillers or that we had a grandfather clock, or even that we had a couch Dad and I used to take naps on.

But I couldn't think straight. My world was a fiery

nightmare, and I couldn't leave it.

Cool hands wrapped around my hot wrists. Breath, fresh and crisp like an autumn breeze, tickled my cheeks. Words, soft and urgent, whispered in my ear over and over, pulling me away from the fire. Out of the memory.

I opened my eyes and found myself staring into another pair. They were a soft summer green, positioned on either side of a thin, straight nose and above high cheekbones. It was a face. A face of a boy—blond, tan, and handsome.

His lips moved, speaking sentences that hadn't yet registered in my brain.

Dazed, I glanced down to see that he supported the upper half of my body with an arm that wrapped tightly around my shoulders. His forearm muscles pressed against the back of my neck, and I marveled at how his cool temperature relieved my burning skin. My legs curved in a way that had suggested I'd fallen somehow. Did I trip on a loose floorboard?

"What?" I breathed, the question passing across my lips like the simmering heat in a desert.

"...all right?"

His voice finally reached me, and I blinked hard, focusing on the solidity of the stranger and the fact that he was holding me so close I could count the sparks of light in his eyes.

I flexed my fingers, and when the numbness retreated and the strength returned to my arms, I pushed out against the stranger's chest. He dropped me—probably from surprise rather than from my own force—and I landed on the burned wood, wincing as splinters pierced my arms, elbows, and palms.

"Careful," the stranger said, watching my movements in obvious concern.

I scooted away inch by inch, my shorts snagging on the splintered wood. "Who are you doing here?"

The boy tilted his head, his lips twitching in what seemed to be amusement. "That sounds like two separate questions."

I gritted my teeth. "You know what I meant. *Who* are you? And *what* are you doing here?"

All trace of amusement disappeared, and his gold eyebrows pushed together into a V. "What are *you* doing back here?"

Back. What am I doing *back* here? Had he…known me?

It certainly was possible. Apart from my family, I hadn't really thought of anyone else I could've forgotten thanks to my amnesia. I hadn't even considered it.

"This was my house…once," I said slowly, my gaze meticulously noting every detail of his appearance in hopes of remembering *something*. He wore a plain navy shirt with olive green shorts, and he was barefoot. Odd… I observed his eyes again and the planes of his face. Nothing struck a chord, but that didn't necessarily mean anything.

"Did…did I know you?" I finally asked.

It was like I'd pulled a gun on him or something. He abruptly stood and took a step back. His eyes were wide, and he looked from me to the charred walls then back to me. "No. I mean, it's not safe here. You should leave."

"Hey, why do *I* have to go?" I stood, rubbing my arms that were irritated and scratched from the wood. "You're the one who creeped up on me."

"I didn't creep— " He stopped, his lips twisting into a scowl. "You were passed out on the floor. I was just checking to make sure you were okay."

Had I really passed out? I'd gotten some weird flashbacks and the next thing I knew I was on the floor and this stranger was holding me.

But just who the heck was this guy? A nice, upstanding citizen who happened to be passing by an old burned house… randomly…in the middle of the mountains. Without any shoes? Yeah, I wasn't buying it.

In fact, it felt borderline dangerous. Whoever he was, whatever he wanted, *why* he was here, I knew it wasn't smart to be around him. Stranger danger and all that.

"It's fine, *I'm* fine, so thanks for your concern, but I'm good. You're right. You should go. Or I should go—both of us. But not together!" I backed away, clearly rambling. But as terrible timing would have it, my right foot came down on a rotted floorboard and the charred wood scraped against my skin as my leg went straight through.

The boy lunged, first catching my wrist, then grabbing my waist and hoisting me out of the newly made crater.

The moment he touched me, the ever-present void in my chest seemed to expand, sucking in my breath like a black hole—a vortex. All the ache and loss and confusion increased exponentially. The feeling came so fast it was like someone had knocked the wind out of me.

As he set me on safe ground and began to remove his hands from my waist, I latched on to them, hoping to cling to the lingering feeling, despite how intensely painful it was. Because it *meant* something. I wouldn't have had this reaction touching just anyone. Maybe this boy was a clue. And maybe if I held on to him longer, something would return.

When I looked up into the boy's face, it was with a new set of eyes.

"I *did* know you," I whispered.

I searched his face, watching his expression morph into panic. His eyes widened and his cheeks paled. When his mouth opened, nothing came out except the strange coolness of his breath, reminding me once again of an autumn breeze.

"No," he said at last, after long seconds had passed while I kept hold of his hands. "You didn't."

"You're lying," I said. The sensation he'd incited was painful to breathe through now. It was like someone was standing on my chest.

I didn't recognize *him*, but I recognized the feeling. And it hadn't left me since the second I'd stepped outside Izzie's car at Gran's. Nostalgia.

But a hundredfold.

I longed for this stranger like I longed for the taste of Mom's special chocolate chip cookies with rock salt on top. I longed for this stranger like I longed to hear Dad read me my favorite picture book, or the way the crickets chirped outside in the twilight, or sticky fingers from watermelon juice.

I don't remember eating Mom's rock-salt chocolate chip cookies, and I don't remember which book was my favorite. But I longed for them.

How could I long for something I couldn't remember?

"I have to go." The boy ripped his hands from my gasp, and as he did, my fingers grazed thread on his wrist.

I glanced down and my suspicions were confirmed. I'd known this boy once. No, not only known him, I'd cared about him. He'd been important to me.

It wasn't just the void inside me, longing for memories I no longer possessed. It was what was attached to his wrist that gave me rock-solid proof.

Indisputable proof.

Around the boy's wrist was a very old, worn, blue-and-orange friendship bracelet.

Chapter Five

The first time I ever remember making a friendship bracelet was after moving to Knoxville. It was a fad that girls in my class had started doing during recess or study periods. When Izzie invited me to try knotting the multicolored threads, my fingers moved on their own, creating a pattern much different than any other girl's bracelet.

It was a unique pattern that I'd known how to make without ever having to learn it.

And here it was, attached to the wrist of a boy whose mere touch evoked such a powerful sense of nostalgia that the black hole inside me roared with pain.

Without thinking, I reached for his bracelet. He tucked his wrist behind his back and stepped to the side, his eyes wider with fear or shock—I couldn't tell which.

"Where did you get that?" I demanded.

"None of your business," he replied the second the words were out of my mouth, as if he'd anticipated my question before I'd even asked.

He swallowed, his Adam's apple bobbing once in his throat, and then his expression shifted into a perfect mask of annoyance. It was the face you gave to someone when you were standing in the Starbucks line, talking with your friend, and the guy behind you interrupts you to put in *his* two cents about what had happened on *Riverdale* last night.

"It is, actually, since I made it for you." If he still wore this bracelet then it had to mean something to him. So had *I* meant something to him six years ago?

His green eyes narrowed. "Do you remember doing it?"

"Well, no, but—"

"You should leave," he repeated.

"Why do you want to get rid of me so badly?"

A brief flash of pain rippled across his features and he took a step back. "Go, *please*."

He seemed to be at war with himself, or an actor trying to figure out two completely different roles. One minute he was aloof, feigning ignorance, and the next he was pleading with me to leave as if he cared about my safety, deeply. "Who *are* you?" I asked again.

He turned to go, but I caught hold of his shirt.

"I made that bracelet for you, didn't I?"

He tried to yank his shirt from my grasp. "You have to let go," he said, voice gruff with frustration.

"Not until you tell me who you are. Look, I lost my memories. From when I was a kid. I *know* you, I just don't remember you. Please—" My voice went much too high on the last part, but the pain was back, and it was kicking me in the heart with steel-toed boots.

His hand closed around mine on his shirt, slowly, gently, prying my fingers away from the fabric. "You shouldn't be here, Briony," he said. His voice had lost its edge. There was no angry undertone, just one of deep despair.

At the sound of my name, which I'd never said to him, my fingers loosened, and he slipped away. While I stood there, shocked, he fled from the house, through the scorched, cracked doorway. I didn't snap out of it until he jumped from the slanting porch.

I went after him. "Wait!"

His warning burned through me like the fire that had destroyed this house. *He knows my name and I never told him.*

He was the clue. He was the piece that I didn't know I'd been searching for.

And I wouldn't let him get away.

His feet pounded against the ground as he headed into the surrounding woods, and I jumped from the porch and followed. There was no clear path through the trees, but the boy didn't seem to care. It was as if he made his own, weaving his way between the basswood trees and cutting through the sweetshrub, wild hydrangea, and tall deerberry bushes.

I ran as fast as I could, ignoring the bushes and undergrowth as well, my steps mirroring his and following the path he crafted. His speed felt almost inhuman, or like that of an Olympic gold medalist. But the strangest thing was that I somehow kept up. I gained on him and felt the air shift around me, as if I'd just entered into a sort of slipstream.

I'd learned the term in a science class—it was the area behind a moving object in which the state of matter around it sped at the same velocity. The very air around him was moving as fast as he was. And I was caught inside—inside the slipstream—with the air bending around us.

Wind rippled through my shirt and shorts, while branches whacked and scraped at my bare arms and legs. Going at this speed was impossible—*should* have been impossible.

The minute I'd realized it, my body seemed to reject the physics of the slipstream and my own momentum. My feet slowed and the boy disappeared ahead of me. I could no longer keep up. Like a deer escaping a mountain lion, he moved too fast and too gracefully. He disappeared into the forest in a matter of seconds, and I came to a dead stop, my pulse going wild.

"Oh, c'mon!" I shouted into the trees, bending over and placing my palms on my knees.

Swearing under my breath, I waited for my asthma to punish me for sprinting, but it never did. The mountain air that filled my lungs was sweet, and clean. Every breath I took, I waited for it to turn against me, but it didn't.

Smoothing my hair away from my forehead and sweaty cheeks, I stared in the direction he disappeared and then noticed something odd.

The trees looked different.

The whole forest did.

It…glowed.

Rotating slowly in place, I took in the sight of a forest that looked *otherworldly.*

Every tree and plant seemed to be alive with a sort of energy that pulsed around it in a wide spectrum of color. No, *radiating* was more accurate. The woods radiated a hued glow—neither liquid nor gas. In fact, this *energy* seemed to be a different state of matter entirely.

"What the hell?" I breathed, stumbling back on trembling legs.

Hugging my arms, I rubbed them, and goose bumps peppered my skin. I slowly lowered myself to the forest floor and took deep, steady breaths. Grass prickled my thighs and crunched under my sneakers. Wind whistled through the leaves above me, and when the leaves moved, the green energy moved with them, smearing the sky and air in a sort of watercolor effect.

It was beautiful, but unreal.

Unreal.

I squeezed my eyes closed. I was queasy, despite the fact that physically, I'd never felt stronger.

My eyes had been closed for no more than a few seconds when a soft chirping sound reached my ears. At first, I didn't think anything of it. It was a bird, surely, even though it sounded like a very strange bird call.

Then it got closer.

And closer.

Chiiirrrppp.

I opened one eye. And screamed.

Crouched by the toe of my right sneaker was a creature that was not of this world.

It would be one thing if it was, like, a weird-looking squirrel, but it was much more than that. It was chipmunk-sized with a face, underbelly, and limbs covered in rich auburn fur, but then…green clover petals sprouted from its back, covering it like the shell of a turtle.

Clovers literally *growing* from its back.

It nipped the air with a tiny mouth, sniffing my sneaker, and then chirruped again.

Chiirrrrpp.

Letting out a squeak myself—of terror—I scrambled to my feet and began running again. It didn't matter to *where*, just as long as I put as much distance between myself and the strange creature.

As I glanced behind my shoulder to check if it was following me, I ran into something. No, someone.

Hands grabbed me and, heart pounding, I looked up.

It was the boy.

He looked as scared as I felt.

"What are you… How did you…" He gasped, his eyes huge and wide. "Did you *follow* me?"

"There was this *thing*," I cried, trying to twist from side to side to see if the tiny alien was around my feet.

"*How* did you follow me?" he asked, raising his own voice to meet my panic level.

Satisfied that the little green gremlin was nowhere to be seen, I looked back at the boy. "What do you mean *how*? I just did."

"That shouldn't be possible."

"I mean, I ran after you as fast as I could, but then I lost you—"

I stopped mid-sentence as what I was seeing caught up with what I was processing. The forest wasn't the only thing that was glowing. The *boy* was, too.

Energy pulsed and moved around him like an extension of his body. Like an aura.

The gold mist-like energy around him seemed to be bleeding into my skin as his fingers pressed into my arms. As the energy swirled against my skin and seeped underneath, my senses exploded.

Sweet and sour juice of wild blackberries. Pounding mountain rain against wet skin. Whistling leaves in the trees. Heavenly wildflower scent.

The Smokies invaded my whole body.

From this boy's mere touch, I could feel the mountains themselves.

I ripped away from his grasp, violent shivers climbing up and down my body.

Even more scared of him and his touch than the strange clover creature, I ran. Again, the where didn't matter, I just had to get away.

The irony that I had been following him five minutes ago and was now running away from him was not lost on me. But I could still feel the remnants of his strange aura on my skin, lingering there like the moisture in the air after an afternoon summer rain. It was too much. Too much to understand. Too much to *feel.*

I couldn't hear him coming after me, but I knew he was somehow. The way he'd moved through the forest before... He could travel through the woods like some sort of ghost. His presence wove through the giant elms that glowed copper, mixing with the gold of the sun.

As I rounded a bend in the path, he shouted my name. "Briony!"

That only made me run faster. My leg muscles burned as they carried me out of the forest full of elms and to a cliff face.

White-and-pink mountain laurel climbed skyward, threading through cracks in a rust-colored mountain wall directly before me.

I tried to stop, but I was running too fast and skidded through the brambles of the path, a cloud of dirt erupting around my ankles. In just a brief glance, I could see how far up I was—and yet, I didn't remember hiking up to this elevation.

The tops of trees stretched out before me, and a lake glittered with reflected sunlight. Emerald colliding with sapphire.

Unfortunately my stop wasn't hard or graceful. My shoulder collided with the sharp rock of the mountainside, and my left foot wobbled. I teetered. A small cry escaped my throat as my fingers scrambled for purchase against the orange and gray stone-face, but there was none. I came away with dust and air, and the mysterious orange energy coating my fingertips, as my ankle folded and I fell off the edge.

The fall was epic. Blue, blue sky filled my vision as my body became level with the earth and the wind screamed and roared.

The boy was suddenly above me, sliding down the cliff in a storm of dust and leaves. He jumped off the side of the ledge and reached for me.

The same second, a gust of mist buffeted me from behind.

The quintessential "smoke" of the Smoky Mountains uncurled beneath me, the wispy clouds forming a blanket of fog that hid the world below.

The last thing I saw before I fell through was desperation in the boy's face, his braceleted hand stretching for me, strained muscles pulled tight under his skin.

Chapter Six

Falling through the mist, I expected to feel wet, or at the very least, damp, but I stayed dry.

I also expected to die.

That I didn't was a surprise, too.

Opening my eyes, I stared up at the blanket of white, silvery "smoke" above me. Pushing myself up onto my elbows, I wondered why my crash had never come. Somehow I had been falling from a height of a hundred feet and then I just…hadn't.

It was more like I'd just appeared on the ground. One second, I'd been about to crash into branches and the next, I was lying in a field of…

A field?

I leaped to my feet and spun in a circle. I was in a field with not a tree, a mountain, or a lake in sight.

Where had the lake gone? Hadn't one been right under me?

Side note: I also didn't feel any pain. Not a single ache or bruise.

Glancing down, I inspected the tall grass poking up between my sneakers. It was varying shades of emerald to amber to gold as fine and as brilliant as real gemstones.

The blades brushed against my shins lighter than a whisper.

The mysterious aura was still there but diluted somehow. Not as alive and pulsing, but merely a soft radiance, like the haze around the flame of a candle.

How was this all possible? Where…was I?

Before more panic could set in, I spotted a figure in the distance. The silhouette grew into sharper focus as it—as *she* came toward me, fast.

Dark-brown hair flew behind her as she ran through the meadow. She wore light-washed jeans and a shirt that was a soft yellow with sunflowers decorating its hem.

She was still too far away to make out that detail, but I was sure that's what it was. Because that was what my mother had been wearing the day before she'd left.

At about five feet away, she slowed, the breeze rippling across the grass and blowing her hair around her face, making wisps of it catch against her lips and hide her green eyes.

"You…you're," I breathed, too stunned to move.

"Briony," she said.

In a few short steps, she closed the distance between us, her arms wrapping around to squeeze me close. Her scent was how I remembered it—citrus, from the hand lotion she used, and a hint of hay. She'd worked with horses at a ranch down the road, and she would come home smelling like their stables.

These small details, like what she smelled like to the blouse she'd been wearing when she'd left, meant that her leaving had been a deeper scar than I'd ever acknowledged. She was my fifth scar—the one that wasn't on my back.

Maybe I didn't remember distinct childhood memories of her before the fire, but she was ingrained in my existence. A piece of the gaping hole inside me.

Her breathing as she held me was slow and rhythmic,

and she was warm.

"I've missed you so much, Briony," she said, her voice right next to my ear. I could feel the vibrations in her throat and chest.

Slowly, my trembling hands rose and gently pushed away her arms. I stepped back. No matter how good that hug had felt, this was still the woman who'd left me. Abandoned her husband and child. "You… I remember you leaving," I said, my voice hoarse, unable to work right. "Where did you go? Here?" I glanced up at the veil of mist that still hung above our heads. "And where is here?"

"Listen to me." Her sharp tone brought my gaze downward, away from the smoky ceiling, and back to her face. "You've passed into the spirit world, Briony," she said, her green eyes boring into mine.

A horrible spark of terror ricocheted through me. "You mean I'm *dead*?"

That fall *had* killed me. Oh my God, then that meant Mom was dead, too.

"No, you're not dead," she said with an impatient sigh. "This valley holds an energy that only a few places in the world possess. It allows spirits to dwell here. Not spirits of the dead, spirits of nature."

The strange creature with green clovers growing out of its back came to mind.

My brain just wanted to shut off.

"What…how…?" I stammered.

"There are places in the world that are special…" she began slowly, her gaze tracing my face, as if she were trying to memorize every detail. Her stare was intense, and somehow persuasive. I found myself desperate to hear more. "There are places that are so mystical and beautiful that the lines between what's real and what's not are blurred. It's in those places where the boundary between the physical and astral plane becomes so thin…that spirits dwell."

Her words went off like a gong within the void in my chest. I'd heard them before. I didn't remember them exactly, or who said them, but I remembered the cadence of them. The magic behind them.

For a few long seconds, I couldn't speak.

"That's not…that's not possible."

"I'm trying to tell you, we are in a place where it *is* possible. You passed through the boundary of the physical world into the ethereal world somehow. Don't you remember getting here?"

I'd been following that strange boy, but I'd only been running after him in the woods, not like walking through a magical wardrobe or anything. The only thing that had been weird was the air trick—the slipstream.

Could that have been me passing through something? A boundary of sorts? A portal?

"It doesn't matter," Mom said, her tone becoming more urgent. "We don't have time. What I need you to understand is that you have crossed over into another plane of existence, a world not bound by matter but controlled by energy."

I thought of the way the special colorful aura extended over plants and trees, *and that boy*, like a layer of radiation.

"It's where the two combine and it's where spirits—"

"Dwell. Got it." I was finally beginning to believe the unbelievable. "But, how did *you* get here?"

Mom shook her head, her grip on my arms tightening uncomfortably. "I don't have time to explain everything, but what I can tell you is that I can't leave this world—*he* won't let me. I need *your* help to escape."

A powerful shock, like sticking a fork in an outlet, ripped through me. "I… *What*?"

"Briony," she said, her voice growing stern, sharp, "right now, I need you to *listen*." She gave me a little shake by the shoulders, and I swallowed, meeting her eyes again. This time, I noticed their shape—angled like that of a fox's.

Like mine.

"Now that you're here, you can *save* me."

Save her from what?

I wanted to demand she tell me how she wound up here, and why she'd walked out that door six years ago in the first place. But if she really was in danger, which everything about her panicked expression told me was true, I had to put those questions aside for now.

And if I managed to rescue her from this weird world, then I could finally get the answers I'd been asking my whole life. How did the fire start? What all had I forgotten? Did she leave because she couldn't handle raising a kid with amnesia?

"Okay, tell me how," I answered, trying to keep my voice calm.

A tiny smile tugged at her lips. "That's my girl. Now, listen carefully, because we don't have much time before he finds me."

"Before *who* finds you?"

"There are spirit gates that need to be unlocked in order for me to pass through the planes of existence. An emissary from the spirit world will help you find the gates and teach you how to unlock them."

An emissary? Were there other spirits that were more capable than me and had…fancy nature powers to unlock the gates? "Well, why can't the emissary just unlock them?"

"No." She squeezed my shoulders again, her eyes bulging. "It *has* to be you."

"I don't understand. Why me?"

"You're special," she said matter-of-factly. "You can pass through the boundary to the spiritual plane. Normal humans cannot."

As if that explains anything. Before I could tell her that, my attention was immediately drawn to her hands on my shoulders. They had begun to glow with a white light, and the radiance traveled up her arms and into her neck and chest.

"What's happening to you?" I whispered, breathless, as chills raced through me.

She ignored the glow and kept her gaze locked on my face. Unfortunately, I couldn't help but watch the rest of her body be swallowed up by it.

"*You must listen, Briony.*"

I jerked my head up from staring at her glowing bare feet. "I am," I said, though my voice cracked. *This is so bizarre.*

"You must unlock the gates by the sunset of the summer solstice. It's the time the barrier is thinnest and will allow a normal human like me to pass through. If you don't—"

A great roar overtook her voice.

Not an animalistic roar but an elemental one. Fire erupted across the fields behind us, igniting the dry meadow grass as if the Human Torch had just sneezed. Orange, red, and gold flames uncurled and reached fiery fingers toward the canopy of mist.

Mom turned back to me. Her eyes were wild, too white, and shining against the flickering light of the inferno. "He's here," she whispered.

If I hadn't been frozen stiff, I might have asked again who this mysterious "he" was she kept referring to. But the fire was hot, and the smoke was thick, and everything about it had me physically shaking from traumatic memories.

He's here for me. Don't let him take me.

It took me a moment to realize that those words weren't

Mom's... They were mine.

From six years ago.

I could only see the fire before me, with my mind blank and my limbs frozen, and feel the burns and taste the ash from that night. Mom was calling to me now, shaking me, the glow on her hands vibrant and unreal, but I couldn't think or respond. I was trapped in my own world. In my own nightmare.

I stared into the flames rippling across the meadow, watching them weave and churn into some sort of figure—but I couldn't be sure if that's what it was. Just like six years ago. Curled up on my couch, watching the flames eat the wood walls and rafters and form a distorted face.

There was no escaping. The fire skipped from blade to blade, coming toward me.

He's going to get me this time.

No sooner had I accepted this, when a gale-force wind blew across the meadow, flattening the grass. Our hair whipped about, clothes flapping and beating our skin. But the flames seemed to retreat, roaring upward instead of forward, taking the shape of a tidal wave.

Mom and I looked up as the mist above us began to swirl counterclockwise, like the beginnings of a tornado. Sure enough, the faster it turned, it became just that. The mist descended toward the field in a funnel-like shape, coming closer and closer toward me.

Meanwhile the fire and the flame-figure within retreated farther, leaving grass unburned and untouched, as if it had never been consumed by the fire in the first place.

The farther away the fire moved, the easier I could breathe and hear my mother speaking to me again. "Listen to what the emissary says, trust him, and you'll be able to do it, Briony," Mom said, gripping my hands tightly. She smiled, but it didn't reach her eyes. The wind batted her hair against her cheeks.

I squeezed her hands back, if only just to convince to myself that she was really here. "What *was* that just now?" I asked, my voice trembling so bad I could barely get the words out.

"Unlock the gates, Briony."

The tornado was now right above my head, and I almost jumped out of my skin at the disembodied arm coming directly out of the eye of the mist-storm.

The arm stretched toward me…a blue and orange bracelet tied to the wrist.

The world around me blurred as his fingers wrapped around my upper arm. Still, I kept hold of Mom's hand and she held strong onto mine as I was lifted from the spiritual meadow. Her whole body was glowing white now—her hand, the one I held, the brightest part of her.

In one strong tug, the boy yanked at my arm and mist closed before me, buffeting my hair and clothes, strangling the air from my lungs. I could still somehow feel Mom's hand in mine, and I didn't let go.

Then the mist was blown away, like the smoke from a bonfire, billowing and dispersing into the tops of the trees.

Trees.

I gasped, stumbling back as I registered the sights and sounds of the forest around me. I would've tripped and fallen if not for a solid body catching me from behind. The mystical aura that had once been everywhere was now gone and it was darker outside. The sun was just beginning its descent behind the mountains and the shadows of the trees stretched impossible lengths across the forest undergrowth.

The hands supporting me drew away, but I ignored them altogether.

Instead of turning to see *him*, I kept my eyes trained on my closed fist, where Mom's hand had been seconds before. Slowly, I uncurled my fingers and a firefly hovered above my palm. *Weird*.

It had been ages since I'd seen a firefly. In the city, they were few and far between.

It pulsed bright yellow then zipped away into the shadows of the forest before I had time to give it another thought.

"Briony?"

I craned my neck to look over my shoulder.

The boy stood there, tan, tall, and handsome, his navy shirt blending into the dark green of the forest. His face, half hidden in shadows, was all smooth lines and distinct angles, and it made him a little…intimidating. He reminded me of a thunderstorm that you saw off in the distance coming across the Appalachians—traveling over rolling peaks with lightning veining across the dark smearing of rain.

A terrifying force of nature, yes, but beautiful.

In opposition to his intense look, his hands were gentle. They came up to rest on my face, and his thumbs swept across my cheeks as his index finger lowered to check my pounding pulse.

The ache of longing grew inside me, but this time I pushed it away and focused on the fact that I'd just seen my mother, and the fire. *The fire.*

I swallowed back a fresh wave of terror and took a few steps away from the boy.

His eyebrows knitted together as his jaw muscles worked against unspoken words.

More questions sprang to mind, new ones. Did this boy know about my mother trapped in this spirit world? How had that fire suddenly ignited? What was *his* connection to this world?

But first things first.

"What are you?" I demanded.

Not *who* this time. *What.* Because a normal human could not pull people out of a spiritual realm the way he'd just done.

He stared down at me then lowered his gaze from my face to the ground. "You were never supposed to come back."

Even though I was dying to drill him with questions, I didn't want him to run away again. He was skittish as a deer. No sudden movements.

"I never expected to come back," I admitted, "but my grandmother broke her leg, and I needed to take care of her."

The boy didn't say anything. His fists clenched and unclenched.

"Look, can I at least get your name?" I asked.

He frowned, his gaze still directed at the ground. "You want my name?"

"Well, yeah…unless you want me to guess. Is it Chris? That's a good guess. A lot of hot guys are named Chris."

He half laughed, half sighed and rubbed the heel of his palm against his hairline. "It's Alder."

"Okay, Alder, tell me how I know you, and how I followed you into that…that spirit world."

"You know…that's the—" His green eyes widened, all trace of any humor I'd earned from him gone as he glanced around at the darkening forest. "Go *home*, Brye, please."

If he thought using my nickname was going to convince me, his plan totally backfired. So few people called me that. So few people I *let* call me that.

"No can do," I said, my voice low but forceful. "I want answers, and I'm not leaving until I get them. What *was* that place? You led me there. Then you pulled me out of it.

I know you know. Please, tell me."

Both of us, entreating each other. Both of us, desperate.

I didn't think either of us breathed in those seconds.

Just when I thought we'd be there forever, a floating yellow light drifted between us, diverting both of our attentions. Another firefly.

As soon as it appeared, a dozen more seemed to emerge out of nowhere. The firefly lights synchronized as the sun's light vanished almost entirely beyond the mountain ridges. The bulbs flashed as one—as if they were part of one consciousness, or one song. I'd never seen so many in my life. I stared in awe, jaw slack as goose bumps erupted over my chilled skin.

Alder twisted to the side, following the sun's disappearance, his green eyes somehow lighter and brighter in the darkness. He cursed under his breath. Then he turned and wove his way through the rest of the forest. I followed, able to keep up this time, probably because he let me. We emerged into a clearing with a large lake stretching out beyond. It was so distant that a line formed at the collision of the water and the base of blue mountains stretching into the twilight sky.

He cast me a worried glance then turned his face back to the dark-blue silhouette of the mountains against the thin gold line—the remnants of the sunset.

I licked my lips, hoping I could convince him to talk to me. If he had allowed me to follow him, then he was willing to talk, right? "Please, just tell me what's going on. I know we used to know each other. And I'm sorry I can't remember you. Really, I am. But if you could just—"

"I really hope I don't regret this..."

"Regret what?"

He was staring at the lakeshore, as if the answers were

written in pebbles. "No turning back now," he whispered to himself. He closed his eyes, as if he was silently accepting some kind of fate.

More fireflies drifted out of the forest, gathering around us in a swarm.

"What…is happening?" I breathed.

Alder turned to face me, hands back to fists at his sides, every visible muscle in his body strained.

At first, I was confused. What was he trying to tell me? Or show me? But then I noticed the subtle transformation.

His already tan skin grew darker, changing into a deep copper. His hair turned lighter and lighter until it looked like it had been dyed in silver moonlight. Then his eyes, once such a rich green, became brighter and yellower until they glowed like the fireflies that flitted around us.

My forgotten childhood friend was a freaking nature spirit.

Chapter Seven

I raised a hand to my mouth, stifling a cry.

Then my attention was stolen away from Alder's strange transformation to the fireflies. At first, their pulsing light seemed normal, despite the sheer abundance of them, but their forms had flickered into something else. They weren't just brief flashes of yellow light, but floating mist-like glowing spheres. Their bodies were translucent and shimmery in the moonlight reflected off the lake.

"Oh...my...God..."

Alder watched me, his gold eyes locked on my face, gauging my reaction.

As if he knew I'd freak out.

I did not disappoint, because at that moment reality came crashing down on me.

Even though I'd just been in a whole other plane of existence, there was a part of me that had been clinging to everything I'd just seen as some crazy dream. In a dream, I could just accept that Izzie turned into Beyoncé with wings, and we went on her world tour with centaur Justin Timberlake as he serenaded "Can't Stop the Feeling" to me on top of the Eiffel Tower—totally not a real example.

Air caught in my chest, struggling to get out, but I

couldn't release it. I couldn't do anything but stare at the scene before me.

I needed my inhaler.

"The fireflies…they…" I choked.

The strange beings floated and pulsed with multi-colored ethereal light illuminating the lake and its shore and the trees around us.

My chest heaved, but I wasn't getting any air.

It was too much. Running into a spirit realm, finding my mother, seeing the field of fire, meeting this boy, and now even the freaking fireflies were changing. They were no longer insects but literal balls of light that seemed to be made of the same strange aura from the world I'd just escaped.

Alder's silver brows furrowed in concern. He took a step forward and I took one back. "Briony, you need to breathe, all right?"

"No…*duh*…." I wheezed.

This doesn't feel like my asthma. My lungs were clearer, better than they'd ever been. Superhuman lungs. But I still couldn't get any air into them.

In three steps, Alder crossed to me and wrapped his hands around my neck. Suddenly air stalled inside my chest. Like he was controlling it somehow.

He held my breath. Literally.

In those seemingly long seconds, the balls of ethereal light retreated into the background, and the mountains and sky caught up with me, slowing under my feet and coming to a stop.

Everything came to a grinding halt.

After looking up into his strange eyes, I closed mine, and when I did, air flew through me again. Into my lungs, oxygenating them, then flowing out. Slowly. Deeply.

I could breathe normally.

"How did you do that?" I asked as he removed his hands from my throat.

Alder scanned my face. "Holding your breath stops a panic attack."

"Well, sure, but not that. I meant how did you—never mind." Out of all the things I had to ask him, how he had controlled my breathing didn't even break the top twenty.

The "fireflies" continued their hypnotic dance, and my gaze bounced from looking at them over his shoulder back to his face, then back to them.

"Are you a spirit?"

He stepped back. "Yes."

"Had…" I swallowed, struggling to organize my thoughts. My gaze dropped to the friendship bracelet. It was tight around his wrist as if he had grown into it. And by the appearance of the knots, I could tell he had even loosened it and re-knotted it a couple times. It was well cared for. "Had I known that before?"

Alder looked away, the tension leaving his body, and replacing it with defeat. "Yes."

I took a minute to process that *yes*. Such a simple answer contained a world's worth of implications and hidden meanings. I'd always longed to know what my missing memories had been, but now the pain of not knowing hurt like a physical wound.

"And did I know of these…" I gestured around to the floating lights. "These…" My voice climbed another octave, high and helpless.

The hole in my chest throbbed and ached with pain that now felt intolerable.

My missing piece.

It wasn't just Mom leaving, or forgetting my childhood,

that had created this void inside me. It was this world. It was Alder. It was the spirits in this valley.

It was the hidden world that my mother said only *I* had access to.

"Wisps," he said softly. "They're called wisps, and yes, you did."

I backed up until I bumped into the trunk of a tree and then slid down the bark, my clothes catching on the rough texture before my backside hit the ground. Resting my head against the trunk, I stared up at the night sky. There were so, so many stars, even this early in the evening. It was strange that something so mystical and distant as the infinity of space was more normal to me than something that was five feet away.

Scrubbing my hand up into my hair, I tugged at the roots, gasping through the sob that I struggled to suppress in my chest. The stars grew blurry above me.

I'd lost this whole world, this amazing, luminous world—I'd lost it all. And somehow that was more devastating than anything I could've ever imagined.

"Wisps." Their name passed my lips without much of a sound at all. My mouth merely formed it. Maybe it should feel familiar to me, but it didn't. It was foreign and strange.

The pebbles of the lakeshore crunched underfoot as Alder-the-spirit knelt before me. I recalled his grip on my arm and the warm, solid hands on my face, checking my pulse, brushing my cheeks… He certainly hadn't felt like a spirit then.

"Briony?" he said, his gaze concerned and yielding. His hand hovered above my knee, as if he wanted to touch me but didn't dare.

"I forgot all this." I dropped my hands to my face, covering my nose and mouth, and concentrated on breathing in, breathing out.

"Okay, you're a spirit. *These*"—I gestured to the things that had once been fireflies around us—"are these spirits, too? How did they get here from the spirit world? And if you're a spirit, how come you look like a human?"

Alder sat back on his heels, squeezing the space between his eyebrows. "This is going to be difficult." Then he sighed and lifted his head to fix me with his unreal, gold stare. "Yes, you did travel to the spirit world, but the more accurate term for it is the ethereal plane. It is the boundary between two planes of existence—the physical plane and the astral plane. The physical is made entirely of matter, while the astral plane is made entirely of energy. So the ethereal plane is—"

"A combination of the two," I said, thinking of the solid trees encased in magical energy.

Alder gave a tight nod. "And wisps are proof that this valley is connected to the spirit world. Places in the world that contain ethereal planes, like this valley, can't exist without energy from the planes bleeding over—that's the wisps."

"So you're saying they're…spirits of pure energy?"

"Yes, mana."

"Mana?"

"The aura that you saw. It's what we call energy from the astral plane."

"*We?*"

"Myself and other spirits."

"Right. Okay, sure," I muttered, lifting my gaze to the stars again. "So that creature I saw, with the clover growing out of its back, that was a spirit?"

"Yes."

I was dying to know more about the little spirit squirrel—if it talked, if it had any powers—but I held back. That wasn't what was important. I had to focus on rescuing Mom so I could learn more about my past and the night of the fire.

As a breeze picked up and whistled through the trees, I could've sworn I heard her voice echo softly, *"You must unlock the gates by the sunset of the summer solstice."*

My nerves spiked, like I'd just forgotten a test I'd had to study for—yet a thousand times worse. I had less than a week to find these spirit gates and I knew absolutely nothing about them.

Focus, Brye.

"What are spirit gates, and how do I unlock them?"

At that, Alder blinked and stood, his mouth opening and closing. "Who told you about them? What spirit did you meet?"

"It wasn't a spirit. When I fell off the cliff," I said, suppressing a shiver at the fear the memory induced, "I met…my mom."

"Your…your mother? But I thought she left you…left the valley."

"Well, you're half right. She did leave me," I said, somewhat bitterly, "but apparently she never got out of the valley. She said that she can't leave the spirit world and that the only way to save her is for me to open these spirit gates. Do you know what she's talking about?"

Alder was already shaking his head before I'd even finished. "Brye, humans aren't able to exist in the spirit world. That's just not possible."

I scowled, standing up, too. "You're talking to a human who was there *literally ten minutes ago.*"

"You're different!" he protested, raising his hands, palms up.

I wasn't buying it. If I was going to help Mom, I had to figure out what made me "special" as she'd called it. Maybe

I could use that to help her escape.

Besides, I'd come here to learn about myself. Who I'd been. And this was it.

"Are you aware of how ridiculous that sounds?" I pressed. "There has to be a *reason,* all right? Tell me!"

"It's difficult to explain—"

"Is it because a dark wizard used a killing curse on me as a baby and I survived?" It was a joke, of course, but I did have scars.

Alder rolled his eyes, making a sound of exasperation in his throat.

"Am I actually a Jedi? A demigod? A lost moon princess? *What?*" I pushed, each question getting louder.

"It's because of ME!" Alder exploded, throwing his hands up. A gust of wind blew around us, tossing my hair off my shoulders and scattering the wisps in every direction.

Breathing hard, Alder lowered his hands, while his chest rose and fell with each labored breath, and his eyes burned like the sun. "It's because of *me*, all right?"

I was a little thrown off by the wind trick, but I could see from his pained expression that his anger wasn't directed at me. It was at himself. "What do you mean?"

He sighed, holding out his hand. "Give me your hand. I'll show you."

Tentatively, I took a step toward him and reached for his hand. Then hesitated.

"Don't worry," Alder said quietly. "I'd never hurt you."

Glancing at the bracelet around his wrist, I said, "Okay." Then I placed my hand in his.

At first, I felt nothing.

Then I gasped, my fingers tightening around his involuntarily, reacting to the senses coursing inside me.

Pounding of deer hooves against hard-packed earth. Taste of mint and sassafras. Leaves brushing against skin. Scent of dogwood and elm.

The Smokies.

Alder dropped my hand. I was glad he did, because I wasn't sure if I would've been able to. I was still trembling slightly at the intense rush of feelings. "What was *that*?"

"That," he said, "was a healthy dose of mana."

"Mana? As in the astral energy?"

"Yes, every spirit possesses it, but I have more than most, since I'm the only spirit allowed to walk in the physical plane. When we were kids, I couldn't control it as well as I do now. Every time we played tag, or anytime we touched, you would absorb some of my mana." He paused, looking off in the distance, seeing something I couldn't. "Some days you had so much that it was hard to tell the difference between you and any other spirit."

"So because I had the mana of a nature spirit, I was able to pass into the spirit realm?"

Alder nodded.

"Then how is my mom there now? Did she get mana, too?"

He folded his arms. "I never gave any to her. That's why I'm saying she can't be there."

"Well, she was," I snapped. *Wasn't she?* It had been six years, and maybe I'd hallucinated that part while the rest had been real… *No.* If anything, she had been the *most* real.

"Look, just tell me how to open these spirit gates so I can get her out of there by the time of the summer solstice."

Alder dropped his arms, his jaw tightening as he stared back at me. "Are you sure she said summer solstice?"

"As sure as I am that there needed to be a Black Widow movie. Why?"

"That's when the boundary is the thinnest between the three worlds."

"So you believe me?"

"It was never that I didn't..." Alder sighed and cast his eyes skyward. After a few moments, he looked back at me in what seemed to be his cat-five intensity stare. "Brye, having this mana inside you...it's dangerous. You should go. Let me try to find your mom myself."

"No." That came out a little harsh, but there was no way I was relying on a *stranger* to do this for me. I had too much on the line. "I'm not leaving here until I get answers. So while I appreciate your concern for me, I'm going to open these spirit gates myself."

Chapter Eight

"You don't know how to open them," Alder pointed out. "Or where they even are."

I scowled at him. "My mother said she'd send me some kind of...um, what are those people called that are like representatives? Ambassadors?"

"An emissary?"

"Sure, one of those," I said, waving my hand in dismissal as I turned on my heel to head toward the charred house not far off, set against the darkening sky. "When my helper shows up, he'll take me to the gates. Until then, I'm going home." As much as I wanted to get moving on my mission, Gran and Izzie were waiting for me, and I'd left in such a rush. If I wasn't careful, they'd have a missing person report filed on me soon.

Behind me, Alder's footsteps quickened to catch up. "What answers are you looking for?"

"Are you serious?" I twisted around so suddenly he almost ran into me, and he took a step back. "For starters, I want to know why Mom left. And then I want to know more about this whole..." I gestured at the surrounding firefly-wisps. "I mean, I lost the first ten years of my life. How would *you* feel?"

Alder's brows scrunched together in what looked like pity. "Brye, you can't get those memories back."

"I know," I said quickly, turning back toward the car. "I know that."

We were quiet as we walked, but the rest of the forest was not. Owls hooted, crickets chirped, and the flap of wings made me wonder if a cave was nearby with a family of bats. The wisps, meanwhile, hadn't left us. They followed Alder as if tethered by invisible leashes. The sight was strange, but incredibly beautiful.

At last, my old house, burned and half destroyed, loomed over us as we picked our way through the overgrowth toward Izzie's car.

When I got to the car door, I felt Alder's hand on my arm. Turning back to tell him I had to get going, my voice failed me at the look on his face.

It was so open, vulnerable, and pleading that I couldn't *not* let him talk.

"You really should leave," Alder said. "It's safer for you away from here."

I could tell he meant it. That he truly was worried. And to be honest, I wasn't exactly stoked about the idea of roaming around a valley and a spirit world, where things erupted into flames at a moment's notice. But now that my past was within reach, I wasn't going anywhere. Not this time.

"Good night, Alder," I said, getting into the car.

"Brye..." As I was about to close the door, he caught it, and with his other arm on the top of the door frame, he leaned down. His navy shirt pulled up only slightly to reveal a thin strip of copper skin. "Look, I honestly don't know much about them myself. But I do know they're not what you think they are. These gates... Each one is controlled by an element."

"Like earth, water, and all that?"

He nodded. "Yes, there are four of them, and each one is protected by a guardian."

"What kind of guardian?"

Alder's lips twisted to the side, clearly reluctant to say more.

Frustrated, I started to close the door on him. My mystery emissary would be more helpful.

"Wait." He stopped the door again. "I don't think this is a good idea, but if you insist on going through with this, then let me go with you. I can help. Meet me back here. Tomorrow morning."

I started to tell him I didn't need him, but then he moved a bit closer. His eyes roamed my face, and I could bet that he was comparing the ten-year-old me with the sixteen-year-old me. Straight teeth, fewer freckles, tamer hair, though still wild.

"I really missed you," he murmured, his autumn breath against my cheeks. "What made you come back?"

My pulse was weirdly erratic, with him so near. "I told you, my gran broke her—"

"No, to this house. What made you come back here?"

"Oh," I said, remembering. "They're going to bulldoze it down tomorrow. I figured this was my last chance."

"What?" Alder's tan skin seemed to pale significantly. After a moment, he pounded his fist on the roof of the car. Before I could ask him anything else, he turned and headed back into the growth of the forest.

• • •

The drive back to Gran's was a blur. Thank God my brain was actually working in the background, telling me what highway to get on, and what road to turn off. When I finally did pull into her gravel driveway, the sound of the rocks under my tires reminded me of the crunch of Alder's steps on the pebbled lakeshore.

I wished he were a stranger to me. I wished I could start from square one, get to know him, and determine my opinion of him. Like anyone else. I *definitely* wished he was just any other human.

But it wasn't that simple, because the void in my chest seemed to respond to him like a moon to a planet—there seemed to be this unexplainable gravitational pull. It was somehow *painful* to be next to him, to talk to him, and yet I had never felt more comfortable with someone I'd just met. He was a walking personification of the contradiction between my heart and mind. And I knew that everything he'd said was true.

We had been friends. The best of friends. It wasn't just the proof of the friendship bracelet, but the way he looked at me and the concern in his voice. The use of my nickname and my own weird, inexplicable feelings.

I rested my head against the steering wheel, trying to drive his face out of my mind.

A light to my left suddenly came on.

For a moment, I was terrified that the firefly spirits had formed into a much larger spirit, but it was just the front porch light.

Izzie emerged from the house, and I could tell from her face that I was in *huge* trouble.

After getting out of the CRV, I climbed the porch steps, preparing myself for the lecture of my life.

Izzie wacked me on my arm with a dish towel. "Good grief, Brye, when I handed you that phone I thought you'd be gone three hours—tops. Not the whole damn day!"

"I know, I'm sorry. I got lost," I said, finding it too easy to sound guilty. "These road signs are hard to make out, and you don't exactly get great reception out here."

Izzie's eyes narrowed and she was quiet for so long, I thought for sure she'd grill me with more questions, but then she sighed and shoved the towel into my hands. "You're washing dishes, and good luck, there's a mountain of them. By the way, I told Willa that your dad had forgotten something for his business trip so you had to go all the way back to Knoxville and FedEx it to him."

I blinked, surprised. It was a reasonable excuse, and I was grateful to her. But I could tell when my best friend was pissed. And why shouldn't she be? I wasn't being honest with her. I was a rotten liar.

"Izzie..."

She stopped, her hand on the door. Without turning around to look at me, she said, "Look, Brye, you don't have to tell me everything. Lord knows you have your reasons for being as closed off as you are. But I've been your friend long enough to know when you're not telling me the whole story. I don't like being lied to, even if it's just a lie by omission, but...know that I'm here for you. Whenever you're ready to talk, I'm ready to listen."

In that moment, I *did* want to tell her. About everything—Alder, Mom, the wisps, the ethereal plane, the spirit gates...

But what if she didn't believe me? I barely believed it myself. How could I prove it to her? I didn't know if all humans could see spirits like I could. Was that part of what made me "special"? And what if she never looked at me the same way again?

I *couldn't* lose Izzie.

I took a deep breath. "Thanks, Iz. I appreciate it."

After making sure Gran had everything she needed for bed, I took a long hot shower and turned toward my attic bedroom, the one Gran was letting me use. Seeing the door at the top of the steps, another feeling of nostalgia crept up my back and squeezed my shoulders.

Rolling them back to get rid of the strange sensation, I climbed the steps. As the stairs creaked underfoot, I remembered each sound so clearly that I must've gone up these at least a million times before.

The attic wasn't a "suburban attic" with boxes and insulation everywhere. Instead, it was a finished room with sloped ceilings and a braided rug on the wood floors. There was a twin bed in the corner with a bedside table and a reading lamp. A shelf with old toys and picture books huddled in the other corner, along with a dresser with an old mirror on top. I crossed to a window, pushed it open, and let the musty air out and the fresh air in. Although it was dark, thanks to the light of the moon and stars I could see beyond Gran's garden. The same lake stretched from the shores of the nearest mountain all the way to a large meadow. Along its edges were more trees, more flowers—nature as far as the eye could see.

The attic obviously hadn't been used for some time. The entire room seemed to be covered in a thick layer of dust. It was so bad I was about to grab my inhaler from my bag, when I remembered I no longer needed it.

I sat on my bed and the springs squeaked beneath me.

Groaning, I collapsed sideways onto the pillow. As much as I didn't want to sleep on a bed that was noisy, I knew I'd rather sleep up here than where Izzie was—in the bed of the woman who'd abandoned me and my dad.

I doubted that I'd ever be able to fall asleep after everything that had happened, but as soon as I closed my eyes, I passed out.

The couch cushions were well worn and loved. They were big fluffy things. I felt like I could get sucked into the cracks of the couch, like the remote control sometimes did, or loose change out of Dad's pockets.

I cuddled into the throw pillows, nuzzling my cheek against the soft tassels, and as I did, a strange smell tickled my nose. For a moment, I couldn't place it. It smelled like a fireplace, or the stove after Mom left the bacon on too long.

Burning.

Tearing the pillow away from my face, I flung it against the wall, the whole thing smoking. The tassels that had once been against my face now burned, smoldering black and red like embers.

The smell got stronger. I looked down—I really was sinking into the couch. But the cushions were burning, too.

I wrenched my eyes open with a sharp gasp. The attic rafters, turned a hazy gold with the early morning sunlight, stared back down at me, reminding me where I was. Sighing, I scrubbed my hand over my face, trying to pull myself out of the remnants of the dream.

Just a nightmare. I was used to them, but this one had been more detailed than ever before. My body felt heavy with sleep. As I began to lift myself on my elbows, yawning, I dropped my gaze—and found a fox sleeping on top of me.

Chapter Nine

"Holy shit!" I twisted and jerked, falling off the narrow twin bed with a *thump*, twisted in the covers. Meanwhile, the fox leaped gracefully to the floor.

I clapped my hand over my mouth, listening for any sounds of movement downstairs from Izzie or Gran. Nothing. Apparently they hadn't heard me. Hopefully they were still sleeping.

The fox lazily blinked eyes that were dark emerald green, similar to the human version of Alder, and slanted, vixen-like, same as Mom's and mine.

But its body was *see-through.*

It was a spirit. A large spirit fox had been sleeping on top of me.

"It's about time you woke up."

Luckily my hands were still over my mouth, because I let out another scream—this one muffled.

The words had come from the fox. Its translucent body had glowed brighter as it tilted its head in the way that animals do.

It *talked.*

The fox arched its back like a cat and stretched. Then it yawned, its long pink tongue rolling out to reveal glistening white fangs.

"Calm down, Briony. Weren't you expecting me?"

Once again, the voice clearly came from the fox, but his mouth hadn't moved. Of course, I wasn't sure if that would make the experience any less creepy.

I tried to focus on what he had said. I was expecting… "Oh! You're the emissary."

"Well done. How clever of you."

Great, he'd been blessed with sarcasm. "Excuse me for freaking out when I find a nature spirit using me for a bed," I grumbled, ripping off my cocoon of covers, and then stood. "So you're here to show me how to open the spirit gates?"

The fox looped around me and headed for the attic door, his little spirit paws not making a sound as he padded across the rug. *"Yes, so let's get started."*

I darted to cover the door to prevent the fox from going downstairs and scaring my grandmother into cardiac arrest. "Whoa, slow down there, Mr. Fox. I need to put on actual clothes first. I'll meet you outside."

The fox huffed and shook his head. *"Humans are such a bother. Hurry up. We don't have much time before the solstice."*

I was about to ask him just how long opening these gates would take, when he vanished entirely. His body had grown more and more translucent until it was gone altogether.

Now alone in my attic bedroom, I rushed around, breathless, throwing on clothes and sneakers. I could hardly believe this was happening. Yesterday when I'd said I was going to open the gates, it already seemed like it had been a dream. But it hadn't. Now I had a see-through fox telling me to hurry my ass up so we could get moving.

As I was creeping down the steps, trying not to make a noise that would wake up Izzie or Gran, I thought about Alder and his offer to help me.

As immensely curious as I was about him, his warnings weighed on me heavily. He said he wanted me to leave this valley. Who's to say he wouldn't try to thwart me somehow? If this fox showed me where to go, I could skip out on my meeting with Alder at my old house. I'd never said I'd meet him there anyway. He'd just told me to and assumed I would.

After scribbling a quick note to Izzie that I was going back to my old house, I grabbed her keys and headed out the door, wincing at the slow creak of the screen door as it closed.

I absolutely hated dodging and sneaking around my best friend, and I knew that this couldn't be my solution forever, but as this fox had reminded me, I had so little time. The summer solstice was less than a week away and no one had yet shared how far these gates were away or how difficult they would be to open.

The idea of leaving Izzie disappointed and hurt made my gut twist, so I promised myself that I would tell her as soon as I saw her again. So what if she looked at me like I was crazy? I had to take that chance. She was the closest friend I had, like a sister even.

Moving through Gran's garden toward Izzie's car, I scanned the rhododendrons and black-eyed Susans and the rest of her overgrown weeds and flowers, looking for my new orange, green-eyed friend. "Psst. Mr. Fox? Where are you?" I hissed.

After moving around the garden for far too long looking for him, I stomped over to the car and yanked the door open. Maybe I would have to rely on Alder after all.

Scratch that.

The fox was in the passenger seat.

"Son of a—" I gasped, jumping back and banging my hip against the open door. "You *must* stop that."

"Stop what?"

I slid into the car, buckling my seat belt. "Forget it, just tell me where to go. Is there some magical rainbow highway that will take us to the spirit world?"

"Just go north. I'll tell you when to stop."

North. As if everyone knew where north was. But even if there hadn't been a compass on Izzie's dashboard, I actually would've known. The sunrise was telling, how the sun was still working its way over the eastern mountain ridge to my left, but I could also just *feel* it. I didn't know how.

I shifted the car in reverse, did a three-point turn, and then started down the long gravel driveway, taking a left onto the highway.

As we drove, the fox was silent and immobile. His green eyes were set on the moving forest, and his translucent body would sometimes get lost in a passing shadow.

Unnerved, I decided I had to talk to him. If he wasn't going to offer any information, I needed to ask as much as I could. "So my mom called you an emissary. What does that mean exactly?"

"I'm your link to the spirit world. I'll guide you on finding the gates and opening them."

"You mean like a spirit guide?"

The fox huffed out a breath through his nose, fogging up the window glass. *"Well, I am a spirit, and I am your guide, but I wouldn't use that term. Putting aside that it can mean different things to different human cultures, it implies that I care about your spiritual well-being and the path your life is taking… I don't."*

"Gee, thanks."

"I'm here to ensure you open the gates. What happens afterward for you is not my concern."

Well, at least he was honest about it. "Okay, do you at

least have a name that I can call you?"

The fox turned away from the window to face me. *"I have many names, as do most spirits, but you may call me Raysh. As for what I am, I am a projection of a spirit from the ethereal plane. My true body cannot exist in the physical plane."*

Hence the see-through factor.

"But Alder can walk in the physical plane and *he's* a spirit," I said. In fact, I recalled Alder had mentioned that he was the *only* spirit, apart from the wisps, that could walk in the physical plane. "So like…what's his deal?" I asked, "How can *he* be here but other spirits can't?"

Raysh's tail swished and his eyes narrowed, as if the mention of Alder was irritating.

"That boy is an anchor to the planes of existence. Think of them as three leaves fluttering in the wind. Alone, they twist and twirl midair, apart from each other. But when on a branch, they are connected, and a bug can travel from one leaf to another. Alder is that branch."

"Okay, he's a branch. Sure." Keeping one hand on the steering wheel, I rubbed my temple, where a headache began to form. "So what's in it for you? Why did you agree to be my emissary?"

Raysh looked back out the window. *"I'm almost as old as time itself. You cannot imagine the monotony of seeing the same things day after day. Being an emissary allows me to see a new world."* His voice felt heavier somehow, laced with longing.

Sensing that was a delicate topic, I moved past it. "Can you tell me more about how these gates work? For example, how am I supposed to unlock one?"

"Each gate is attached to an element of the physical world. The elements are the building blocks of the physical world, but

they cannot exist without mana. So the gates are essentially pools of mana that make up the elements in the physical world. They serve as pillars to the astral realm."

"So how will opening them allow Mom to come home?"

"Unlocking the gates merely allows the mana to flow freely. Humans can then pass through the barriers that would have otherwise been blocked off to them."

"But how did she get there in the first place?" I asked. "Did she go there on purpose? Did she leave and then just accidentally fall down a rabbit hole?"

"Rabbit holes would be too big for humans."

Why would I have thought a spirit fox would get that reference? "No, I just meant, did she actually stumble upon it through some weird portal?"

"You'd have to ask your mother. Stop here and turn."

Almost slamming on my brakes, I just barely managed to swerve down a side road. *Hummingbird Road.*

Chills danced across my arms as I thought of Alder waiting for me there. "Hold up. Why are we going to my old house?"

"We need the human spirit to assist you in opening the gates."

More chills. "You mean Alder. Why?"

Raysh's lips rippled back, baring his white teeth. *"I don't like it, either, girl, but we need him. He is a product of all three worlds, and since the gates are as well, they require his touch."*

"So you're saying I can't open the gates without his help?"

"Yes."

"But Mom said only *I* could unlock the gates."

"Yes."

Finally, I stopped the car entirely to turn and stare at the fox in my front seat. "*Both* of us have to?"

"Yes."

I leaned back, trying to process this new information. I had to work with him to open the gates. Had to. There was no way this would go well. For one thing, Alder hadn't been too thrilled about this whole quest. It seemed like the only reason he was coming was because he wanted to make sure I didn't get myself lost or eaten by some spirit. For another, I didn't even trust my classmate to write half of our science report, how the hell was I going to trust a tight-lipped, ethereal nature boy who kept telling me to get lost to do something he didn't even want to do in the first place?

"Where the hell is my house?" I exploded, slapping my palms on the dashboard. I couldn't explain it. I'd been here *just* yesterday. I was already at the end of the road and I didn't see a single gravel path to turn down.

Raysh stood on his hind legs, placing his paws on the window. *"We don't need the house. Just him."*

I looked to the right and, sure enough, Alder stood off the side of the road, under the shade of a large tulip tree, leaning against the trunk.

As I parked Izzie's CRV on the shoulder, I could see that he had reverted back to his more human-looking self. Gone were silver and gold, replaced with blond hair and eyes the color of the leaves he stood under.

While I had been grilling Raysh, I had gone up and down the street twice, and the burned house was nowhere in sight. Had the bulldozers come early? Was my house already leveled, its rubble transported away? That fast?

But then my gaze caught on a strip of white gravel running along the side of the road not far from where we were standing. The beginnings of a driveway. The only problem, of course, was that there was no driveway, just an entire wall of thick trees.

Had he…? How…?

Alder watched me carefully, clearly waiting for my reaction while I put two and two together. I opened my mouth and then closed it, pressing my tongue to the roof of my mouth to prevent myself from saying anything I would regret.

The truth was I wasn't sure what to say or how to feel. I didn't need to see it myself to know Alder had somehow caused an entire copse of trees to grow overnight. Obviously a nature spirit would be able to make plants grow, but a miniature forest? That was impressive. His trees now shielded my house from view—all to keep the bulldozers from finding it and tearing it down.

At least, that felt like the only plausible explanation.

Alder's eyes narrowed at the fox sitting by my ankles. "The emissary, I take it?"

I glanced down at Raysh, who didn't seem thrilled to meet Alder either. Did spirits get along? "Um, yeah, this is Raysh. He said he can show us where the gates are."

Alder tore his gaze away from the fox to look at me, his brows lifting. "Us? So you do want me to come along?"

My stomach flipped. "Well, apparently, I need your help to be able to open them."

Alder tilted his head, his brow furrowing. "How's that?"

"Good question," I muttered.

Like Alder had said last night, he really didn't know much about the gates, including, apparently, the fact that I needed his help to unlock them in the first place. He'd offered his help last night purely on an *I don't want you to do this alone* mentality.

Nice of him, but unnecessary. I'd rather trust myself to do something than trust a total stranger.

Only now it looked like I was forced to work with not one, but two strangers.

I turned to the fox. "You want to walk us through how this is supposed to work, O furry one?"

"A gate can only be opened by bringing its key into the physical world."

I folded my arms. This endeavor seemed to get more daunting by the minute. "No one mentioned a key."

Raysh shot me an annoyed look. *"All gates have keys. Unfortunately, the key cannot be stolen by a spirit."*

"Why not?"

"The guardians that hold the keys are powerful, ancient beings. Stealing from one of them is taboo for a spirit, and besides, we are bound to the elements they control. So only you can get the key, Briony."

I folded my arms. "Then why do I need Alder?"

"Bringing the key to the physical world is only part of the process of unlocking the gate. It must also be combined with the mana of its element. Alder is the only one able to infuse the key with enough mana to unlock the gate."

I imagined opening an old treasure chest under a giant tree, and then a little victory tune went off as I pulled out an old-fashioned brass key and held it up over my head—like in one of those old video games that Izzie's older brother played. It was what had come to mind, but truthfully, I didn't know what to expect. I glanced at Alder to gauge his reaction.

He was already staring at me with an unreadable expression. "You *need* me to help you, but you don't *want* me to."

My cheeks burned for some reason, because it wasn't that I didn't... My history with Alder had to be the definition of *complicated*. That feeling that I kept having whenever he'd touch my arm or hand, or even being in the same presence as me? It wasn't just nostalgia. It was loss. I'd lost something very dear when I'd forgotten this boy in front of me.

And I wasn't quite ready to face it.

Hugging my arms, I muttered, "What do you expect? I don't remember you and you haven't exactly been helpful. All of yesterday you told me to get lost."

"That's only because I don't want to see you hurt again."

The void in my chest gave another groan of pain. I took a breath. "Well, this might be the one chance I have to actually… heal. Living with over half my life missing hasn't exactly been easy."

Silence followed my confession, and he stared down at me. I could only return his intense look with one of my own.

"Might I remind you both we have a gate to open? Or shall the two of you just keep gazing at each other?" Raysh's voice floated up as he licked his paw nonchalantly.

Both of us flinched and looked away. My cheeks were hot, and Alder's neck was red. Dumb fox.

Clearing his throat, Alder stepped through the tree line and was swallowed by the shadows of the thick canopy of leaves above. "Then let's get going."

Twenty minutes of walking later, we came to a grove of yellow birch trees. I could almost picture this place in the fall months when the trees would be a golden yellow. Leaves would shiver in the autumn wind, one gust away from floating to the forest floor, but right now, they were a soft lime-green and shaped like teardrops with strong veins running horizontally across.

Raysh stopped in the middle of the grove, sitting down

and swishing his wispy tail right through the grass. *"Here is good."*

I looked around, trying to find some mystical gate. For whatever reason, I almost expected a gate made of clouds. "Good for what? Is the first gate invisible or something?"

"The gate is in the ethereal plane," Alder explained. "Although, I don't know where exactly. Luckily, the fox does." If I wasn't mistaken, I could trace a small amount of bitterness there.

"There are many things you don't know," Raysh huffed. *"Spirit though you might be, you have the heart of a human. And because of that, you will never be one of us."*

Alder said nothing in reply to the odd comment, but I noticed the brief look of pain cross his face, and I found myself wondering what that had meant. He could look like a human, sure, but what parts of him specifically were spirit?

"Whatever. Let's just cross over," Alder said, his tone short with irritation. He paused then held his hand out to me. "You'll need to hang on."

I stared at his hand, remembering what I'd felt the last time I held it. The Smokies coursing through me like oxygen in my bloodstream. The effect had been addicting and intoxicating—thrilling. I hadn't wanted to let go of him.

It had also been slightly terrifying. Too intense.

My gaze drifted to the friendship bracelet around his wrist.

I'd trusted him once. Enough to go into the world with him when I'd been a little kid. I had to do it again.

I reached for his hand and, like a magnet, I latched onto him. His fingers laced with mine.

The autumn chill going through me. The smell of flowering mountain laurel and dogwood in my nose. A warm fluttering in my stomach.

Before I could place the last sensation, Alder moved forward and I followed, my feet clumsy and heavy with awareness of my own physical body. It had never felt like a burden before, but it did now. I was like a weight falling to the bottom of a pool.

I was about to open my mouth to ask Alder to slow down, when I felt the slipstream encase us once more. Wind rippled around me, like I was breaking through something—a net or a web—made of a substance lighter than air. Mist curled around our calves, reaching our hips, blowing up into my hair and painting my skin with the energy. It made my body buzz and my pulse race. It felt so *alive.*

It whirled and curled around my limbs, and Alder tightened his hold on my hand.

Then all of a sudden, he stopped—so quick and so fast that I fell against him. His arm curled around my shoulders and steadied me against his chest. His heart thudded under my ear and Raysh's words came to mind: *you have the heart of a human.*

Pushing the thought aside, I stepped forward, away from Alder's chest.

"You okay?" he asked.

"I'm fine," I answered, blinking against the bright glow of the surrounding trees. Immediately I recognized that they were the same birch trees as the grove we'd been standing in a half minute before, but instead of green, they were now yellow. The color of their name.

The entire grove glowed gold, the mana pulsing gently around tree bark and leaves.

"They changed," I breathed, watching as a mustard-yellow leaf trembled and fluttered to the ground.

"In the ethereal plane, the trees take on their best form. For the yellow birch, it's in the autumn, where the leaves stop photosynthesis and rest, and the trees can finally relax."

Instead of staring at the forest around us, I took in Alder's appearance. He was back to being shades of copper, gold, and silver. His spirit form.

"Is that what happens with you?"

He glanced down at me, raising an eyebrow. "What?"

I gestured to his silvery-white hair. "Is this your best form?"

That earned me a tiny smile as he shook his head. "It's my true form. I hide it during the day in case humans see me."

"Can you not control it at night?" I asked, thinking of the moment by the lakeshore when he had transformed before me as the sun went down.

"I could, but it already takes a lot of concentration to hide the wisps."

I drew in a sharp breath, realization hitting me. "That's why they're disguised as fireflies—you hide them."

Alder nodded. "The wisps can easily be seen at night—so I hide them as fireflies. But in the daytime, it's me who needs to be hidden."

"This way," Raysh said, trotting up the path, not bothering to wait for us.

"Stick close. Do *not* wander and…try not to touch anything," Alder instructed as we wove our way through the gold trees. Their mana brushed against my skin, and I could taste their fresh winter mint scent and feel the sun on their leaves. My whole body grew warm with it.

From the grove emerged a path that curved this way and that, serpentining upward at a slight incline. Growth was absolutely everywhere, making the forest much darker than the yellow grove of birches. The trees seemed to get larger with each step I took, and as I peered farther into the woods, I could've sworn they were so thick and large that they felt closer to the size of California redwoods, rather than the slimmer sugar maple trees I knew them to be. Their unique leaf shape of five points, smaller than the normal Canadian maple leaf, was familiar to me, even though I knew I'd never really come across any sugar maples in Knoxville.

It was then I realized why I was able to identify plants with just a glance. Maybe having the astral energy of a nature spirit made you a botanist without the fancy PhD. Go figure.

Or maybe Alder had just taught them all to me and I'd retained them somehow.

Either way, I was able to tell when the scenery became… unnatural.

For the most part, the changes of the forest within the ethereal plane were subtle, besides the obvious increase in size. The moss climbing the trees wasn't just green, but a rich aquamarine, a full-color spectrum from lime to violet. The flowers themselves were illuminated, glowing with a mystical aura.

We passed bishop's cap, tiny white flowers that grew up long green stems. They shined so bright white that it was like walking through a forest of Christmas lights. Several times I had to force my feet forward when all I wanted to do was stand and gawk at the resplendent world around me. More colorful flowers, like fire pinks, purple phacelias, and blue phloxes decorated the trail that Alder led us down. The colors were more saturated, more vibrant than what should've been real.

I ached to touch one. To bend down and smell their petals and *feel* their mana. Surely each one was unique and special in their own right.

As if Alder sensed my temptation, he kept glancing back at me.

Finally, I couldn't take it anymore. "Okay, *why* can't I touch anything?"

"Because you're a human."

"So?"

"You don't belong here."

"Raysh." Alder glared at the fox then gave me a sheepish glance. "There are parts of this world that could harm you."

I glanced at the glowing flowers and sugar maple leaves surrounded by the soft green mist. They certainly didn't look threatening.

"*Flowers* are dangerous?"

"Let's just say you shouldn't risk it."

"Huh. That's comforting."

He chuckled. "Hey, you asked." He paused ahead to lift a branch for me. As I made my way between the trees and under the canopy of branches, I found a rabbit sitting where I'd been just about to step. If it had been any other *normal*-looking rabbit, I might not have leaped a foot in the air, but as this one was covered in moss and had purple flowers where its tail should be, I couldn't help it.

With a yelp, I jumped back, the top of my head hitting Alder in the chin. Rubbing his jaw, he steadied me. "It's just a sprite."

"Which is what exactly?" I planted a hand over my racing heart.

The rabbit tilted its head. Did it know we were talking about it? Could it understand us?

"It's a nature spirit but doesn't possess much mana," Alder explained, then added, "It's not, um, cognizant."

"You mean it's not like Raysh. It can't talk."

"It can't talk to humans," Raysh sniffed. *"I can hear it talking just fine."*

I started to kneel to get a closer look at the sprite, when

the ground shook under my feet. At the tremor, the bunny sprite scampered off into the undergrowth.

Alder and I froze while Raysh continued along as if nothing were amiss.

"Was that..." I started as the earth once again trembled.

"I'm guessing we're close," Alder said, reaching for my hand.

When he took it, I didn't feel anything this time—no Smoky Mountain senses running through me, or anything at all, actually. Merely his pressure and his hold.

I glanced at him, confused as to why I couldn't feel *any* of him. Not the texture or warmth of his skin. It was as if he cut off *all* sensation from me. Was that the only way to prevent him from giving any mana to me?

The ground shook again, and I refocused. "What the hell is happening? Is this an earthquake?"

Earthquakes were common in Tennessee, but barely noticeable—nothing like *this.*

Geography class taught me that the Madrid Fault ran right through West Tennessee, and the Eastern Tennessee Seismic Zone was a hotbed of activity. Seismographs in the Tuckaleechee Caverns outside of Townsend often recorded quakes with a magnitude of two or smaller, but most people didn't feel them at all.

"Remember how I told you there were guardians?" Alder asked as we cleared the bend in the trees and came to the edge of a vast green meadow.

I gasped, involuntarily squeezing Alder's hand.

A beautiful buck stood in the middle of the meadow, easily larger than any deer I'd ever seen. From this distance it looked more the size of a moose—big, powerful, imposing. A king of the forest.

Other than the creature's antlers, and its unnatural size,

it appeared to be a normal white-tailed deer. The antlers, though...were not antlers at all. They were branches. Branches that extended outward at least two feet, decorated with leaves, vines, and budding flowers.

The great buck reared back on its haunches and came down hard on its front hooves, and the earth...trembled.

Chapter Ten

I lost my balance as the ground shook with the force of an earthquake.

Alder caught me easily, wrapping his arm around my waist, his gaze concentrated on the buck in front of us. "Welcome to the source of all the seismic activity in South Appalachia, Brye."

"Otherwise known as the earth gate," Raysh said, moving around my calves.

"That's…incredible," I breathed, reeling over the fact that the Eastern Tennessee Seismic Zone was all the work of a single nature spirit. As much as I was dying to find out more about that, the monstrous buck was a tad more pressing. "Please don't tell me we have to beat this guy to get this so-called key you mentioned?" Now it *really* felt like a video game. A big boss battle to claim the key to escaping the dungeon.

The buck reared and slammed its hooves onto the ground, causing a larger, angrier tremor to run under our feet. This time, the force was enough to cause leaves to shower down on us, and I reflexively squeezed Alder's arm around my waist. How could he be so unaffected? He was like a tree, standing solid and strong.

Well, he *was* a nature spirit. I was still getting used to that fact.

"The key is part of the guardian itself and that of its element. Something that can be removed. Stolen."

"Part of the..." I scanned the great buck, from his powerful onyx hooves to the sharp prongs of his wood-antlers, realizing it could only be one thing. "Oh, no freaking way. I have to take its freaking *antler*?"

"Technically it's a branch."

"How in the three-planes-of-existence am I supposed to take an *antler*?"

"I'm sure you'll think of something," Raysh replied. *"Unless you don't."*

Great, this fox was both sarcastic *and* condescending.

"Yeah? Well, right now I'm thinking you'd make a nice fur coat," I snapped.

"They see us," Alder murmured by my ear, voice tense but still calm.

With a chill, I lifted my gaze to the large nature spirit in the middle of the meadow. Sure enough, the buck was glaring right at us, and its breath came out in angry puffs through its wet black nose. But the breath wasn't just air—it looked like clouds of shimmering energy, blowing out like a snorting bull in a cartoon.

I needed to figure out a way to get the key, but my mind was drawing a blank. Should we have waited till it slept? Did guardians sleep? I could loop around through the forest and find a way to come up behind it. Or climb a tree and somehow jump onto its back.

Before I could really think through either one of these plans, the buck charged.

Alder set me aside, stepping forward then crouching to place his hands on the ground. "Go!"

From his hands a shimmery mist rushed out like water from a faucet, pouring mana into the earth. The trees and flowers vibrated with a different kind of energy—Alder's energy.

Raysh nipped at my ankles, and I snapped out of my trance. Heart pounding, I backed into the nearest tree, my hands scrabbling to find purchase against the bark.

"What's the worst that thing could do? It's just a really large deer," I muttered to myself.

"You're right. It's completely harmless with its earth-shaking hooves and sharpened wooden stakes attached to its head."

And those wooden stakes were racing right toward Alder at an unnatural speed.

The instinct to run to him propelled my legs forward, but Raysh tugged on my shorts with his teeth, stopping me. *"Don't you dare,"* he growled.

I was about to swat the fox away when Alder's mana rippled throughout the meadow like a wave swelling across an ocean.

And like an ocean, a tsunami followed.

The ground *moved* under Alder's command. Not just a tremor like an earthquake, but an entire layer of earth shifted and rose upward, as if being pushed by some sort of creature underneath. The churning mound of dirt, grass, roots, rocks, and all rushed toward the guardian, but it didn't stop its charge. Didn't even blink. It rammed head-on into the mound of earth.

For a split second, I was worried the attack might've harmed the stag, but the next second the ground exploded from the collision of the buck's branches and the pack of hard earth. Dirt, pebbles, flecks of grass, and even the wildflowers on top flew apart like bomb fragments. And it *felt* like a bomb explosion. A blast of force—magical or physical—seemed to shake the trees and rumble the meadow. It even made my ears ring. But the guardian merely shook its head in irritation, a few flowers, leaves, and twigs falling from its branches.

The moment the twig-antlers fell to the earth, grass grew, flowers sprouted, tree saplings broke through the ground.

Chills raced through me. The stag's antlers held mana, probably specific to the earth gate, and whenever it made contact with its element—in this case, the meadow—there was growth. That couldn't be normal—even in the spirit world.

Raysh was right. It really was the key. But… I had to wonder: if a single twig could hold that much power then maybe that was all I needed.

My gaze darted from the new growth to the buck snorting and blinking in confusion, huffing great puffs of iridescent mana. It stamped its hooves in irritation, sending more tremors. I wobbled but managed to stay upright.

Alder, on the other hand, was on his hands and knees, his head bent down and his shoulders rising and falling with exertion. Just how much energy had that little stunt cost him?

"You said I needed a branch, right?" I asked Raysh. "But you never said how big."

"If you're thinking what I think you are, it won't work. As soon as a piece of the antler touches the ground, it is transformed into growth. Absorbed into the earth gate. You must get it from the guardian directly."

"Or right before it falls."

The buck trotted back, green eyes narrowing at Alder, and a spike of fear surged through me.

Alder was still hunched over, breathing hard, and I knew

he wasn't going to get up in time, let alone send another magical spirit attack toward the buck.

It wasn't like I had been relying on Alder to stop the deer with his nature powers, but he had limits just like anyone else. I'd never forgive myself if he got hurt because of *my* quest.

I was the only one who could get this key, and I had to do something, and fast.

The stag lowered its antlers, readying for another charge.

If I'd had more time, I could've figured out a better plan. A plan that would get me that key and save Alder in the process. But I didn't have time for both. I chose to save him.

Without thinking further, I ran forward, out of the tree line and to the meadow's edge. Immediately the power of the earth gate hit me like a physical punch to the gut. I staggered backward as a rush of sensations overtook me.

The smell of grass. The dankness of a cavern. The hard-packed dirt underfoot. The rough, sunbaked stone of the mountainside.

Instead of resisting their pull, I took it all in. The mana empowered me, making me feel stronger, sturdier. I waved my arms, yelling, "Hey! Bambi's dad! Over here!"

The buck's head jerked in my direction, the leaves and flowers quivering with the sudden movement.

Alder raised his head, still heaving, one eye open and the other closed. "Brye—get back!"

His words came to me from a great distance, like I was in some kind of tunnel and he was at the very end of it, calling to me. All I saw, or heard, was the giant spirit guardian before me.

About to charge.

Swallowing, I took a step back.

The buck lowered its branches and charged like a bull. This time there was no advancing mound of rubble to stop it.

Dimly, I heard Alder call my name again.

I turned and sprinted back into the trees, ducking behind a large poplar.

With a rush of hooves that sounded like rocks tumbling over one another, the buck leaped to the side of the tree, digging its hooves into the earth to stop its powerful momentum. I flinched at the wave of wind and mana that came with its arrival.

Up close, the nature spirit was gorgeous. Soft caramel fur, big eyes, black nose, powerful muscles, and deadly hooves.

For a brief moment, the spirit stared back at me. Distrustful, confused, but not exactly…angry.

"I suppose I couldn't have one of your branches, could I?" I asked.

This was the wrong thing to say, because the buck reared back and thrust its antlers at me. I screamed and dropped down as the branches stabbed into the tree trunk behind me.

Twigs snapped off, leaves fluttered, petals rained down, but I was so scared I didn't snatch up a single one of them. Cursing myself, I tried to crawl around the trunk on my hands and knees.

Just as I thought one of the hooves was going to bash my skull in, Alder appeared, wrapping two fists around the base of the deer's antler-branches and pushing it back.

"Get…out…of…here…" Alder grunted, wrestling with the great buck's antlers. The muscles in his back and shoulders tightened and flexed as he poured all his strength into keeping the rageful creature at bay.

There was no way we could beat the earth guardian in a battle of brawn. Alder would wear out long before it did, and I couldn't do much more than run the hell away.

Oh… *Run.* An idea formed in my mind. One that was hopefully clever enough to escape with the key in hand and our bodies unbroken.

"I've got an idea," I wheezed. "Come with me to the meadow."

"The meadow is the central location of the gate itself. The guardian is more powerful there." Raysh was up in a nearby tree, out of danger, content to watch us struggle.

"The fox is right," Alder said through a grunt.

"I know. Will you trust me?" I knew I was asking a lot, but there was hardly time to explain my plan.

"Yes." Alder wrenched the antlers back, giving it one more big shove, and twisted away to grab my hand.

As we ran into the meadow, my head reeled at how easily he followed. How could he do that? He may have known me as a kid, but that was over six years ago. I was different now. For all he knew, I was reckless. Impulsive. Not thinking anything through.

He didn't even know *what* my idea was.

But he trusted me anyway?

In the middle of the meadow, Alder and I turned around, hand in hand. Alder let his mana flow through me, filling me with all the sights, sounds, and tastes of the Smokies. And this time, I could feel *him*, too. The rough calluses of his fingers and the smoothness of his palm.

The guardian emerged from the forest seconds later and stamped the ground. An earthquake rumbled, its effects surely recorded by the seismograph in the Tuckaleechee Caverns.

I grabbed Alder's arm, steadying myself, and moved closer to him, feeding him instructions.

Alder's jaw clenched, but he nodded, raising his hand that was covered in mana. Green mist swirled around his wrist and between his fingers.

The buck reared back and charged for a third time.

I squeezed Alder's arm, whispering, "Wait..."

Alder's hand trembled, the bracelet I'd made him quivering.

It got closer and closer.

"Now?" Alder breathed.

"Wait."

The hooves thundered toward us, and when I saw the green of its eyes, I screamed, "Now!"

Alder jerked his hand in an upward motion and a fully grown tree burst forth from the ground, climbing skyward like Jack's beanstalk.

The buck barely had time to leap around the growing tree, and its antlers scraped against bark. I lunged for a twig and snatched it as it fell, right before it touched the blades of the meadow grass.

Alder grabbed my arm above the elbow, hoisting me up as I felt the twig's mana ripple through me like an electrical current, sending shivers and spikes of energy through my entire body. Together, we ran through the meadow, Alder casting his arm out behind him, and three more trees shot up out of the ground in a zig-zag pattern, forcing the buck to slow down and dodge and weave through them.

We headed for the tree line, still running—running and running until I could no longer feel the earthquakes underfoot.

Chapter Eleven

We collapsed in a clearing. Unsurprisingly, Alder stopped first. He stumbled forward, his hands on his knees, chest heaving, and sank to the ground. He rolled onto his back, and I watched as his chest rose and fell with effort. There was a sheen of sweat on his skin, making his brow, neck, collarbone, and arms shine in the sunlight filtered through the birch leaves.

I wanted to help him, but I didn't know how. He'd used up so much mana. First, literally moving an entire mound of earth, and then, making full-grown trees pop up out of nowhere. And we must've run half a mile through forests after that.

Dropping down next to him, I lay on my back, too. For some reason, I was tempted to take his hand. But I worried I might end up stealing more mana from him, and it was clear he needed as much as he could get. So I moved my arm close, my knuckles just a breath from his.

While we lay there, I noticed shades of green mist flowing from the earth directly into his skin.

Did he draw mana from this world simply by existing in it?

Alder moved his forearm over his eyes, as a soft rumble

started in his chest. The rumble turned into a chuckle, then full-blown laughter. He laughed without abandon, rich and loud and just…happy.

I sat up, gaping at him. "What the heck is so funny?"

I didn't really see the comedy in getting almost trampled or punctured to death by wooden stakes.

Slowly, his laughter faded, then he lifted his arm a little to reveal one green eye. He grinned at me. "You called the guardian spirit of the earth gate *Bambi's dad.*"

For too long, I stared at him. My silly reference hadn't even been the least bit hilarious. And yet he'd laughed like it was the closing joke on a comedy special.

My gaze darted to the bracelet on his wrist, remembering how he'd took off running with me. Trusting me wholly. I swallowed, but something caught in my throat. Why did I feel this ache to know that this boy—a stranger in many ways—laughed at my corny jokes?

"Oh, good. You survived."

We both looked to the side to find Raysh sitting on a rock covered in moss, licking his paws. It reminded me of the way a human would check their nails—an air of indifference around them.

"Yes, no thanks to you." Alder heaved himself up to his feet, no longer as shaky or as pale as before. He seemed to have soaked up enough energy to feel normal again.

"I guided you to the key, didn't I? Speaking of which, do you have it?"

"What? Oh!" I glanced down at my enclosed fist. Concerned with Alder's weak state, I'd totally forgotten that we'd retrieved what we came for. Uncurling my fingers to reveal the small brown twig, I held it up for Alder. "I sure hope this is it," I muttered, then cradled the twig in my hand, hoping not to squeeze it too tight in case I accidentally snapped it.

He held out his hand to help me up. "One way to find out."

I took his hand and got to my feet. Then I glanced at Raysh, looking at my guide expectantly. "So we have to take it back to the physical plane now, right?"

"Yes, and Alder must infuse it with his mana."

"Okay, so how do we get back…?"

Silently, Alder wrapped an arm around my waist, bringing me close to his chest.

Startled, I was about to push him away and tell him to leave room for the holy spirit, when a tunnel of wind erupted at our feet.

I gasped, pressing my face into his collarbone and wrapping my arms tightly around his neck, as the wind blew my hair and batted my clothes against my body.

But as soon as it began, it was over. As the vortex of wind died down to a soft breeze that whirled around our feet, kicking up leaves and shredded grass, Alder stepped away from me. Hands on my shoulders, he ducked his head to meet my gaze. "Sorry—I should've warned you. Thought you'd remember from the last time."

Now of course, I remembered the tunnel of wind and the hand that had pulled me back to the physical world, after I'd met my mom.

But my head was so full of things that I felt like I was beginning to forget everything, and for a girl with retrograde amnesia, that was probably the scariest thing that could happen.

I took a steadying breath, tucking pieces of flyaway hair behind my ears. "No, it's okay. I'm good."

"Are you ready to use the key?"

Glancing down, I found the fox curled around my shins.

The emissary pawed at my sneakers, except its paw slipped right through them.

I looked around at the forest. It was a different place than where we had entered the ethereal world. The trees around us were a collection of wild crabapple and hawthorn—both trees that grew in mid-to-low elevations. The sky was still blue with a tinge of orange and gold coming from the west. The sun was just beginning to set, and its light spilling across the mountains made the valley look truly angelic. Celestial. Divine… Whatever you wanted to call it. No surprise that spirits dwelled here.

"Right here?" I asked Raysh.

"Should be safe enough. It's well out of the reach of any humans or nature trails," Alder said, hands on his hips, as he glanced around the area.

"How do you know?" I asked.

Alder just smiled.

I tilted my chin and returned his smirk with one of my own. "Oh, a nature spirit thing. Well, aren't you handy?"

Alder just chuckled and shook his head. "Glad you think so."

Then I frowned, thinking about any humans being nearby. "But is that a concern? Humans being close by, I mean."

"*No,*" Raysh said at the same time Alder said, "Yes."

With an irritated glare at the fox, Alder explained, "I'm not sure what will happen when we use this key, so yes, it's a concern. But, we're a good distance away. We should be fine."

The twig was strangely warm in my hand, warm like it had some life in it. But then again, it *had* been part of the guardian itself, even if it was a branch. And I knew enough now to realize that everything in these mountains was alive.

"What happens to the guardian after I use this key?" I asked, curious.

I hadn't thought about what it would do to the gates within the ethereal plane once I opened them in the physical.

"Nothing terrible, if that is what you are worried about."

"Just humor us, Raysh," Alder said, folding his arms. He must be worried about its effects as well. Clearly, he was way more connected to this ethereal plane than I was.

Raysh huffed, the breath from his black nose stirring the grass at his feet. *"Fine. Without a gate to watch over, the guardians obviously cease to be guardians. They revert to normal, yet still powerful, spirits. The gates merely become another place within the ethereal plane. Think about it like a dam. The gate is holding the mana in one concentrated place, so once you open it, the water spreads and evens out."*

The fox lifted his orange and red face to meet my eyes. *"You can't have it both ways, Briony Redwrell. You either remove these barriers preventing your mother from returning, or you leave them as they are and go home."*

I blew out a breath and opened my fist, then dropped the now green-glowing twig into Alder's outstretched palm.

He enclosed his hand around the key, and green mana—vibrant and varying cool shades of color—wrapped around his fingers and wrists.

The astral energy grew brighter and brighter until a flash of green light went off within his closed fist.

Alder and I both leaned in to look at the "key."

Laying in the center of my palm was not a twig, but an acorn.

"It—it changed," I stammered.

"Unsurprising. The key takes on whatever form it needs to join with the element of its source."

Alder looked from Raysh to the acorn. "He's right. It changed to a seed. To plant it into the earth." He then flicked his fingers and the grass and dirt shifted, moving around to create a small hole in the ground.

"Like I said, handy," I told him, unable to stop a smile touching my lips.

He grinned in response. Bending down to the newly made hole, he dropped the acorn and moved the dirt over it, packing it flat.

At first, nothing happened.

Then the entire ground...shook.

I got up, wobbly on my feet, and Alder grasped my hand, tugging me closer. The tension radiating off him felt like a second energy.

"Is—is that the earth guardian?" I asked over the sound of the rumbling.

Alder didn't respond, his gaze directed at the place where I'd just planted the key. Then he looked up—reminding me of a dog who hears a high-pitched sound.

"Shit," he breathed. "*Shit.*"

I didn't even have time to ask what was wrong before another rumble followed. This time, directly from above.

The moment I looked up, lightning bolts of fear struck my limbs.

Rocks tumbled down the mountainside, heading toward us in an avalanche. A rockslide.

It was coming up fast—we'd be buried underneath tons and tons of boulders and forest debris. This wasn't just any landslide. It was a direct result of the spirit gate opening. But even if it was a normal natural phenomenon, we'd never be able to outrun it.

Still frozen, I barely noticed Alder lift me into his arms. My breath locked in my chest as he ran forward. But where could he run fast enough to escape the shower of earth racing for us at a magical speed?

But he wasn't running into the forest. He was running

into another world.

The slipstream came upon us faster than before. The barrier of mana crashed through me like an ocean wave at the beach. The sensations and the energy almost too much—I felt like I was drowning in it.

For some reason, it faded away faster than before. Was I getting used to it or was that simply because I was in Alder's arms this time?

As I caught my breath, Alder set me down on a collapsed tree covered with moss and vibrant green ivy wrapping around the trunk in clusters of three tear-shaped leaves. The ivy looked familiar, but my brain was too foggy with magical nature adrenaline to identify the plant properly.

"I'm sorry, Brye, are you okay? Running into the ethereal plane was the only thing I could think of to escape the rockslide."

"I'm fine," I rasped, still trying to regulate my breathing. "It was brilliant."

Except as I said it, my pulse jumped erratically. The mana sparked through my veins like an electrical current. Even with some of Alder's mana allowing me to pass through the barrier, the full brunt of it had been too much for me.

His hands cradled my neck and, once again, oxygen moved through my lungs, and my pulse slowed to a regulated, normal rhythm.

I lifted my gaze to his as the smell of mint and laurel, the chill of the morning in the mountains, and the taste of chicory ensnared my senses…but there was something else there, too. Beyond the Smokies, there was guilt—a churning, restless feeling.

Alder was sharing more than mana with me. He was sharing a bit of himself, including his emotions.

I didn't just see the regret in his furrowed brow or

downturned lips. I felt it inside.

"Thanks," I said in a soft exhale.

He drew his hands away, leaving the skin on my neck hot. "No problem."

Shoving his hands into his khaki shorts, he glanced around. "Where's Raysh?"

It took me a moment to shed the sensations and feelings that coursed through me—all Alder's. "Beats me," I finally said, silently urging my blush to disappear. When the fox spirit didn't show up for the next minute or so, I started looking around the clearing as well.

"He couldn't have...gotten crushed in the rockslide, right? I mean, he passes through stuff in the physical world."

Alder shook his head. "I'm sure he's fine. Maybe he went to go tell your mother we unlocked the first gate."

"Right, the earth gate," I said with a nod. "So what do we have left? There's earth, water, air, and..."

I hesitated, the next element unwilling to come to my lips. Why hadn't I thought of it before?

I took so long that Alder said it instead. "Fire."

Staring down at the forest floor, I saw flames erupt in the brush. Saw them climb and jump and leap up the bark of the trees. Saw the glow of mana flicker and die as the energy was consumed by something greedier.

It was like the ethereal plane, no, maybe just this valley, had triggered something inside of me. It brought me back to that awful day six years ago.

The realization that I would have to face a *gate* of fire was...all consuming.

The fire in my vision surged upward. Heat licked at my skin and embers flew at my clothes. Amidst the crackling of flames and their hiss and pop, I could've sworn I saw another face and heard a voice calling my name. Meanwhile, the scars on my lower back throbbed with pain. It was like someone was clawing at my skin, reopening wounds that had been closed long ago.

I slapped at my shirt and shorts, hoping to put out the embers, but I couldn't. They grew and grew, and my breath shorted—

Hands grabbed mine, stopping them from beating against my clothes.

"Brye—Briony!"

I blinked to find Alder kneeling before me, clutching my trembling hands. Chest heaving, I hunched over, the pain in my lower back echoing up and down my spine.

"There was fire. In the grass, on the trees, there—" I stopped midsentence as I was able to tell that it wasn't real. All the plants and trees were alive and well, just as they had been before my vision.

"Fire? Where? What did you see?"

"I…" I swallowed thickly, still trying to get my bearings. Trying to convince myself that there was no fire. No face in the flames. No sinister voice. But the soft whisper of pain through my scars was proof that *something* had shaken me.

Was this PTSD or something, or an actual spirit haunting me? Why did I keep seeing fire everywhere? "It…it's nothing."

"No, Briony, *tell me*."

Alder's jaw was clenched, his eyes hard and level, as if mentally preparing himself for what I was about to say.

I licked my lips, dropping my gaze from his face. "Ever since the fire, I've had nightmares. Just smoke and flames and not much more than that. But since I came back here, I had a dream that was an actual memory of the fire, and then in the meadow with my mother there was a wall of flames. It was like it was coming for both of us. And just now, I saw fire in the grass and…" I dropped my head into my hands. "I don't know if what I'm seeing is real or not. Was that just a vision? Was it all in my head?"

Alder's hands rested on my shoulders. They were warm, comforting. "This is why I didn't want you here."

I looked up, my eyes narrowing in suspicion. "What do you mean?"

He sighed, his gaze searching my face in desperate concern and obvious regret. "I didn't mention it because I was hoping that you didn't remember anything about the fire."

My eyes widened. "Were you there that day? Do you know what happened?"

Alder dropped his head, sighed, then looked back up at me, gaze hooded. "It happened the day after I brought you to the ethereal plane for the first time. You were ten, I was twelve. Just kids. Naive, ignorant kids," he said, a trace of bitterness in his voice. "I should've known better, but I wanted to show you something amazing. I had…no idea what I was getting you into.

"By then, you had more than enough mana to cross over. We'd been playing together for over five years, so you were almost as much a spirit as I was." His hand raked through his short silver hair. "I should've never taken you there, but I…I didn't know. No one told me…" He paused and closed his eyes, then opened them. "Anyway, I didn't realize it at the time, but a spirit followed us out of the ethereal plane to the physical world."

"What? You said spirits can't—"

"When a spirit *tries* to travel through the boundary, one that doesn't possess a physical body like I do, it's either an emissary that's able to manifest a projection of itself, or…"

Like Raysh. After he paused far too long, I prompted, "*Or?*"

He lifted his head fully to look me in the eye again. "Or the spirit's astral energy takes on a physical form."

This sounded eerily familiar. I licked my lips. "Which is?"

"Fire."

I felt like I couldn't breathe again—even though I could. Better than ever. It wasn't my asthma and it wasn't a panic attack, either. I just felt smothered. The sun, sky, mountains, and forest all around us seemed to press down on me and swallow me whole.

"So a spirit *did* start the fire," I whispered in a strangled voice, covering my face with my palms.

Alder said nothing. I couldn't see his face, but I could imagine the tortured look.

Move on, Brye. You're only confirming what you already suspected.

Reining in my emotions, I dropped my hands and asked, "Do you think the fire gate and this spirit that came for me have anything to do with each other? Or could it just be another spirit turning into flames when it crossed into the physical world?"

Alder suddenly stood, letting out a growl of frustration. "I don't know. Raysh was right. I don't know very much at all about the spirit world." He paced back and forth across the grass. Watching him made me so restless that I had to stand, too. "It's not like I have spirit parents or even my own emissary teaching me," he continued. "I was created as a bridge between the worlds, so mana can flow from plane to plane freely. And it's not like there is a manual for me. I'm not as old as Raysh. I live and die like a human."

He said all this in a rush of breath, frustrated, tortured, and even bitter. Not that I could blame him.

I couldn't imagine being the only one of my kind, trapped between worlds, a part of both but belonging in neither. It seemed impossibly, incredibly lonely.

Breathing hard, he turned back and crossed to me, meeting my eyes with a forlorn stare. "Honestly, Brye, do you think if I'd known all this was possible—that you could absorb my mana and be chased by a spirit—that I would've let any of this happen to you?"

Standing so close, I could feel his mana radiating off him. The essence of the Smokies…the world's best aftershave. I hated to admit it, but it was distractingly intoxicating.

But I managed to concentrate on his words and hear the pain. The regret. It was real and unquestionable. "I believe you."

At that, Alder's shoulders relaxed slightly, as if a weight had just been lifted.

"But I'm not going to stop searching for answers," I said. "I think Mom knows something. I think the same spirit that was after me might have her."

Alder nodded, his expression transforming into one of anger. "Then we'll get her back, and we'll get the spirit that went after you."

A rush of relief swept through me. It was nice to know that he was truly on my side while we went after the rest of these gates. *One down at least.*

But it was still just one. The solstice was three days away and I had two days left. Hopefully, the other gates didn't take longer than a day. Izzie would have a conniption if I was gone so long that…

I gasped, reeling back. "Shit! Izzie!"

Alder blinked. "Who?"

"My friend—my friend is with my grandmother. I've been gone for way too long. She's gonna freak. And I left her car back on Hummingbird Road. *Crap*."

"I can show you a shortcut through the ethereal world."

Following Alder through the mystical glowing forest seemed completely normal to me now. After only a day in the mana-charged woods with strange noises and strange creatures darting in and out of the underbrush, I was already used to it.

It even felt somewhat...comfortable to me?

Or maybe it was just because Alder and I were walking side by side. He felt like this enormous presence beside me—and it was hard to concentrate on anything but him. I barely noticed the growing itchiness along the back of my calves and along my wrists. It was such a normal sensation to me, thanks to my constantly chlorinated skin, that I didn't think much of it. Probably just a few mosquito bites from last night's escapades, traipsing through the woods without decent insect repellent.

Finally, Alder came to a stop by a brook with crystal clear water flowing with blue mana weaving in and out a small but swift current. Smaller Carolina willows dotted the opposite shore, their leaves gently fluttering in the breeze. "This is it. Stand close, okay?"

As I moved into his side and Alder drew an arm around my shoulders, I couldn't stop the rush of heat to my cheeks and neck. He, of course, gave absolutely no indication that this was the least bit flustering.

At once, wind picked up around us, turning and turning into a mini tornado that stretched into the impossibly blue sky. Water from the brook and rogue willow leaves joined the tornado and then—just like that—vanished.

Back in the physical plane it had gotten darker. The sun had dipped below the mountains, fading into the western horizon beginning its surrender to the night sky.

Wisps flitted around us, pulsing in various degrees of brightness and color in harmonious synchronization. Their glow illuminated the forest, and I recognized my old house and Izzie's car through the gaps in the grove of tulip trees Alder had grown. Eager to head back, I took one step forward.

And promptly collapsed.

Chapter Twelve

Pain shot through my legs like nothing I'd ever felt before. It was hot and cold and unreal. I'd never experienced anything like this. It wasn't torturous, physical pain. It was *energetic*. My legs and wrists trembled with mystical adrenaline coursing through every vein under my skin, while my body convulsed from the sparks of pure, unbridled mana.

"Briony!" Alder caught me around my shoulders, his forearm supporting my back. His fingertips traced along the inside of my wrist and his chest pressed against my arm in a sharp gasp.

"Poison ivy," he whispered. "Oh *no*."

Scooping me up, one hand under the back of my knees and the other wrapped around my middle, Alder balanced me easily in his arms. I was so uncomfortable and disoriented from the pain in my legs that I wasn't even in the right state of mind to be embarrassed. I let out an involuntary cry as my legs spasmed again.

He squeezed me gently in response. "I set you down in it. It had to have been on the tree," he muttered, words strained with agony. "Where else did it touch you?"

I sucked in a breath through my teeth as another shock

sparked through me. Cautiously, I lifted a shaky hand. My vision was blurry, but I could see glowing red welts decorating my hands and wrists and splotches on my calves.

"I—I hadn't—" Another shudder went through my system and I clenched my teeth, sticking my tongue to the roof of my mouth, afraid I'd accidentally bite it off.

"Shhh, it's okay. I'll take care of it," he said, though his voice was coated with panic. "You're going to be okay."

Alder cradled me to his chest as he ran through the tulip trees. The wisps followed us, floating like Japanese lanterns and lighting our path.

He stopped at Izzie's car. "I need the keys," he said urgently.

Shaking, hardly able to control my arms, I managed to tug the keys out of my front pocket. Alder unlocked the car, threw open the back hatch and lifted me inside, laying me down.

Leaning over me, he turned on the car's interior lights. Before I could ask what he was about to do, another spike of mana hit the base of my spine, and my back arched. My fingers glowed with a pulsing red energy just below my skin, and I sucked in a breath, whimpering at the aftereffects of the lightning strike inside my body.

"Briony? Can you hear me?" he asked. Light fingers danced across my hot, hot skin.

My very cells seemed to vibrate with all the mana inside me.

Dimly, I nodded, swallowing through the magical adrenaline rush. The welts on my calves, hands, and wrists burned with searing heat and freezing cold, glowing mystically in the stale, halogen light of Izzie's CRV.

"Just hold on to me."

Alder took my trembling hands and guided them to

his cheeks. The cool softness of his skin under my restless fingers gave me a little…relief.

His hands held my wrists and then ran up and down my skin, his fingers grazing the crook of my elbow, running across the luminous, angry red welts.

Immediately, a feeling of serenity resonated within me. His touch was like a salve against the relentless, mystical energy eating me from the inside out. I blinked, my eyelids heavy with exhaustion, and managed to see light blue mana wind around my arms. Mana drained slowly from Alder's fingers as they traveled across my arms. Meanwhile the angry red energy from my own hands leached into his neck and jaw.

A whole different kind of panic hit me as I realized what he was doing. Draining the poisonous mana from my hands. Sucking it out of me like snake's venom.

I tried to move my hands away, but he held them in place. "No," he admonished, "keep them there."

"Alder—" I tried to argue but stopped as tremors seized my legs. While my arms felt better, my calves were still in agony. I twisted, my side pressing against the back seat, and ripped my hands away from him, letting out a cry of pain.

"I'm so sorry," he murmured as his hands moved to the back of my calves. "Poisonous plants are stronger in the ethereal plane, and they were bound to affect humans differently. I can't believe I didn't notice it."

I wanted to tell him that we'd both been shaken after the landslide, and that it wasn't his fault, but I couldn't. I could only cover my mouth with my hands as I whimpered through the strange sensations of pain and energy spasms down my legs.

But Alder's mana was soothing. A shudder went through me as his blue mana calmed the mind-numbing sensations of fire and ice, adrenaline and agony, panic and pain.

During it all, I thought: *Thank God I shaved my legs last night.*

Breathing out, I lifted my arm to lay it across my forehead and squeezed my eyes closed. Only when the poisonous mana receded to a tolerable level of itchy, irritating throbs of soreness, did I open my eyes.

Alder was concentrating on his work, his hand on my leg literally bleeding mana into my skin.

I watched him for a moment before I felt strong enough to speak without my teeth chattering. "I'm okay now—it's better."

His brow furrowed and he looked paler as compared to when he'd started. "It's not all gone yet," he mumbled.

"Why did you take me to the car?" I asked, my heart rate finally slowing to a somewhat normal pace.

"The forest has mana, too. You needed to get away from *all* of it, until I could..." His breath stuttered, and I knew then I had to force him to stop. Sucking out the poisonous mana, giving me his had been too much for him. Like I saw back in the earth gate, he had his limits.

I grabbed his hands and tugged them away from my spirit rash, forcing his gaze to mine. "*Alder.* You've done enough."

Backlit against the car's overhead light, his features were impossible to discern. "No, you're wrong." The way he contradicted me sounded like it hurt him. "It'll never be enough. What I've taken from you..."

Taken from me? Was he referring to my memories?

The pain and regret in his voice seemed to pull and tear at the void in my chest, making it expand until it threatened to swallow my heart as well. How could I feel such anguish from someone I'd met just yesterday?

My fingertips skimmed his soft, silvery hair as I took his cheeks in my hands and pulled his face closer. Close enough for his cool autumn breath to fan against my cheeks. "You haven't—"

A bright light hit our eyes and we both threw our hands up against its onslaught. Squinting, I pulled myself up on my elbows to find the high beams of a pickup truck shining at us like we were two criminals caught sneaking out of prison.

My organs seemed to rearrange themselves as a slim figure with brown skin and coiled curls stepped out of Gran's old pickup truck. *Son of a sea biscuit.*

"Briony Margaret Redwrell," Izzie called, slamming the truck's door, "you better not be making out with some guy in the back of my car!"

Alder jerked back so fast he bumped his head against the car's roof with a *thud.*

I sat up straight, ignoring the residual sparks of pain, to watch my best friend stomp across the gravel and come to a halt. I glanced back at Alder to find that he had resumed his human disguise. He was all blond hair and green eyes again. I wondered if Izzie had noticed his ethereal form.

Something about the way she had her gaze honed on me told me she hadn't.

"Iz, this isn't what it looks like," I said hurriedly.

She got two feet away from the hatchback and stopped. "Really? Because it looks like you were just about to *kiss* him."

"I wasn't! Listen—" I said, trying to keep my voice calm as I swung my legs around to jump out.

Izzie gasped, her eyes glued to my calves and wrists. "Girl, you are *covered* in poison ivy."

Frowning, I looked at my skin. The red welts weren't completely gone yet, and they still glowed subtly. I was surprised Izzie wasn't screaming about *glowing skin*, then I caught Alder's eye, and he barely shook his head.

Izzie couldn't see the mana like I could. All she saw was a rash.

"I know. Alder was helping me," I said.

Izzie's eyes narrowed. "Helping you? How? Mouth-to-mouth doesn't work on rashes."

"For the last time," I groaned, "we *weren't* kissing."

"Briony, I've been worried *sick* about you all day. I finally got so scared I took your Gran's truck to look for you at your old house—my next stop would've been the sheriff by the way—and then I find you tangled up with some Ralph Lauren model? I would like answers. *Now*, please."

"We..." My words trailed off, unable to keep up with the lie any longer. I couldn't think of what to tell her that would make sense, but more than anything, I was tired of lying to my best friend.

I looked over to Alder and he seemed to be staring at me, somewhat alarmed, as if to say, *you're not thinking what I think you're thinking.*

"Is there a way you could show her, please?" I asked him.

Bathed in the yellow glow of the headlights, Alder opened and closed his mouth, his gaze jumping from me to Izzie.

"Show me *what*?" she said.

"Briony..." Alder trailed off, clearing his throat, his eyes silently communicating to me that this *wasn't a good idea.*

"You said you trusted me. Well, I trust Izzie. Ipso facto you can trust her."

Alder and I locked gazes, a silent war going on between us.

"Will someone *please* tell me what is going on?" Izzie hissed, stomping her sneaker into the gravel.

"Where is Gran?" I asked.

"She fell asleep watching *Dateline*," Izzie said, folding her arms. "Now *what is going on*?"

"So yesterday, when I went to my old house, I hadn't exactly gotten lost," I started.

"No shit, Brye."

"I met Alder, and he…" I directed my gaze back to Alder, pressing my palms together and pleading. "Please will you just show her? It'll make this so much easier."

Heaving a large breath, Alder took a cautious step forward, thrusting out his hand. "Hi, I'm Alder. Um, Briony's childhood friend."

Izzie cocked an eyebrow at me as if to say *are you for real with this*?

"Iz, please."

Lip curling, Izzie stepped forward and shook his hand.

At once, silver mana roared up and off his skin, merging into Izzie's. She gasped, tearing away from Alder and stumbling backward. She waved her hands as if trying to shake off the sensations that I knew she'd just felt.

"I can hear hawks and smell pine needles and taste wild honeysuckle—" Izzie rattled off, her breath coming out in short quick bursts. Then her gaze swiveled toward me, and she squeaked. "Brye! You're glowing!"

No question she could now see the red mana rash luminous on my skin.

Isabelle Jennison now possessed a small dose of nature spirit mana.

"Oh my *God.* What is *happening*?"

"Iz." I glanced down the lone dark road and back to my friend. "Why don't we get off the side of the road? This could take a while."

Chapter Thirteen

To Izzie's credit, she took the whole story fairly well. She only freaked out twice.

Izzie sat in the front seat while Alder and I occupied the back. The three of us had gotten into the CRV and pulled it off the shoulder into the grass. There, we sat in the dark of the car and I talked until my throat got sore. She'd been silent for a solid six minutes now, just staring ahead and watching the wisps float about in the dark outside the car. At some point, Alder had taken my hand again, sending gentle waves of mana across my skin.

At least he no longer seemed to be drawing out any poisonous mana. The red welts had stopped glowing twenty minutes ago. In fact, I had a sneaking suspicion that all the mana was gone and it was just a regular poison ivy rash now.

But I kept my hand where it was.

"A landslide. A landslide was the opening of a spirit gate?" Izzie finally muttered, rubbing her forehead.

"The earth one," Alder clarified.

Izzie stopped, turning all the way around in her car seat and glaring at Alder. "Yeah, I remember hearing about the scary deer monster that almost skewered my friend."

"It wasn't a monster, it was—"

"*So* not the point!" Izzie snapped. She turned to me. "You still have to unlock more of these things? What's the next one? I want to come."

I gaped at her. "You... Why?"

"I don't want you doing this alone."

"She's not going to be alone," Alder countered.

"Does this guy have an off switch?" Izzie asked. Then her eyes snapped pointedly to my hand in his.

I slipped out of his grasp, swallowing. "Alder, can you give us a minute?"

Something passed across Alder's face that I couldn't quite pinpoint. "I'll see you tomorrow." He paused on the way out the door. "Don't use calamine lotion—it'll irritate your skin."

How did he know that? Was that a nature spirit thing?

"Use the all-natural stuff." After opening the car door, he stepped out into the darkness and the wisps seemed to swim around him the moment his foot touched the ground. The glowing spheres followed him, reminding me of tiny fairy lights from *Fantasia,* as his silhouette disappeared into the woods.

Izzie let out a low whistle. "It's like a scene from... What's that movie with the blue people called?"

"*Avatar*." I frowned at her as I climbed up into the passenger seat. "You were rather rude."

Izzie raised her eyebrows, placing a hand on her chest. "*Moi?*"

"Iz."

"C'mon, Brye. The guy pumped you full of spirit energy when you were a little kid, then next thing you know, there's a spirit after you that lights your house on fire. And *now* he leads you into the spirit world, takes you to a gate with an all-powerful creature that almost kills you, *then* he sets you in magical poison ivy. What I wanna know is: why aren't *you* angry with him?"

It was a good question. Why didn't even the smallest part of me blame him for my lost past? If he had just left me alone as a child, I might've never lost my memories. A mysterious spirit never would've followed us out of the ethereal plane and gone after me, and destroyed my house, and later, my family.

But whatever had happened, the truth was I didn't blame Alder. I didn't *trust* him, but I didn't blame him, either. Just within the last hour, I'd experienced his own worry—the fear and anxiety he had for me—and more and more I was beginning to see just how close we had been. Through his eyes. And I had to imagine that "ten-year-old Briony" would never have blamed him for anything that had happened.

As for the "current Briony," my heart simply wouldn't let me. Every time he was near, that gap in my chest reverberated with longing and loss.

Like Alder had said, we'd both been kids. We hadn't known any better. Alder didn't seem to know much at all about the spirit world, and I was reminded of Raysh's words, *"You'll never be one of us."*

While I was struggling to find an answer to Izzie's question, a car zoomed past us, shining its high beams across the dark road. We both jumped, suddenly and cruelly reminded that real life moved on outside the car.

Izzie stayed in her CRV while I took Gran's pickup. We drove slowly back to Gran's house and parked. As we came through the back kitchen door, *Dateline* blared from the den.

We peeked into the room to find Gran snoozing in her chair. Izzie and I headed back into the kitchen. She gestured to my poison ivy rash. "Go put on some of that all-natural lotion and change into your pajamas. I told your gran that you were sick, and it's been ridiculously difficult trying to keep her from climbing the stairs to check on you."

As I hurried up the steps, I heard Izzie turn off the TV, then Gran's groggy voice say, "I was watching that, Isabelle."

"Sorry, Mrs. Kaftan. Do you want me to turn it back on?"

"No, no, that's all right. How's Briony? Is she feeling better? Maybe I should call her father."

"Oh, she's feeling a lot better. In fact, she said she'd be down in a bit."

I shut the attic door with a soft *snap*, then quickly rubbed lotion up and down my arms and calves. It helped calm the itch, but it didn't come close to the soothing touch of Alder's hands and nourishing mana. My ears grew hot, thinking about...everything.

After I was sure the red welts had reduced to nothing more than light pink splotches, I changed out of my T-shirt and jean shorts and threw on a night shirt and athletic shorts. I couldn't let Gran think I was lying in bed all day in normal clothes—that was just inhuman.

Trudging down the steps, trying to look as sick as I could, which wasn't exactly hard—I was pretty darn exhausted—I found Izzie and Gran sitting in the living room.

Gran had a Sudoku puzzle in her lap. Her brow furrowed when she saw me. "Sugar pea, how are you feeling?"

The look on her face and the term of endearment jolted me. It was what she'd called me in that very faint memory. The one with the fairy figurine.

I bit my bottom lip in an attempt to hold back a tide of emotion.

She really had been worried about me all day.

"I'm feeling much better, thanks," I said, collapsing into an armchair across from her. The lie sat uncomfortably in my stomach. "What did you guys do today?"

"Mrs. Kaftan taught me how to knit." Izzie held up what I *assumed* to be a potholder.

I smothered a bubble of laughter, and Izzie scowled at me.

"It's harder than it looks."

Gran leaned back in her chair, smiling. "She's doing very well."

"I have no doubt, but don't get any ideas for Christmas, all right? I'm all set on sweaters."

Izzie stuck her tongue out at me, and I laughed.

"Your father called for you today, Briony. I told him you weren't feeling well." Gran closed her puzzle book and nodded toward the kitchen. "He wants you to call as soon as you're better. He sounded quite worried, so I told him that it would be all right for you two to go home. As I've been trying to tell Izzie, I could easily hire a home nurse to come help me."

She was worried about me, and yet she still continued to push me away. Not wanting to start an argument, I got up and crossed into the kitchen to the only phone in the house. I dialed Dad's number by heart—he'd made me memorize it when I was eleven—and waited for the voicemail. I guessed he was probably working late for the business trip. To my surprise, he answered on the second ring.

"Brye?"

"Hey, Dad," I said, hoping to sound as chipper as possible.

His breath of relief crackled over the receiver. "Are you all right? Willa said that you weren't feeling well?"

"I'm fine, I—"

"Is it that place? I'm starting to think this was a bad idea. I mean, you had such a trauma there, and asking you to go back—"

"Dad!" I interrupted, terrified he'd say I needed to go

home. I didn't need *another* person wanting me to leave.

"I'm fine, I swear, it was…just really bad cramps." Again, I didn't relish lying to my father, but I couldn't imagine telling him I'd found the love of his life, the woman that had left us both, trapped in a spirit world nestled within the Smokies.

"Oh. *Oh.*" Dad's voice went up a little, as it usually did when we needed to talk about feminine hygiene and health. He'd been really great about it growing up, but it still made him a tad uncomfortable.

"Well, do I need to call the gynecologist?" he said.

Quickly I explained that I'd forgotten my usual painkillers, and all Gran had was stuff for her leg, and I hadn't wanted to take any of that. "Izzie and I will run to the drugstore tomorrow."

After promising to call again soon, we said our good-byes and I hung up. Walking back into the living room, I caught Gran showing Izzie how to redo her knots in her mess-of-a-potholder.

Seeing the two of them together, I was actually *jealous*. I wanted to be with Gran, sitting and learning how to knit. While I was happy to hear her call me "sugar pea" and know how worried she'd been about me, I could still feel this wall between us.

I just wished I knew why.

For the millionth time, I wondered what my time in this valley had been like. What my relationship with my Gran had been like and what my time with Alder and the spirits had been like. Besides the spirit that had gone after me, the other spirits didn't seem evil…just…

I thought of the charging buck, the vines and leaves decorating its branches, the chaotic green eyes, and the unrestrained power of its hooves.

It had been wild.

"Briony?"

I looked up, realizing that I'd been staring at nothing, lost in the events of today and the mystery of my past, present, and future.

Gran peered at me from over her readers.

"Are you hungry? Izzie made some excellent chicken noodle soup."

Wow. They'd even fixed something for the "sick" me. "Izzie only knows how to make spaghetti."

"Not anymore. Willa taught me. So get ready for *two* perfected meals."

I grinned. "Make way for the next Top Chef."

"So..." Izzie said, as she put away the large soup pot under the counter. "How are we going to swing tomorrow? We could say that I need to drive you back home to get something—"

"Iz, you're not coming," I said with a sigh, turning off the faucet.

"What? Of course I am."

I looked up from the sink to peer outside the window, seeing the wisps drift around lazily in the garden. In the window's reflection I could see the look of frustration on my friend's face.

"Let's sit on the porch," I suggested.

Out in the Tennessee summer night air, the anxiety that came with the chaos from the day and the unknown smacking me in the face at every turn, seemed to fade. The temperature was warm, but not stuffy or intolerable thanks to the mountains, and the music of the crickets and frogs was a distant background buzz—calming like an air conditioner's soft whir. The wisps flitted here and there, drifting to the bushes and alighting the plants with sparks of mana. Transferring energy, like bees with pollen, from flower to flower.

Izzie and I sat on the rocking bench and I pulled my legs up, hugging my knees. "So, be honest. How much are you regretting being my friend at the moment?"

Thwack—Izzie hit my arm with a bench pillow. "If you ask me another question like that, I'll block you on Instagram. You got that?"

"Got it," I chuckled. "I just, if you weren't friends with me, you wouldn't be in this mess in the first place. You wouldn't be giving up your summer to…to learn how to knit."

"First, your gran is delightful, and second, that's not the way friendship works, Brye. You can't pick and choose the things you want in a friend. You have to accept all their burdens and baggage and annoying tendencies. If you love them enough, they'll even become endearing. Like how you always, *always* sing the wrong lyrics to Maroon 5 songs."

"Adam Levine is *impossible* to understand."

"My point is I accept all of you, Briony Redwrell. Nature spirit powers, dangerous missions, terrible at lyrics, and all."

I twisted my hands in my lap. "And what about Alder?"

Izzie's teasing smile turned into a frown. "What about him?"

"Do you accept him, too?"

"That's different—"

"It's not, actually. You *just* said you can't pick and choose the burdens of a friend. Well, Alder and I were friends. And I didn't pick and choose only the human part of him. I accepted the nature spirit part of him, too."

"But you were a kid."

"Exactly. We *both* were. He didn't know what he was doing to me. In fact, when I came back here, he tried desperately to get me to leave. And it's *my* decision to unlock these gates and go after my mom."

Izzie was quiet for a long time. A wisp twirled through the air in a delicate pirouette and landed on a shrub of bright red begonias.

"Okay, I get it," she said softly. "Using my own argument against me. Clever girl."

Laughing, I bumped my shoulder against hers. "Thanks."

She scowled. "I'm still coming, though."

"I don't think that's going to be possible. You need a *lot* of mana to be able to pass through the barrier into the ethereal world, and Alder only gave you a little."

"Then he can give me more."

"He won't."

"Uh-huh. And why wouldn't he?"

"Because," I said confidently, though my heart ached at what I was about to admit, "he regrets bringing even me. There's no way he'll want to bring another human along into danger. He's...a good guy."

Feeling Izzie's stare on me, I looked back at her. "What?"

"Giiiirrrl, you better not be falling for him."

My cheeks lit with heat and I almost fell off the rocking sofa. "I'm not falling for him, and I *wasn't* kissing him!"

She raised her hands into the air in mock innocence. "I'm not saying you were—I'm saying you *wanted* to."

"No, I didn't." But that didn't sound believable, even to me.

Izzie raised one eyebrow. "Look, all I'm saying is, in all the time I've known you, you've never had sparks like that fly with any other guy. And that includes Eric—mister-I'm-too-good-for-musicals."

I laughed, remembering Izzie's rivalry with the last guy I'd been close to dating. "Izzie, you've got to let that go."

"Never. *Hamilton* is the voice of our generation. Anyway, my point is...*you* had your hands on *his* face."

"That was..." I drummed my fingers on the edge of the bench, now not even remembering how or why I'd done that. "Iz, I barely know him and he's...he's not even human."

"So? He *looks* human, and he's fine as hell."

"I'm so done talking about this. C'mon, let's go to bed."

We headed back inside, and I was glad the house's conditioned air cooled my inflamed cheeks. In a way, Izzie's accusation had left me with the same sensation of vertigo—of my world tilting—as the first time I'd set foot in this valley. Our conversation replayed in my mind as I climbed the stairs to my bedroom, reinforcing my already growing fear that I was beginning to feel something for the boy I'd left behind.

Chapter Fourteen

Dad tossed another log on top of the burning pile. The flames crackled and popped at the new fuel. They danced hungrily across the dry wood, eating at it faster than termites, transforming the once vibrant tree bark full of life and energy into ash. Embers exploded in a shower of sparks, climbing high into the night sky.

I held out a stick with a marshmallow attached over the flames. All too quickly, the marshmallow went from fluffy white to charred black.

The fire on the sweet treat traveled up my stick, and the heat burned my fingers. I couldn't drop it in time. The flames touched my fingers, curling around them in red and gold shades.

I tried to shake my hand to get it off, and sparks flew to the grass at my feet. Igniting.

I wanted to stamp on the growing fire around my toes, but I was barefoot and my hand was already burning. My breath came out in panicky bursts.

Make it stop! Make it stop!

Whispers came from behind me and I felt the need to run, but I couldn't because the fire at my feet was too high to jump over.

A hand touched my shoulder, and I jerked away, screaming, the hand raking downward in sharp, blinding pain against my lower back.

Cold sweat coated my skin as I forced my eyes open in the darkness of my attic bedroom. Tossing the covers to the side, I groaned, threading my fingers into my hair and feeling the beads of sweat along my temples.

Yet another nightmare. But this time, not a memory. Or maybe, it had started out as one. Perhaps they became mixed together like dreams do.

Either way, I hadn't woken up because of it. I woke up because the scars on my lower back were *killing* me. They throbbed and pulsed as if they were freshly made and not six years old.

It was strange. These scars had never hurt me before. Not even an ache. I would've remembered that after the fire.

Thirsty after a dream where I'd been surrounded by heat and having sweated through my night shirt, I got up, changed, and headed downstairs for a glass of water.

At the sink, I took a cup out of the dish rack and filled it with water. As the water filled my glass, I glanced up and froze in awe at the scene through the window.

I abandoned my water and went out the back door, letting it shut behind me with a slight creak on its hinges.

The garden was alight with wisps.

They were all varying shades of pastel colors. Light pink, lavender, periwinkle, sky blue, lime green, rose gold, pearly white—it was as if the wisps took on softer versions of the colors of the nature around them. Of the pinkish red rhododendrons, deep orange black-eyed Susans, and vibrant green leaves and vines.

Moving through the garden, my bare feet crunching over weeds and pebbles and discarded flower petals but feeling no discomfort, I admired these so-called fireflies. These wisps that were evidence of a world beyond our own.

They were so beautiful.

Had I seen these every night as a child? Had they been so normal to me that they'd lost their novelty?

A wisp floated in front of me, doing a loop-de-loop in midair.

No, that wasn't possible. Nothing could take away their magic.

"Brye?"

I stopped moving through the garden and turned in the direction of my nickname. To my right, Alder stood in the yard, a few steps from the tree line, just near enough to see his face but not read his expression.

He moved closer, the wisps twirling around him, lighting up his features and shining their own multicolored light on his silver hair.

"What are you doing up? Is that rash still bothering you?"

I glanced down at my arms. I'd already forgotten about the magical poison ivy. "No, it feels fine. Why? Were you here to check on me?"

Alder was now at the edge of the garden and only a low bush of magenta geraniums stood between us, while a few light pink wisps floated around our knees. He shrugged and glanced away, maybe a little embarrassed to have been called out. "I guess I was worried."

I smiled, tucking a piece of hair behind my ear. "That seems to be your constant state."

Alder let out a quick, exhausted laugh, rubbing the back of his neck. "I guess you're right. I didn't always used to be like this, though."

"So what were you like?" I blurted. "I mean, what were *we* like?"

Alder's gaze lifted to meet mine, and then lowered to the bracelet I'd made for him. "We were…"

This wasn't going to be easy for him. I'm sure it had to be painful, talking to an old friend and telling them what they'd forgotten even though you remembered it all like it was yesterday. But I couldn't bring myself to stop my questions and my desire to know. To remember.

"How did we meet?" I asked, my fingers brushing against the butter-soft geranium petals.

"You'd gotten lost."

"Really?"

His mouth hooked into a half smile, his gaze far off as if caught by the memory. "Yeah. You were five, I guess. Old enough to have been able to wander into the woods outside your house. I found you crying under a poplar tree and then I led you back home. And I guess I"—he stuffed his hands in his pockets, lifted shoulders to ears in a shrug—"kept coming back."

We were quiet for a moment as warmth seemed to spread from my chest and into my cheeks and palms. I wiped my hands on my old night shirt and cursed that I was in my pajamas.

"How did you know where I lived?" I asked.

"I may not know everyone's name, but if all you do is hike through this valley for eighteen years, you begin to know it like the back of your hand, including where people live and what they do. But it's almost impossible to keep track of the spirits in the ethereal plane. They wander around a lot."

Trapped between worlds.

I swallowed, folding my arms across my chest. "I guess

my parents hadn't been all that worried about me."

Alder ducked his head, meeting my gaze. "No, they were incredibly worried."

I stared back at him. "Well, maybe my dad was."

"Your dad wasn't even home. Your mother and gran were beside themselves with worry."

Then why did she leave? And I knew she had, because I'd seen her walk out the back door that night. It was the one memory I wish I could forget. I remembered her tone of anger and frustration, bordering on desperation.

But I couldn't ask Alder that. For one I didn't want to show him how vulnerable I was. And for another, he wouldn't know in the first place. Instead, I asked, "How do you think Mom got into the spirit world? Is there a way for humans to pass through without your mana?"

Alder nodded. "There is. It's a hiking trail. It's closed to most humans, though. Those truly connected to this valley can enter, but they can only stay in the ethereal plane, and most find their way out anyway. I've led a few hikers out that accidentally wandered in."

"Why just the ethereal plane? Why not the astral plane, too?"

"Nothing physical can exist in the astral plane, remember?"

"So…wait, are you telling me Mom is still somewhere in the ethereal world?" Come to think of it, Mom had never said exactly *where* she was in the spirit world, only that she was trapped by some spirit—the mysterious "*he*."

"Well, yes, but—"

"Then we can just go *get* her!" I exploded, throwing my hands in the air. "Who cares about the gates! We can just go rescue her and take her back through the pathway. She was in a meadow."

I grabbed his arm, pulling him through the garden, my

pulse racing. Mom probably had been convinced by Raysh that these gates needed to be open, which was why she asked me to open them. When in reality I could just go find her in the ethereal meadow. *This is such bullshit.* This was why I didn't trust anyone. They were always out for themselves. Raysh just wanted to see the physical world, so he made up this nonsense about having to open gates.

"No, Brye—" Alder dug his heels into the loose soil of the garden, planting himself like a massive oak. "That's not how it works."

"What do you know?" I whirled around to glare at him. "You've said yourself you hardly know anything."

Pain flashed across his face and immediately I regretted snapping at him.

I dropped my hand from his arm. "I'm sorry. I'm just frustrated."

He folded his arms then ran one hand up his shoulder to wrap around his neck. The muscles in his forearm strained, and I wondered what kind of war was going on in his head. Finally he said, quietly, "I know you are, but let me explain. The ethereal plane is not meant to contain humans for a long period of time. They either find their own way out, or their spirit—their soul, rather—is pulled toward the astral plane."

"Their soul?"

"A human's soul is pure life and energy. It is mana in a raw form, not bound by elements or anything else. If your mother was kidnapped by this spirit that had gone after you, or if she wandered into the spirit world and stayed there for *this long*, then the only way she could still be alive is by her spirit existing in the astral plane. It's why the gates are so important. It will allow her spirit to pass through the barriers to the ethereal plane and rejoin her body."

"So we need to find her body in the ethereal world, too?"

I groaned, leaning against the short white picket fence that ran around Gran's garden.

"I wouldn't worry about that," Alder said, the slightest hint of a smile touching his lips. "I don't know a lot of spirits. But I have some…friends, I guess you could say. They agreed to look for your mother's body. Once we open the gates, we'll have time between when the solstice begins and when it ends to find your mother's spirit and get her back to her body."

Knowing what I was up against, seeing the clear path to success, made the weight on my shoulders lighter and I was able to return his small smile. "So, these friends…have I met them?"

Alder actually laughed. "No, I was content to keep you to myself when we were kids."

My face flushed, but Alder didn't seem to notice that he said anything remotely heart-racing.

"What else?" I asked.

"What else what?"

"What else did we do when we were kids?" I was hungry for more. More of this past that must've been so beautiful and magical.

No wonder the hole in my chest hurt so terribly. No wonder I felt like I'd lost a piece of myself here.

"Come this way." Alder turned and gestured for me to follow him. Together, we moved through the wild jungle that was Gran's garden, pushing aside overgrown shrubs and dandelion weeds that had grown to the size of house cats. Alder stopped at the edge of the porch around the side of the house. Dropping one knee into the dirt, he knelt and stuck his hand underneath the porch.

He grinned. "Thank goodness. I was worried she'd found them and gotten rid of them."

Before I could ask what he meant, he had withdrawn

Chapter Fifteen

The next morning, Izzie was knocking at my door at the butt-crack of dawn. When I let her in, still in my pajamas, she eyed me with an amused smirk. "Is that what you're wearing to go traipsing around in a spirit world with Mr. Cheekbones?"

Deciding not to admit that he'd already seen me in my pajamas, I stepped aside to let her in.

"You're really not coming, Iz," I said with a yawn.

"We'll see about that."

"Okay, but let's say I'm right. How are you going to cover for me with Gran? She won't buy the same excuse twice." I crossed to my suitcase and pulled out a fresh set of clothes.

"Why are you asking *me* that? This is your whole idea," Izzie snapped.

"But you're better at improv," I said, stepping inside the closet to change.

"Is that your way of telling me I'm a good liar?" she asked, her voice carrying through the door.

I tugged the fresh shirt over my head. "No, it's my way of telling you you're a brilliant actress."

"Well, you're not wrong there. What are you *doing*?"

Finished changing, I'd crossed to the window and lifted

his arm from under the porch. In his hand was a silver pail with a few different things inside. Simple household items, but I knew immediately what they had been.

A child's adventuring kit.

I plucked out each and set them on the porch. A pair of binoculars, a small spade, a flashlight, and a mason jar.

"We watched movies, and we played board games, and read books," Alder said, "but more than anything else, we explored. We went all over this valley together."

My fingers raked across the pair of binoculars as if feeling them could somehow bring back their associated memories. It couldn't, but I could imagine.

Bird watching in the trees with binoculars as he would call out the types of birds to me. Blackberry picking with him. More berries in our stomachs than in the silver pail. Catching fireflies, real ones maybe, in mason jars, and letting them go before I was called in for dinner.

A few wisps floated by, illuminating my face and Alder's, and, for a fleeting moment, I saw the face of the boy my mind had forgotten but my heart hadn't.

The next second, the wisps twirled away, and Alder's older, more angular face was swallowed in shadow. He placed a strong hand on top of mine that rested on the pail's rim and my heart skipped.

He said quietly, "You should get some sleep, Brye."

But I didn't want to. What waited for me in my be was possibly more fiery nightmares, and then the followir morning I'd have to go after the next spirit key and fig another deadly powerful guardian.

As I accepted his hand to help me up, I wondered, thou which was more dangerous. An almighty nature spirit or growing feelings for one?

the bug screen. "Sneaking out." I took stock of my options by leaning over the edge and observing the garden and the side of the house. Directly below was a white wooden trellis. Honeysuckle vines wound up the wood, with tiny yellowish-white flowers peeking out in the dark green leaves. I wasn't sure if the old trellis would hold my weight, but I wasn't that heavy and...well, the fall wasn't that far.

"Through the *window*?" Izzie hissed, hurrying over to grab my elbow.

"I just heard Gran downstairs. She can't see me leaving or she'll get upset. This is better, trust me," I said, thinking of the worried look she'd had yesterday.

"I'm coming down, too, then."

Rolling my eyes, I hoisted my leg over the window sill, my bare foot finding purchase with the diamond shape of the trellis. "Okay, fine. You do you."

Slowly, I lowered myself down the trellis. It trembled slightly, but it held strong. I hopped down the last few feet, my sneakers finding a cushioned landing in the soft grass and dandelion weeds curling up from under the edges of the house. Izzie dropped down next to me and together we snuck across the garden to the tree line.

We didn't have to wait long for Alder to show up, and much to Izzie's aggravation, Alder took my side, saying exactly what I'd predicted. "There's no way I'm giving you any more," he said.

Izzie glared at the two of us, like we were somehow in on the whole thing together. As if I'd *choose* to join up with an estranged nature spirit and unlock mystical gates guarded by giant magic animals for funsies.

"I don't like any of this," she growled, then turned to Alder, sticking a finger in his face. "If you let anything happen to her, I swear to Beyoncé—"

"What are you going to tell Gran?" I asked, interjecting before Izzie could describe a creative way to castrate my childhood friend.

She sighed, her shoulders slumping. "I guess I'll have to think of something. She mentioned something about her Bridge Club yesterday. So we might go play cards with some old biddies who smell like Mary Kay products."

I gave my friend a swift hug. "No amount of Starbucks gift cards in the world can thank you enough."

"Oh, there's an amount, you just can't afford it."

As Izzie headed up the porch steps, Alder and I turned toward the forest. After we passed through the bushes of pastel-colored chrysanthemum, Alder muttered, "She scares me a little."

Laughing, I jogged into the trees, Alder following behind me. I could've sworn I heard him chuckle, too.

We emerged into a clearing with a stream. Blue mana flowed everywhere, weaving into the grass and up the trees, winding around the branches and coating the leaves with it. The mana's origin seemed to be the stream, with the mist-like energy clouding above the water like the bottom of a waterfall.

Edging closer to the creek's bank, I could see the mana move like it was the current itself, and maybe it was. Under the glassy surface, tiny minnows swam, following the mana's and the water's flow as if they were merely passengers. Perhaps they weren't swimming at all. Dipping my hand into the stream, the blue mana wound around my fingertips and I could actually taste the water. The chill temperature and its freshness coated my tongue and bled into the reservoir of mana that was building within me.

At the earth gate, I had felt the mana simply by stepping into the meadow, and now I could feel the water's mana—its energy—like a tangible thing, stirring deep inside my chest and pooling in my gut. It was the first time that I truly identified this mana Alder claimed I possessed. Would I be able to use it somehow? Or was collecting it all I was able to do?

I glanced over my shoulder to find Alder watching me intently, his eyes back to gold and his silver hair white in the sunlight.

"Have you seen Raysh recently?" I asked him, though that hadn't really been the question on my mind.

He scanned the forest, hands flexing at his sides. Mana sparked from his fingertips like smoke from electrical charges. "No, I haven't. I can lead us in the general direction, but beyond that, we could go around in circles for a while."

I ground my teeth together, irritated. Both at myself for not thinking to look for Raysh sooner, and at the arrogant fox for not being here to carry out his emissary duties. But even if I had thought to find him sooner, I'm not sure I could've. He had simply appeared on my chest and appeared in my car before.

The only option was to wait for him.

Alder seemed to reach this conclusion as well, because he stuffed his hands in his pockets and shrugged. "I'm sure he'll find us," he said, though I could detect just a hint of doubt in his voice. "We should get moving in the right direction at least. It may take us a while to reach the water gate."

A jumble of nerves and excitement coiled tight in my chest. *The next spirit gate.* I could picture Mom in the meadow, pleading for me to save her. To unlock the gates in time for the solstice. We still had two days left. It had better be enough time.

The weight of our deadline hung over me and my stomach flipped with apprehension. We *needed* Raysh to show us the way.

Unfortunately, it wasn't like we had any other option than to just move forward without him and…pray.

We walked for a while, the stream we followed widening to the size of a small river. It still wasn't very large, but it was shallow with big, sharp rocks sticking up from the bed, tossing the water up and out, making it froth in white water rapids.

Alder grew tense beside me, his eyes glued to the crystal water racing over the rocks and exploding in bright white bubbles.

Partly to set him at ease, and partly because I wanted to, I took his hand, interlacing our fingers. He didn't say anything, but the muscles in his arms seemed to ease slightly. And his cheeks reddened.

At his palm against mine, I felt that gaping wound in my chest yawn wide and tremble inside me.

I thought of what Izzie said last night. *You better not be falling for him.*

I'd never trusted a boy enough to give him the label of boyfriend. After hearing all the rumors of how boyfriends and girlfriends cheated on one another and the nasty things they said behind their back, I'd always opted for what was safe. No one could abandon me if they didn't get close in the first place, right?

Of course, that hadn't stopped the pain of losing someone who was *supposed* to be there for me forever. No matter what. When I'd gotten amnesia and was taken to the hospital, I was told that I had parents who were worried about me and loved me and were going to take me home. I'd been relieved. I might not have known these people, but it was better than being completely alone in the world.

But then I'd watched her leave one night out the back door after a shouting match with my father that had woken me up in the first place.

It shouldn't have hurt as bad as it had. Had I even loved her yet? Maybe not then, but I'd trusted her. Trusted her to be there for me, to help me navigate a world without memories, without a past. Without an identity.

And she'd failed me.

"Briony?"

I looked up and Alder's face was close. His autumn breath chilled my hot, wet cheeks.

Once again, I hadn't even realized I was crying in the first place. It was like stepping down from Izzie's car all over again, nostalgia and longing kicking me in the gut at once, leaving me completely stunned.

"What's wrong?" he asked, his gaze raking over my face in open, deep concern.

"Nothing, I'm good. Just allergies." I sniffed, wiping at my eyes and cheeks, thoroughly humiliated. I couldn't remember crying when Mom had even left that night. But I was now, apparently.

Out of *freaking* nowhere.

"Briony—"

I ducked my head away and cleared my throat. "I'm fine."

Alder hooked my chin and wiped at a rogue tear with his thumb, continuing to look at me in a way that somehow ripped me in two. "Your *fine* is definitely not *fine*. We talked about everything when we were kids. And I know it's not really like that between us anymore, but…" He sighed. "I'm just saying, if you need to talk, I want to listen."

His offer was tempting, extremely tempting, but then I

remembered the poison ivy episode. How worried he'd been then and was now. I'd felt his guilt like it had been my own emotion. "I really am fine."

He studied me, then shook his head. "Of course you're not. How can you be? You lost ten years of your life and now you're on a rescue mission for your mom, all because of me."

"No, stop." I threw my hands up. "I knew you'd do this. It's why I didn't want to say anything. I don't blame you. None of this is your fault. You were just a *kid.*"

"It doesn't matter. I should've never gotten involved in your life—"

I took a step back, like I'd just had a drink thrown in my face—nineties sitcom style. Except there was no laugh track in the background, just a devastating silence. It reminded me of my conversation with Izzie, but for some reason this hurt a thousand, million times worse. "What? So you're *regretting* being my friend?"

Alder winced. "That's not what I said."

I folded my arms. "It's what you just implied."

"Briony, I'm just saying that it would've been easier for you, and safer, and we wouldn't be caught up in all this mess if we'd never—"

"Just. Stop." My growl was that of a mountain lion's. I'd never once blamed him for all this. He'd been a stranger to me, but earnest, and kind. And seemed to have truly *missed* me. Missed me like I was the reason that maybe he had a gaping hole in his chest, too.

But this...this stung like a rejection. It was like finding my father crying at the kitchen table, with my mom nowhere to be seen.

A long silence stretched between us. Then, after what felt like eternity, Alder spoke. "Honestly, I wish I *could* regret it. I think it would make me a better person if I did, but..."

With my chin still tilted downward, I raised my gaze to watch his expression carefully, waiting for the rest.

"I loved being with you. Every day was an adventure when we were together. There's no way I could really regret it. I'm just too selfish."

Before I realized what I was doing, I had taken his face in my hands once more. "Please, always be selfish." My thumbs brushed his cheeks, and my fingertips lightly raked across his jaw.

"My, my, am I interrupting something?"

Alder and I jerked apart, whirling around to find Raysh standing on the other side of the stream. His paws poised daintily on an old oak's roots that stretched a few feet and disappeared into the side of the river bank.

"Where have you been?" I snapped.

"I was finding the water gate and its key," he said, jumping down from the tree roots and leaping effortlessly across the creek.

"You didn't already know?" I asked as the fox trotted over to us.

"Must I remind you that I am very *old, and it has been five hundred years since I have visited the water gate? Besides"*—Raysh sniffed—*"foxes don't like water."*

"How far away?" Alder asked.

"It's still a ways up the river. You'll know when we get there."

Groves of hemlocks and American beech, even more rare trees, like the elusive white willow with its long draping curtains of leaves or gray poplars, lined our trail to the gate.

Sprites—a raccoon with ivy woven into its fur, and a possum with a tail covered in brambles—dove into flowering shrubs and scampered up trees when we got too close.

Meanwhile, the river grew wider and calmer. Our first clue that we were getting close was when the river was joined by a smaller brook, then another. It was as if all the streams and brooks and rivers in the ethereal plane were converging into one place.

One central location.

One gate.

The trees around us thinned, eventually revealing a big beautiful lake in the distance. The mist all around us was light blue, full of astral energy. The air was charged with power, and the whole forest was silent, as if holding its breath.

Weeping willows, river birches, poplars, and alders grew along the lake's edge, their leaves fluttering gently, a green mist trickling off to merge with the blue of the lake's mana, creating an aquamarine fog that disappeared into the sky.

It was breathtaking.

I could've stood there forever. The lake's surface reflected the trees and the mountains that seemed to stretch on behind it. What was truly magical was that I'd seen this scene in the physical world.

Even with all the spirit world's mystical and magical energies enhancing its beauty…it wasn't all that different from what was back home.

Yes, my home. The Smokies…this valley…it was my home. My heart thudded at the thought.

Alder's hand brushed mine, and I flinched back to the present to see him pointing at a small island in the middle of the lake. It had a few thin trees, but mostly wildflowers dotted the edge, their petals just barely grazing the water.

"Is that where the guardian is?" I asked.

Raysh chuckled. *"Foolish girl. That* is *the guardian."*

I was about to ask the fox what he meant, when the island *moved*.

Chills danced over my skin as I realized what I was staring at.

A head emerged from the waters of the lake, sending waves through the once calm, placid surface.

The head of a turtle.

"Cowabunga," I whispered.

Alder snorted next to me, obviously amused by my childhood cartoon reference. A tingling warmth spread through me at my ability to make him laugh.

Below us, Raysh pawed my shoelaces irritably. *"Can we focus, please? Getting this key will be challenging."*

"You still haven't told us what the key *is*." I gestured to the island-turtle resting in the middle of the lake. "And how the hell are we supposed to get close to it? I don't suppose you have a canoe?"

Just as the words were out of my mouth, the turtle dropped its head into the water, and blew a stream of ice across the surface of the lake.

"What's it doing?" I asked.

"Keeping the waters cool."

I glanced at Alder, then back at the ice bleeding into the lake. It wasn't the rivers feeding into the lake. It was the lake feeding the rivers. All of the chilled water of the Smokies could be traced back to here.

"That's why all of the waters in the Smokies are so cold. Even during the summer," I whispered.

Alder smiled. "Yep, it's a constant fifty-two degrees. You can thank the water guardian for that."

Once it was done blowing its icy breath over the water,

it dipped its head all the way under and the island started to move—fast, given its massive size—toward the rocky shore that was a quarter of a mile away. Its powerful legs, the size of an oak tree's trunk, thudded onto land, and waterfalls cascaded over the edges of its shell. Slowly, it turned, showing the shell's underside—smooth, pearly pink, like stone. Or was it an actual shell?

It was impossible to tell without getting closer.

"There's…there's no way. I mean, it's *huge.* How can we get around that thing?" My voice got higher with each word, all trace of my earlier humor gone.

"You have to, the key is the guardian's shell."

I stared at the fox, dumbfounded. "The whole *thing*?"

"You didn't have to use the whole rack of antlers on the earth guardian, did you? So, only a piece of its shell should work."

"Then how…" My words trailed off as I noticed the light pink, purple, peach, and gray stone fragments littering the shore. Most were probably too heavy and large for me to pick up, but there had to be at least one I could carry. The great turtle moved its giant body to rest against the shore, closing its eyes lazily, as if enjoying the sunlight like a regular turtle. As it settled against the rocky shore, slivers of the shell's underside chipped off, dropping to the ground like discarded flower petals. The lake lapped up the fragments, tossing them into the deep blue depths of the water gate.

"You're a good swimmer, right?" Alder muttered, scanning the shore.

"How did you know that?" I couldn't remember telling him about my swimming before.

He shrugged. "You liked swimming as a kid. I figured you'd keep with it."

I sucked in a breath. It wasn't just that Alder remembered,

but the fact that something from my forgotten childhood had remained the same.

I'd always wondered if I'd been a different person before the fire. If the flames had burned away the first Briony Redwrell and a new Briony Redwrell had walked through them.

And if they had, then was that why Mom had left?

Had she been comparing me to the daughter I'd been to the daughter she now had? Maybe she'd wanted the old me back.

So it was good to know, a relief really, that simple things like my likes and dislikes remained the same. That I was not just a person made of my past, but my own person, and not even the strongest forest spirit in these mountains could take that away from me.

And I wouldn't have known that if I hadn't met Alder. More and more, he was making me understand why we'd been friends in the first place.

He caught me staring and his eyes seemed to spark. "What?" he asked.

"Nothing," I said, jerking my gaze away. "You were saying about swimming?"

"There's a small river that leads closer to the spirit," Alder said, pointing toward another river that flowed out into the Smokies. It cut through the rocky shore that the turtle lounged across. "We can swim down it and get to the shore without it noticing."

"I think you mean swim *up* it. The current is coming away from the lake."

"I can control the current."

"You know, I really should've called that one."

Alder hid a smile as we moved through the forest in the direction of the river, Raysh following behind us, silently slipping through the undergrowth, his tail swishing this way and that. When Alder waved his hand across the river, blue mana trickled out of his fingers like rivulets, merging with the mana in the river and, in turn, adjusting the current.

Leaving Raysh by the bank, Alder and I slipped into the water. I hissed out a breath through my clenched teeth at the freezing temperature and gave a violent shiver. Then we dunked our heads below the surface, submerging ourselves into a world of aquamarine, the plants and water mana blurring together to create a pastel hue that was…well, ethereal.

Alder swam ahead of me, moving through the river like Michael Phelps. I was able to keep up fairly well but had to pull and kick a little harder than normal because of the extra weight of my clothes. Alder was fully clothed, too, but it didn't seem to bother him one bit. Being a nature spirit, able to literally control the current around us, clothes probably didn't weigh him down as they did for a normal human. He didn't think to even take off something as simple as his shirt.

Pity.

Alder stopped swimming, thrusting out his arm and stopping the current. The water stilled to that of a swimming pool and he kicked his way to the surface. I followed, our heads breaking the surface.

Blinking water from my eyes, I noticed that we were still nowhere near the guardian. Why had he stopped?

Then I saw the hint of something stick out from the water. Like a shark fin. Clearly, that was impossible, but the water sloshed around us, like something *big* was coming.

"Briony—get out—" Alder started to yell, but it was too late.

Something knocked against my leg and I was pulled under.

Precious air escaped my lips as two shapes raced past me with the speed of missiles, jet streams of bubbles trailing behind. And then the current was back, pulling me to the right, and I followed it, knowing it was better not to fight it.

But I managed to get my bearings, pulling myself level. I almost wished I hadn't, though.

A whole swarm of gigantic fish charged for us in an underwater stampede, throwing the current of the once-calm river into raging white rapids.

Chapter Sixteen

Fish scales scraped against me, carrying me farther away from the guardian, back up the river, toward sharp rocks. Amidst the bubbles, I could only just make out the spots on the scales and their golden-orange underbellies. They were brook trout, the only native trout species in the Smokies.

Of course, I was quite sure normal brook trout didn't grow to four feet long.

Rocks came up sharply on my right, jutting toward the surface. I had just enough space to avoid being taken up into the rapids, and for one brief moment, I thought, *I can do this.*

Then my elbow slammed into a rogue stone and the pain made me gasp.

Underwater.

Not a good thing to do.

But I couldn't help it. Hitting your elbow standing still was painful enough—all those nerves arcing through your body and freezing you, but this pain was ten thousand times worse. I'd probably sliced open my skin and hit it so hard my shoulder jerked unnaturally. The rest of my body followed, and I lost whatever control I had.

Freezing water slipped down my throat and into my nostrils, too, filling my lungs. It stung and burned, but it wasn't any worse than the constricted, desperate *panic* that had me kicking and thrashing. My vision started to tunnel and as it did, the water around me shifted unnaturally. Like the entire river just...*tilted*.

Instead of sloshing left and right, splashing against the banks, or forward, speeding ahead, it went...up.

From its center, the river parted like the Red Sea. Great towers of water surged up to the sky on either side, creating walls of churning liquid against the banks, the trees and brambles and grass doused by showers and icy water.

I rolled over onto the river bed and coughed, my body surrendering the small amount of water I'd swallowed. Then I looked up.

Alder stood in the middle of the river, water stretching toward the sky, his eyes glowing bright like two wisps and his hand outstretched and trembling.

A few trout had been caught in the walls of water, and their fins flapped and splashed. The force of the river strained behind the strong blue mana barrier that flowed out of Alder's outstretched hands.

He took careful steps toward me and then crouched down. "Brye? Can you move?"

The towers of water shuddered and Alder's eyes flared gold again, mana pouring out of his arm to strengthen the barrier that held off tons of raging, angry, icy water.

My body felt beaten and bruised, but no bone seemed to be truly broken. Trembling, I lifted myself on my good elbow and let out a groan. My elbow still screamed in agony and my left side was in an immense amount of pain. "My side," I rasped. I didn't know what a broken rib felt like, but if it felt worse than this then I definitely never wanted one.

"I've got you." His other hand waved through the air right over the left side of my rib cage.

His mana, silver this time, rose up from his skin and spread onto mine. Like the steam off a teacup, it whirled and teased and disappeared under my skin.

I could *feel* the energy—*his* energy—rush through me like a blood transfusion.

It chased away the pain. Curled around my bones, the places where it hurt the most, my elbow and left rib. Pressure, warm and soothing, coated my muscles and nerves, taming my pain and making it bearable.

No, not just bearable. Nonexistent.

In no time, the pain was gone, his mana disappearing like the wisps of smoke from a strong breeze.

Quickly, we climbed the river bank. The moment we were clear, Alder dropped his arm, his whole body shuddering as the river splashed down in a miniature tidal wave. It rained down on us as the trout jumped and twisted in midair, then fell back into the river and swam away.

"That was…incredible." My heart was still racing from being overrun by giant trout, almost drowning, and then witnessing Alder move an entire river.

Alder hunched over, panting with strain as he rested his palms on his knees. "That took a lot of energy."

I rested a hand on his shoulder. "If you get into the river it'll help restore your mana, right?"

He raised an eyebrow, his breathing slowing. "How did you know that?"

"I saw how you soaked up mana from the ground after the earth gate. That's how it works, right? You draw mana from the ethereal plane. But you should rest for a few minutes."

He nodded, wiping droplets from his chin with the back of his hand. "No, let's keep going."

The trip downstream was trout-free, while swimming

with Alder was almost effortless the second time around. We swam closer together, riding with the current that he manipulated.

When we finally reached the water gate, Alder squeezed my hand, pulling me to the bank. Together, we broke the surface of the water, and I sucked in a breath to see the monster turtle a mere twenty-five yards away. Its head was lying on the smooth rock, warmed by the sun. Its eyes were closed, and I could swear I heard it *snoring*.

"Okay, get ready," Alder said, pushing himself out of the river then kneeling on the shore, water dripping from his silver hair and his shirt clinging to every inch of his body.

"What are you going to do? Lure him out with pizza?" I whispered, pulling myself out of the water as well.

Alder chuckled. "He looks more like a Donatello to me."

"Alder."

"Brye, you have to get the key. I'll distract him. That's how this works."

"I know, but..." I ran a hand through my wet hair. It tangled and snagged, and I mentally groaned knowing it would be a rat's nest by the time it dried.

He shook his head and said simply, "You don't get it."

"I don't get what?" I asked, scowling.

Yes, I had trust issues, and I had trouble being a team player. Relying on someone was difficult for me, but I knew that my hesitation for Alder to be the distraction again wasn't just because I didn't trust him.

I didn't want to see him hurt.

Before I could argue any further, the turtle breathed deeply. The sound made Alder and I freeze, our gazes bouncing from the turtle back to each other.

Yep, this conversation could wait.

Alder took off across the wet boulders covered in water,

algae, and slime. His strong legs jumped from rock to rock, landing smoothly on each. How he didn't fall was beyond me. I certainly would have. He was quiet, too, his feet barely making a sound across the wet stone.

I scrambled up the bank, but not nearly as gracefully, and kept my gaze locked on the prize: a pearly pink shell fragment the size of a dinner plate nestled right next to the guardian's leathery front toe. It was about the only one within decent reach that I could carry easily.

As I balanced on the rocks, carefully jumping from one to the next, I checked Alder's progress. He was already nearing the turtle's face.

I prayed that he wouldn't have to do anything, that it would continue to sleep the day away, and I could merely tip-toe over, grab its broken piece of shell, and make like a tree and leaf.

Damnit, no one is ever around for my good ones.

Once I hit the part of the shore where the rocks flattened out, I moved faster, my sneakers slipping and sliding on the wet, slimy stones. Ducking under the lip of his shell, where a curtain of moss and vines dangled off the side, I felt something heavy hit my shoulder. My pulse jumped as I frantically tried to brush it off. The heavy thing hit the stone at my feet.

Hissing.

I shrieked, the sound echoing along the shore.

The turtle's sapphire reptilian eye snapped open in my direction. The guardian lifted itself on its trunk-sized legs and delivered a loud roar. A Jurassic Park roar.

While the snake—an eastern black kingsnake—elongated, stretching in a way that indicated it was about to strike. A small voice in my head reminded me that this snake wasn't poisonous. Only northern copperheads and timber rattlesnakes were the two species of snakes that were poisonous out of the twenty-three species found in the Smokies.

Still.

Poison ivy wasn't supposed to have almost killed me, either.

The snake was already irritated after being tossed from its dry island down to a shore covered with water. It gave an angry hiss, revealing two long fangs.

Above, the guardian swiveled its soft, leathery neck toward me. The upper part of the mouth was shaped like a triangle. A snapping turtle.

And snap it did.

I fell backward, the mouth coming up short by just a few feet—thanks to a strand of vines around his neck acting like a lasso. Alder was on the other end of the vines, pulling back on the neck of the guardian with all his strength.

"Get the shell!" he yelled.

I bolted for it, but the snake hissed angrily, its body coiling around the shell as if it knew exactly what I was after.

Cursing, I tried to lunge for it anyway, but Raysh's voice pierced the air. *"Don't let it touch you!"*

I froze, my hand outstretched, and the snake's unnatural green glowing eyes latched onto it. Just waiting to sink its fangs in deep.

My pulse pounded in my ears as Alder's grunts from holding back the neck of the turtle reverberated in my muscles and nerve-endings.

Aggravated, the snapping turtle grabbed the vines in its mouth and whipped its head to the side. The momentum of the vines coming from the guardian's great tug sent Alder flying into the lake with a large splash.

As Alder sank into its depths, the snake and the giant

turtle turned their glowing eyes toward me.

"Use your mana, Briony."

Raysh's voice whispered in my ear, like the spirit was right beside me. Guiding me.

"Use it?" I muttered.

But I couldn't use mana like Alder. I wasn't a nature spirit.

Then I remembered Alder's words.

"Some days it was hard to tell the difference between you and any other spirit."

I raised my hand, my fingers flexing as I focused on this reservoir of mana inside me. Reaching deep into this pool of astral energy, I imagined the water from the surrounding rocks congealing, coagulating, *converging* into one giant wave. Blue mana trickled out of my fingertips, trembling and shaking. Weak, but there. I fed it more strength, pouring as much mana as I could from my reservoir into a river of my own making.

The blue energy pulled millions of droplets off the rocks, floating them in midair, and when I felt I had enough power behind it, I flicked my wrist forward.

And splashed the spirit guardian right in the face.

Oops. I *had* been aiming for the snake—the creature that hated water.

The water spirit didn't even blink, but luckily the movement did surprise the snake enough to uncoil itself from the shell and dart into the shadows of the guardian's underbelly.

I dove for the shell fragment, scooped it up, and raced back toward the lake.

The guardian roared again and jerked its neck forward. Icy cold air blew at my back like the arctic wind. Its mouth was right behind me. Mere seconds from closing in.

At the same moment, the water receded from the shore, like an ocean tide pulling in. It built and built, rearing back into a gigantic wave that rose high above the turtle.

Within the wave was Alder. He reached his hand out to me, his fingertips emerging from the stirring curtain of blue mana and restrained water. Without a second thought, I launched myself into the wave, diving off the rocky shore just as I would off a block at the rec center pool. My streamlined arms pierced through the wave's wall and Alder's hand wrapped around my middle, pulling me tight against him.

In one fluid movement, Alder let go of the mana and the force of the displaced water shot us away from the shore, into the center of the lake, buffeting our bodies against the strong magical currents.

We had to get to the mouth of a river. Still being within the water gate was too dangerous. The guardian could come after us and chomp us up for a midafternoon snack. But Alder had used up almost everything he had with that wave. I could feel it from his touch and the mana mixing with mine.

I still had some, though.

But was I strong enough to get us to a river?

I had to try. I tightened my grip on the shell fragment and on Alder's waist as he had mine. Once again summoning the reservoir of mana inside, and pushing it down around my legs, I gave one powerful kick.

We shot through the water like a missile straight into the closest river mouth. I'd forgotten how powerful the current had been and, too late, I worried we'd hit rocks and rapids.

Just as I was trying to figure out how to slow down and get safely to the river bank, three dark shapes darted around us.

Chapter Seventeen

The shadows within the water spun around us like sleek eels, and I worried, for a brief moment, if they actually *were* eels. If they were electric, I shuddered to think what would happen if they shocked me. Judging from the effect of the poison ivy, a spirit eel's mystical energy could stop my heart in one second flat.

Still holding onto Alder, I tried twisting around in the water, feet first, thrusting my other hand out holding the shell to stop our wild momentum. But then a furry body shoved my wrist.

Jerking my head to the side, I caught a glimpse of a small brown fluffy face with black eyes and algae whiskers.

An…otter?

Another one pushed against Alder's side, guiding us into the mouth of the river. As the current slowed around us, I realized that the otters were doing that, too.

They were helping us.

In calmer waters, I kicked up and gasped as oxygen filled my burning lungs. Thankfully, we had traveled far enough downstream to safely get to shore. I focused on guiding Alder's limp body back up the bank, ignoring the playful otters that jumped and moved about, pulling on Alder's shirt and nudging my legs, as we crawled up the bank. I knew they were speaking, but I couldn't understand their tittering. It was too fast and too jumbled to decipher anything.

Especially when all I wanted to do was lay my head on my arms and sleep for two years.

Carefully placing the shell on the grass within reach, I maneuvered Alder onto his back, keeping his calves in the river, and watched as blue mana from the river seeped into his skin.

I dipped my toe in and the mana brushed against me, but as I suspected, the energy didn't merge with mine as it did him. If I wanted more mana, and I was pretty sure I did if it would allow me to help open these gates, I would have to get it directly from Alder.

Which would be difficult considering he seemed to cut it off from me each time he touched me. I hadn't felt his skin or the senses of the Smokies inside me unless he allowed me to. It was…frustrating.

"Turtle and pebbles, play, play," an otter squeaked hopping over my legs. So their tittering had been English after all, and not their own little otter language. They had to be more than just sprites then. It was then I noticed its fur and whiskers were covered in algae and its tail was a *cattail,* as in the water plant.

The other two otters joined in, singing and squeaking in jumbles that hardly made any sense.

"River bank, river bank, wet."

"Wet, wet, wet."

"Minnows and pebbles. Minnows."

"Run and jump. Sun and dragonflies."

"Human, human, human," another sang, rubbing his algae whiskers up and down my arm.

"New, new, lord, new," the third one trilled.

It took me a moment to put their meaning together. "Human" and "new."

"New human?" I asked the river spirits. "Is there an *old* one?"

Could that be…Mom?

I tried to grab one, but it danced out of my reach, and they all squeaked louder, excited, thinking it was a game.

Next to me, Alder groaned. Blinking in the bright sunlight, he blew out a long breath. He touched my wrist and wrapped his fingers around it, but to my disappointment, no mana absorbed into my skin.

"Are you okay?" I asked.

The otters continued to squeak and giggle and throw around nonsense words.

"Quiet," Alder growled hoarsely.

Immediately, the otters stopped their prancing and playing, obeying him.

I flicked his arm. "They saved our asses. Be nice."

At that, an otter rubbed his whiskers against Alder's hand, and he petted its head.

The otter purred like a kitten. *"Tikki good, Tikki good."*

Alder chuckled weakly as he sat up. "Yes, Tikki, you did good. Tavi! Rikki! Leave Briony alone," Alder snapped.

The otter that had curled on my lap, digging his paws into my wet shirt, and the other one who had been chewing on the end of my hair, both leaped up and jumped back into the river, their brother quickly following.

For a moment, I sat there, stunned. "Rikki, Tikki, Tavi?"

Alder leaned his head back on the bank and pursed his lips, his cheeks flushing.

"I know that book… Did we read that as kids? Did you name them after it?"

He nodded sheepishly. "It fit."

Laughing, I shook my head. "That's amazing."

His brow furrowed in an almost pained expression, and I thought of when he'd told me how much he missed me, and how every day with me had been an adventure. My throat tightened. He named them from a book we'd read. From a book I was sure we probably loved.

He rubbed his temple and sighed. "I haven't been this dehydrated in a while. And dizzy."

I brushed a blade of grass from the bank off his damp cheek. "Kinda sounds like you're drunk."

Alder raised an eyebrow. "Drunk?"

"It's a human thing, c'mon." I gripped his hand and pulled him up just as Raysh bounded into view.

"I see you retrieved the water key."

Flashbacks of the ordeal came back to me in flickering images, and I realized how much I'd needed the two of them. Alder's mana had once again proved to be incredibly useful, and Raysh had instructed me to use my own, opening myself up to a new power I'd never had before.

I picked the shell up and ran my hand across the sleek, pearly surface. "Thanks for your help back there—both of you, I guess." I tried to keep my tone genuinely grateful, but there was a strong part of me that wished I'd been fast enough and graceful enough to get the shell on my own. Then I stood and turned to Alder.

"Can you get us back to the physical world? We've got a gate to open."

Alder's wind tunnel dropped us next to the lake that he'd led me to after he pulled me out of the ethereal world. I recognized it immediately, with the trees and the mountains in the distance. Gorgeous and real—not made of astral energy or spirits. Magical in itself. Sights like this were the reason the ethereal world existed in the first place.

There are places in the world that are special.

I looked down at the glowing shell, tracing my fingers along the jagged edges, and then passed it to Alder.

For a moment he just held the shell, but then blue mana bled out of his fingers. The astral energy spread like blue arteries, pumping life and Alder's own unique mana into the water gate's key.

When the entire shell was encased in a blue glow, it flashed with light and shrunk to the size and composition of a small pearly-pink stone. Sweeping his thumb across the surface, Alder dropped the stone into my hand.

"Why don't you do the honors?"

"Can I?" I asked Raysh.

"It does not matter who infuses the key into its element, just as long as it has his mana."

A small thrill went through me as I moved my wrist back in a whip-like motion and chucked the stone. It skipped across the surface of the lake, hitting it three times before sinking into the water.

Alder shielded his eyes from the sun and gave a low whistle. "Three skips. Pretty impressive."

"Thanks, I'm hoping to bring back the gold." I grinned. I never remembered learning how to skip rocks, but I must've at some point. "Did you teach me how to do that?"

Alder smirked, shoving his hands into his pockets. "I might've."

A second later, the entire lake rippled.

I grabbed Alder's arm, a sudden alarming thought coming to me. "Do you think—do you think it's going to flood?" I asked, my voice hitching in fear.

Before Alder could answer, the bottom fell out of the sky.

Torrents of rain crashed down upon us and I gasped, water flying into my mouth as it hit my face and cheeks and covered me and everything around me in mere seconds.

Of course. The water in the Smokies didn't just come from the lakes and rivers and brooks.

It came from its storms. They were wild and unpredictable.

Like a spirit itself.

The translucent fox didn't mind it one bit. The emissary just turned and walked away, his glowing form disappearing into the dark downpour. *"Until tomorrow."*

Alder's hand grabbed mine, tugging me forward. "This way!" he called over the pounding rain.

I followed him while trying to keep the water out of my eyes. I expected to never be dry again.

We didn't have to run very far. Through the driving showers, I could make out a structure—an old abandoned home. It was small with red paint peeling off the sides, revealing white worn wood, consumed by time and the elements. Alder tugged me onto the decaying porch and through the rotting door, our footsteps squeaking and creaking across the splintering floorboards.

The rain sounded like it was going to tear through the roof. Pushing back my wet mane of hair from sticking to my cheeks, I eyed the ceiling warily. "How long do you think it'll last?"

Alder hovered in the doorway, looking straight up into the sky. "You can never tell with these storms."

Wild. Unpredictable.

Unable to resist, I took in the navy shirt plastered to his skin, outlining the muscles in his back and shoulders. Everything about him was powerful—wild, mystical, entrancing, a storm in his own right.

Yet he was wonderfully gentle, too. Petting the otter spirits, carrying me, drawing out the poisonous mana from my skin.

Maybe he was more like heat lightning. A storm off in the distance, where the thunder was too far to hear and the summer lightning would flash against high clouds on the horizon, illuminating the sky. He had all the mystery and wonder of a storm, but none of its destruction.

"I don't get what?"

Alder turned away from watching the rain and raised an eyebrow in confusion. "What?"

"Back before the water gate, you said I don't get it. What don't I get?"

"Oh." He paled just slightly, his back-to-blond hair still dripping water down his jaw and neck. "Nothing. Don't worry about it."

"Nope, definitely worrying about it."

Alder hesitated, his arms crossing his chest. "I'm not sure how you'll handle it."

I placed my hands on my hips. "Well, you'll just have to risk it. Tell me."

He let out a puff of air that sounded a bit like a laugh, then glanced around the old house. Well, really, it was more like a shack.

"Briony, you..." He stared at me for a long moment. Like a gentleman, his gaze was locked on my face, but I was keenly aware of my own wet clothes and highly thankful that I'd chosen to wear an olive green shirt today.

"Spit it out, Alder."

"I'm the conduit for all three planes."

"Yeah, and?"

"Even though I go to the ethereal world, I'm not

supposed to *stay* there. I can talk to spirits there, I can even befriend some, but I can't have conversations with them. I can't really argue about something worthwhile, or play Clue, or just relax and eat blackberry pie. *You* were my first friend, Briony. *You* were the person who reached out to me.

"I've talked to the other folks in the valley once or twice. And they're nice. But they look at me strangely on the rare occasions that I pretend to be a hiker, just passing through. It's like they know, on some level, that I'm not really, fully human. And besides, ever since I'd realized what I'd done to you, I never got close to anyone else."

He ran both hands through his wet hair, eyes glassy, jaw clenched, and body coiled tight, reminding me of the kingsnake on the rocks.

Guarding itself.

"It's…I'm…" He swallowed.

"Lonely," I filled in for him.

Without realizing it, I'd moved closer to him. Very subtly, he nodded, as if he couldn't stand to admit it. To say it out loud.

I couldn't blame him. Much of my days following the fire had been lonely. I hadn't known my father very well at that point. The amnesia was fresh. And after this woman, who was supposedly my mother, left us, I was constantly asking myself if she had left because of *me*.

"I'm sorry," I whispered.

"That's not why I told you." He dropped his hand and sighed, still actively avoiding my gaze. "I just want you to understand why I can't *lose* you again. Not to a fire, not to a guardian. Not to a force of nature. Not to anyone or anything. Never again."

While I remained speechless, he turned away to continue watching the storm.

Unable to resist the confession that hit me like a gale strength wind, tossed me around like white water rapids, and crushed me like a landslide…I slid my hands around his chest and hugged him from behind, pressing my cheek against his back, right in the spot in between his shoulder blades.

He was frozen under my hold, his body incredibly stiff. It was like hugging a tree. But I only tightened my hold, the gap inside my chest trembling and aching.

"I wish *I* hadn't lost *you*," I murmured.

The pounding of rain filled the pause that followed, an unrelenting, mindless sound that was almost a relief. A relief that there was something to fill the emptiness following my admission.

I don't think I'd ever said something quite so vulnerable in my life, and the awkwardness of it made me draw away. But before I could step back and place more distance between us, Alder twisted back around, catching hold of my arms.

He intertwined our fingers, and the hint of his mana nudged against my skin. I knew he was holding it back, but I wished he wouldn't. Part of me wanted his mana to fill the reservoir I'd practically emptied at the water gate, but *most* of me just wanted to feel his skin. The warmth and the calluses of his fingers, the smoothness of his palms, and the intimate touch of the inside of his wrist.

"You're holding back," I noted.

His fingers tightened against mine. "For good reason. My mana is what got you into this mess."

I sighed. "You worry too much."

"Also for good reason." He stepped into my space and leaned his head down to rest on my shoulder. His autumn breath chilled my collarbone, goose bumps washing over my skin, even though I'd never felt so warm in my life.

"I really missed you." His lips brushed my skin. I wanted to feel them, too.

Letting go of his hands, I ran mine over his shoulders and upward into his short hair on the nape of his neck. Still, he held back his mana and the real, human touch of him. Human, or spirit, he was cutting himself off from me.

But truthfully, I didn't much care about the mana in that moment. I wanted to feel *him.*

Skating my hands from the back of his neck, I cupped his jaw, and he followed my direction, lifting his face closer to mine.

His mana flared under my touch and in that quick impulse, the Smokies rushed through me like rapids. But I ignored the mountain senses. It was his warm, damp skin that I'd been after. I wanted more of him. Wanted to breathe him in like the air my lungs had been craving for all those years away from this valley.

A thunderclap shook the skies and the shack around us.

It ripped me back to my senses, crashing to reality like the lightning striking a few miles away.

Alder stepped back so quick and fast that the absence of him was what I imagined missing a limb to be like. Turning to the side, I tried to calm my breathing—it was too shallow, too unnatural to pretend that moment hadn't just shaken me to my core.

We stayed apart and didn't say a word for the next half hour while the rain continued its dance across the forests, hitting every surface of leaf and tree, and flower, and stone, and creating an endless, haunting echo throughout the mountains.

Chapter Eighteen

I made it back to Gran's just a few hours before dinner and found the house completely empty and Izzie's CRV gone. Alder had left me outside the garden, so now here I was, standing on the welcome rug, alone, still soaking wet and dripping all over the embroidered sunflowers.

Were they still at Bridge Club?

I took a long, hot shower and changed into capris and a razor-back tank, choosing sandals this time, since my sneakers were practically ruined after traipsing all over the mountains and the ethereal plane. While snacking on some strawberries from the fridge, I took a look around the house. Izzie had done a lot of work, and the guilt of having my best friend take care of *my* grandmother and clean *my* grandmother's house made the usually sweet fruit taste bitter. So I shoved them back in the fridge and moved through the house, hoping to find something to clean or something to do that wouldn't make me feel quite so crappy.

There were little things, like that morning's breakfast dishes and taking in the laundry from the clothesline outside. While my grandmother had invested in a washer, she had not, apparently, bothered with a dryer. It was just lucky that the storm from the water gate had been isolated by the lake and hadn't soaked Gran's drying laundry. Unclipping some of my grandmother's long skirts, I folded them neatly and put them into a wicker basket. I took a moment to smooth my fingers over the woven fibers, feeling a distant memory try to rise to the surface.

But there was nothing.

Sighing, wishing more than anything I could get just a sliver, like the memory of the fairy figurine and the broken wing, I turned back to the clotheslines.

Izzie had even washed sheets. They were white with small blue flowers printed on the edges. A breeze sent waves of white fabric rippling in the wind.

And that's when it came.

A very small memory, but precious.

I was a child, weaving in and out of the sheets blowing with the summer breeze. I was running from someone, maybe hiding. I was trying not to laugh. A tan hand jerked back the white sheet, fingers wrinkling the intricate blue flowers. I dodged away from the blond boy, my seeker, and ducked under another sheet that hung on the opposite clothesline. Giggling. The boy followed, hoisting up the sheets and calling my name.

"Brye, I found you! You're it!"

The sound of my laughter came back to me, sweet and bitter, like the strawberries I'd had, and echoing in the hole inside my chest.

Blinking, I stood there, clutching the clean, dry sheet to my chest and trying to hold onto the memory, to burn every single detail in my brain.

Alder.

We really had been friends. I knew I wouldn't get all my memories back, but this was why I'd been so determined to come and stay here. Answers. Pieces of myself.

Knowing he'd been dear to me was one thing. Actually *seeing* it, felt like my heart was ripping itself in two.

With shaky hands, I stuffed the sheets into the basket and brought them inside to Gran's room to make her bed. I tugged the fitted sheets tight around the edges and then fluffed the main sheet. As it whipped up, the sheet knocked over a glass on Gran's nightstand.

Cursing under my breath, I moved around the bed and let loose a sigh of relief. The cup hadn't broken because it was plastic, but it still had been half filled. Most of the water had gotten on the floor, but some of it had dripped into the drawer of her nightstand.

After grabbing a rag from the kitchen, I mopped up the water on the floor and opened the drawer. Luckily, there wasn't much in it. Gran's reader glasses, a few pill bottles, some pens, and a paperback romance novel with a vampire guy on the cover with his nipple showing. *Fangs of Desire*.

"Good for you, Gran," I muttered, wiping off a few water droplets from the cover and placing it back in the drawer. The one thing that had not gotten wet, thankfully, was a loose sheet of paper.

I meant to shove it back inside the drawer, not wanting to snoop—when the name on it stopped me dead.

This was a letter. Signed by Heather.

Heather as in…my mother.

I devoured it.

Dear Mom,

You'll be angry at me for this. For years and years, probably. But you're also a mother, so I know you will understand on some level. And I know you'll never stop loving me, no matter how angry this makes you.

I have to go. You know I do. Jimmy thinks it's superstitious nonsense, but you and I both know it's not. He'll come for her again and try to take her away from me. I can't let that happen. I will take her place and hopefully that will satisfy him. I pray that it will be enough, but if not, please, keep her away from this Valley. I'm sorry to take you away from your only granddaughter, but you know what's at stake.

Please don't tell Jimmy and Briony. Especially Briony. I don't want this to hang over her all her life. They've already taken her past—I won't let them take her future. She deserves happiness, even if I am not a part of her life. Don't tell Jimmy. I don't want him to worry about me and what I've done. Besides, he will take care of our daughter. He'll move her away and it will be for the best.

I love you to the tops of the mountains, around the moon, and down the slopes of the Valley.

Love,

Your Heather

I wasn't sure how long I sat there, reading the letter. Rereading it. And reading it again. I read it so many times that I'd memorized most of it.

Mom hadn't just left one night because she couldn't handle a daughter with no memory of her with a husband that argued with her all the time. She hadn't just left because she no longer loved me or Dad.

There had been no rabbit hole.

She had gone to the spirit world *because* of me.

To take *my* place. For what, I couldn't even guess.

I felt like throwing up. My stomach heaving, I rushed into Gran's bathroom and splashed water on my face to help get rid of the terrible nausea.

Alder had said it was *his* fault that all this was happening, and I'd tried to tell him that he'd just been a kid, so he couldn't be blamed for that.

But I realized that nothing I said could stop that guilt. That terrible, sickening feeling that you had caused someone so much pain.

Because now I felt it, too. Mom *had* loved me, and it was *my* fault that she was locked in the spirit world in the first place. This whole time I'd thought maybe she'd somehow stumbled into it. Or the same spirit that had gone after me might have just taken her, too. Because that's what this spirit did. Took people.

But it was so much worse than that. She had left to ensure my safety. She had...*sacrificed* herself for me.

Looking up from the sink, I saw my reflection in Gran's mirror. Saw how the water dripped off my face and ran down my throat and passed over my lips.

I wasn't sure how much of that was water from the sink, or my own tears.

Pacing the living room, I got more and more antsy. Gran and Izzie still weren't back yet. Not that it was a cause for concern, but I was desperate to talk to Gran about the letter. To ask her what she'd known.

At last it made sense. This letter was why Gran had never contacted me for six years, and why the minute I'd shown up on her doorstep she wanted to turn me away. Because even though Mom might have sacrificed herself to this spirit, there was no telling if the spirit might want me again if I ever returned.

She'd also never told Dad why she left because she knew he didn't believe in nature spirits. *Jimmy thinks it's superstitious nonsense.*

Finally, I got fed up with waiting and decided to take Gran's truck and go see them at bridge. From my short stay here between the fire and when Dad moved us to Knoxville, I remembered the local town was tiny. Just a cluster of houses and local shops off the well-beaten path of one of Tennessee's many highways. I should be able to find it even without Google Maps.

I couldn't stay in that house alone for one more second. In the back of my mind, I considered going to Alder to tell him what I'd found, but the letter felt fiercely private, and I didn't want to pull him into my guilt spiral as well. I was almost certain he'd blame himself for this, too, even more than he already did.

No, I felt as if this was my burden to bear alone.

Plus, it didn't help that seeing him after that almost-kiss was going to be incredibly awkward.

How could I have been *so stupid*? Izzie literally told me not to get too close. More than that, I barely knew him. Half a week. That was as long as I knew him.

But that wasn't what my heart told me.

My heart told me that at one point, I'd known him better than I knew myself.

Except for that one small memory of hide-and-go seek, my mind came up blank.

It was *unbelievably* frustrating.

Gripping Gran's steering wheel until my knuckles turned white, I pulled out onto the rural highway, turning right. I remembered passing the town's sign on the way to Gran's with Izzie. It was just a simple sign with the words FIREFLY VALLEY carved into the wood, the paint faded and peeling.

Braking slowly and turning off the highway, I guided Gran's pickup down the gravel road into the town of Firefly Valley. Or maybe they called this the "downtown" area of the valley. Who knew? It barely qualified as an actual town anyway.

The old road was worn and lined with small houses-slash-shops. Many of them were extremely familiar. I stepped on the brake and came to a complete stop when I passed a light-yellow house with a sign on the front that said MICK'S VALLEY EGGS. The logo was carved into a wood sign similar to that of the town's, and a low fence of chicken wire ran around the perimeter of the messy yard. Three chickens pecked their way around the house, strutting, then pausing, jerking their heads in staccato movements. Smiling, I continued down the road, going even slower than before, hoping another shop would jump out at me.

Sure enough, a light-green house with a white picket fence and a big ole porch with rocking chairs made me slow to a crawl. The sign on the fence read FARRAFIELD HONEY, and a memory came rushing back to me—Gran spreading a lump of honey on a steaming biscuit then serving it to me. Mom had been in the living room with Dad. They'd been arguing, yet again, about what to do about their destroyed home. Should they rebuild? Dad wanted to move. Mom had said it didn't matter where they went.

"He would find her anyway, Jim."

I came to a full stop, latching onto that memory and trying to pull more from it. But it was faint, buried under six years of me trying to repress the pain and confusion after the fire.

She must have been talking about the spirit. About the one coming after me from the fire, which had to be the same one she went out to sacrifice herself to, because I'd been safe ever since she left.

Swallowing, I eased off the gas and nudged the truck forward. She'd been protecting me, loving me, all along. I hated that I'd wasted so many years being angry and bitter.

Finally, I came to where the road ended in a cul-de-sac. There were about five other houses, one of which seemed pretty busy. And by busy, I mean more than one car parked in front—including Izzie's CRV. I swerved the truck into a spot next to Izzie's and climbed out, noting the sign that read TILLYWATER'S CAFÉ.

Like everything else in this tiny, one-street town, the house seemed to be half cottage, half something else. In this case, a restaurant-slash-coffee shop. I wondered if it was the only one within a twenty-minute drive. On the porch lounged two cats, bathing in the late evening sun. They barely opened their eyes as I mounted the creaky steps and grabbed the front door handle. With a little wave to the tabby whose tail swished by my feet, I stepped inside.

A bell jingled above me, and I closed the door behind me with a *snap*.

Tillywater's Café had once been a large living room, with big bay windows on either end, where ivy hung down from the roof and the leaves lightly tapped the glass. It had shiny, dark wood floors and small tables and chairs with a loveseat and a chintz sofa in front of a coffee table. The space felt like an indie coffee shop where you'd see college kids with hipster glasses and tattoos typing on MacBooks and sipping over-priced coffee while working on their screenplay, novel, or simply a term paper that would one day change the world.

The irony was that this place was probably around long before that scene. Just a place for some neighbors to get together and sip iced tea.

Nestled in a corner with a card table sat Izzie, Gran, and three other sweet-looking older ladies each holding a hand of cards. Everyone looked up at the tinkle of the doorbell, and Gran's smile stretched wide when she saw me. "Briony!

Come over, meet the girls."

Two of "the girls" I recognized almost immediately. There was Mrs. Farrafield, an African-American woman with gray braids and thick glasses, who happened to harvest the best honey in the Smokies. And the other I knew was the wife of Mr. McKlinnon, owner of Mick's Valley Eggs. She was maybe a decade older than the rest—possibly early seventies—with pale, wrinkled skin, short white hair with streaks of gray and strong-looking, callused hands. The third woman wore a beautifully knitted shawl, had tan skin, gray hair, and dark eyes, and she didn't ring any bells.

My gaze moved from each of their faces to Izzie, who gave me a look worth a dozen questions. I mouthed, *"I'll tell you later."*

As soon as I got to the table, women I barely knew stood to hug me, all saying things like, "You got so big!" and "Look how pretty you are!" and "I can't believe it's been so long—how's your daddy?"

I murmured pleasantries, saying "thank you" when required.

"Well, bless my stars and garters! Is that lil' Briony Redwrell?"

Glancing toward the sound of my name, I saw the waitress—well, most likely the owner of Tillywater's Café—walk around the corner of what was probably the kitchen.

She was a lady with big glasses and big hair, and the prettiest smile I'd ever seen.

The moment she reached the table, the woman gave me a hug, her cheek bumping into mine. "So good to see you, darlin'."

I could only nod and smile—I hadn't been expecting to see all these people who would remember me. Firefly Valley had been my *home*. I'd grown up with these women.

Whether or not I remembered little more than their names, they certainly remembered *me* and cared about me.

It was both heartwarming and a little sad.

"Hey, Ms. Tilly, can I get some more tea?" Izzie asked, raising her empty mason jar with ice cubes in it and condensation dripping from the glass.

"Of course, honey. Anything you want. How about you, Briony? Sweet blackberry tea?" Ms. Tilly asked as she pulled out a chair from another table and wedged it on the other side of Gran.

"Yes, please. That sounds amazing."

She booped my nose. "Coming right up, cutie pie."

She bustled back into the kitchen, and I sank into the seat she had pulled out for me. Now that I was here, I wasn't sure what I'd been thinking. I couldn't just demand Gran leave her game because I'd found a letter that made me rethink my entire existence.

It would've been deeply rude, and we had our Tennessee hospitality to maintain.

So I sat back and waited. I had no idea how to play bridge, but that didn't matter. Twenty minutes went by, and the women didn't play a single hand. It was clear the card game was their excuse to sit around and gossip. Of course, with two new visitors, they were probably even more distracted.

"So what are you up to these days, Briony? Your friend Izzie was just telling us how much of an amazing swimmer you are," Mrs. Farrafield asked as she patted me on the knee.

Mrs. McKlinnon nodded sagely. "Oh, she must get that from her momma."

A hush fell over the little table, and I couldn't help but glance at Gran. To her credit, Gran merely cleared her throat and said with a smile, "I've got to use the little girls' room again. That tea runs right through me."

I started to stand to help her with her crutches, but she swatted away my hands. "Just sit, Briony, I'm fine!"

I clenched my fists under the table as Gran hobbled toward the back hallway. Oh, I so desperately wanted to tell her everything—all that I knew and how I was working on getting Mom back. But I couldn't tell her *here*.

"Darla!" the third woman hissed, setting down her hand of cards and glaring at Mrs. McKlinnon.

Mrs. McKlinnon knitted her brows in concern. "Oh, I'm so sorry, Briony dear. That was insensitive of me."

I shook my head. "It's okay. I mean, you don't need to apologize. It's kinda nice to know that we had things in common. I didn't know Mom was a swimmer."

"Oh, she was an everything!" Mrs. McKlinnon laughed. "Such spirit in that girl."

I was *acutely* aware of the fact that she said *was.*

"And such an imagination, too," Mrs. Farrafield mumbled into her tea.

"What do you mean?" I asked, leaning into the table, squeezing its edge tight.

Mrs. Farrafield blinked, her brown eyes slightly magnified by her large glasses. "Nothing, dear."

"Mrs. Farrafield, please tell me." My voice was strong yet gentle. Coaxing.

The two other women shot glances toward the bathroom, while Mrs. Farrafield pursed her lips. Izzie had frozen while sucking up the last bit of her blackberry tea, her straw in her mouth.

"Well, your mother… Let's just say she put more stock into local legends than most folks do around here. And I think Willa believes, too. On some level, at least. S'all just old folklore, though."

"What's all folklore?" I pressed. I'd never considered that the rest of this valley could know about the nature spirits and the ethereal plane. Figuring out more about the valley's history had never even crossed my mind—especially not when I'd been getting all my spiritual information directly from its most credible source: a spirit.

Mrs. Farrafield straightened, obviously feeding off all the attention I was giving her. "It's just something my momma told me and her momma told her. Nothing to worry about, hon."

"It's an old local legend about how a god lives in this valley."

I turned to look at the third woman with the tan skin and beautiful shawl. My pulse stuttered. "A god?"

"What's the legend, Mrs. Jackson?" Izzie asked, shooting her gaze to me then back to Mrs. Jackson.

"Oh yes, a god. Old settlers in the Appalachians told stories about a god that roamed the forests. Every hundred years, the god would come down from these mountains and mark a woman and steal her away to make her his bride."

Clunk.

We all sprang up from the table as Izzie knocked over her glass. Luckily, it was mostly ice, so tea didn't spill everywhere, but it got some of the cards wet and we had to hurriedly pick up the ice cubes before they all melted.

Around the same time, Ms. Tilly returned with my blackberry iced tea and got us a damp towel to mop up any sticky tea residue while Izzie apologized profusely. The older ladies waved her clumsiness away with a laugh, but their words and chuckles were muffled while my brain raced through the possibilities.

A god came down from the mountains to mark a woman and steal her away to make her his bride.

That had to be the mysterious *"he"* Mom had been referring to this entire time. But who was *he*? Not just another spirit, but a god? Well, that could be just part of the local legend. It could simply mean another spirit, or…could it be the guardian of the fire gate? But that would've been inconsistent with the behavior of the other two guardians. They didn't seem to care much about humans. They only wanted to protect their gates.

So what spirit was it?

Of course, I knew who Izzie thought it was.

Mr. Cheekbones.

The idea of it was so ridiculous, it bordered on amusing. Alder didn't want to make me his bride. We were childhood friends.

Okay, so we almost kissed earlier today. That wasn't the best timing. Even so, I was one hundred percent confident that he had no intention of "stealing me away," and I based this off our first meeting, how he'd been desperate to get me away from this valley, not keep me here with him.

How he asked me all the time if I was okay.

The tenderness in how he held me…

I dropped my head into my hands. *Stop thinking about him!*

"Briony? Sweetie, did you hear me?"

I looked up to find Gran balancing on her crutches, a concerned look on her face. "Don't tell me you're feeling bad again?"

"No—no, I'm fine, Gran. I promise."

"Well, regardless, we should be getting home for dinner. It's late, ladies," Gran said, addressing her Bridge Club members.

"Well, I swan! It's nearly dark!" Mrs. McKlinnon said, standing from the table and beginning to pack up her cards.

"Y'all leaving?" Ms. Tilly called from the hallway. "Let me get you a to-go cup for that tea, Briony."

"Thanks, Ms. Tilly."

The women shuffled about, distributing hugs and cheek kisses. Izzie and I accepted them graciously. There was something about a grandma telling you how pretty you were that made you feel all warm and fuzzy.

"Now, we'll see you both for the Firefly Festival, won't we?" Mrs. McKlinnon asked excitedly.

"Firefly Festival?" Izzie and I asked in unison.

Mrs. Farrafield gasped. "Willa! You didn't tell these girls about the festival? Why, it's only our little valley's claim to fame. Best kept secret in the Smokies, we say."

"I didn't think they'd be here that long," Willa said, giving me a side-eye that I rightfully ignored.

"What is it?" I asked.

"Oh you know, typical festival fun. Live band, funnel cakes, festival games, dancing, plus crafters from all over the Smokies come to peddle their wares. I'll have a booth, of course, selling my honey and preserves. And Darla's husband, Mick, will be selling his blue-ribbon eggs."

"That sounds amazing!" Izzie said, her eyes lighting up. She loved events like that.

"Oh, it is. You two will have to come," Mrs. McKlinnon said, patting Izzie's shoulder. "Invite your friends! Or boyfriends," she said, winking.

As we emerged out onto the porch with the rest of the ladies, a pickup truck pulled up in front of the café, and a large, burly mountain man—beard, plaid shirt, and all—stepped out of the truck and tipped an imaginary hat. "Evenin' ladies."

The Bridge Club all said their hellos to the mountain man, but I'd stopped listening. I was too busy staring at the bed of his truck. It was full of chopped wood and spare branches, which *would* have been normal if not for the pearly white mana wrapping around them like a second layer of bark.

I'd never seen anything like it before. The physical world wasn't exactly teeming with mana, at least not that I'd seen. But that was surely what it was—what else could it be? Only I, the girl who could see nature spirits, was staring at the truck bed like a weirdo.

"Ms. Tilly!" he called, "should these go around back?"

Ms. Tilly, who had been trying to hand me a to-go cup while I'd been occupied with the mana-covered wood, waved back. "Oh, hey there, Jasper! Yep, feel free to unload right around on the edge of the meadow. That's where everyone's been putting 'em."

"You got it!" he called back, then hopped back into his truck and pulled it around the cottage.

"What's that wood for?" I asked loudly, unable to stop myself from interrupting the other conversations around me.

"That's for the festival bonfire," Mrs. Jackson explained. "Everyone brings wood from all over the Smokies. Sometimes it's just a branch, or as you can see, sometimes they bring whole truckloads of spare wood. It's a tradition we started. Makes us feel connected, even though we might live far apart. We all love these mountains."

Although the bon*fire* part of it made me shiver with anxiety, I couldn't deny that it was a nice sentiment.

But, more importantly, what was the mana on that wood? Would Alder know? I'd have to ask him later.

"So when is the festival?" Izzie asked.

"Just two days from now," Mrs. Farrafield answered. "This weekend. In fact, setup is supposed to be happening all tomorrow."

Two days from now. The summer solstice. The same day I was supposed to bring my mom back from the spirit world.

I drove Gran home, and Izzie followed us in her CRV. I was trying to find a delicate way to bring up the letter when she asked, "How was your date?"

My heart jumped so big I nearly crashed the truck. "*What?*"

Gran narrowed her eyes at me. "Izzie said you went back to Knoxville for a date today."

That little sneak.

Swallowing, I kept my eyes trained on the road ahead, which was already pretty dark from the sun dipping well below the Blue Ridges.

"Um, it was good."

"Do you like him?"

That was a loaded question. "I don't know yet."

My lips tingled with the blatant lie. Even I couldn't deny that I liked him now.

Crap. Crap. Crap.

"Hmm, well. Sometimes that takes time. And sometimes you just know."

I groaned internally. How could I possibly have admitted that to myself? How could I already "just *know*"? It had never happened to me before.

"Your mother just knew."

My hands clenched involuntarily around the steering wheel. For so long, I'd avoided knowledge like this. I'd had no desire to learn about the woman who abandoned us.

How wrong I'd been.

"Really?" I asked, trying to keep my voice level.

"Oh, yes. She'd just started college in Maryville. Still lived at home to save money, and she met your father at a coffee shop. He'd just moved to the area to start his first job at an engineering firm. She came home from the coffee shop that day and said, 'Momma, I found the man I'm going to marry.'" Gran chuckled, shaking her head. "When your momma put her mind to something, she just did it."

My eyes burned, and the road became blurry. She had put her mind to saving me.

And she just did it.

She'd believed in that old legend. Knew there were spirits in the mountains and believed some kind of god had come to steal her daughter away. So she went to take my place.

Pushing back my tears and steadying my voice, I said softly, "I never knew that before."

"Yes, well, I imagine Jim doesn't talk about your mother much."

My non-response was answer enough.

"She loved you, you know," Gran whispered in the silence of the cab. "I know you may not believe that…after, well, her leaving. But…"

"No, Gran, I do. I know."

She reached over and patted my thigh. "You're a good girl, Briony."

Was I, though? I'd been lying to her most of the weekend. But now that I knew the truth, it made it so much harder.

"Gran…" It was now or never. I could ask her about the letter, whether Mom had ever mentioned what kind of spirit had come to our house within the flames that day.

But her sniffling stopped me.

I glanced over and she was dabbing her eyes with a tissue, weeping as quietly as she could. "Gran? Are you okay?"

"Oh, I'm sorry," she replied, her voice thick with tears as she tried to pull them back. "I don't mean to blubber. I just...sometimes I wonder if there was something I could've done to stop your mother from leaving. I believe she had a good reason, but I wish she would've confided in me more. Maybe there was something we could've done together. But then, I think if I were her..." She sighed and shook her head. "Never mind. It's all in the past. Nothing to be done about it now."

Her words, while painful, accomplished one thing. They told me Gran knew as little as I did. I stayed quiet the rest of the way home. There was no point in making her cry a second time.

Chapter Nineteen

"Iz, I'm not talking about this anymore."

"Oh, c'mon! His bride—his *bride*!" Izzie flicked her wet hands at me, spraying me with soapy droplets.

We were washing dishes after I had made dinner. Pork cutlets with balsamic glaze and wild rice pilaf. I'd be lying if I said Gran's praise that my cooking skills could win *Chopped* didn't make me feel like I'd actually won the real thing. Izzie had then said I could finally upgrade my food truck to a brick-and-mortar restaurant and then cure cancer with my ten thousand dollars. I balled up my napkin and threw it at her.

"I'm telling you," I said, taking a plate from her and wiping it dry with my towel, "he's not trying to steal me away or make me his bride. I mean, he barely touches me unless he has to."

All the times he held my hand in the ethereal plane, made sure to keep me close, and brushed my cheeks to make sure I was all right didn't count. *I didn't feel him at all.* So how could he have felt me, too? Besides, most of our intimate moments *I* had initiated.

Izzie gaped at me. "Do you *want* him to?"

"No!"

"You're such a bad liar. Luckily, you have me to cover your ass."

I frowned, placing the plate on the shelf with the rest of the set. "You're missing the point entirely. I'm just saying, it's not Alder. It has to be some other spirit that was after me. Some other spirit that took Mom."

"Uh-huh, and who told you that?"

"Alder. But—"

"He also told you that when spirits enter the physical plane they turn into fire, right? And that's supposed to explain your house. Well, what about that fox spirit you mentioned? How come he's able to cross into the physical plane and not burst into flames?"

"Because he's an emissary."

"Well, that's convenient."

"Izzie."

"Briony." She turned off the hot water and stared at me.

"What?" I asked, growing uncomfortable under her long stare.

"I've never seen you this way before."

"What way before?"

"Trusting."

Was that what I was doing? Trusting Alder? I mean, in a way, I supposed I did. I believed him. But also, it didn't make sense otherwise. If he truly wanted to take me away, he could've done so already many times. Instead he tried to drive me away from the valley. He tried to convince me not to go after the spirit gates and let him go instead. If his actual plans were to steal me away, he simply didn't have to bring me back to the physical world.

Also, there was an inherent *wrongness* to the idea.

I felt it in my chest, in my gut, and every bone, muscle, vein…

I shrugged, hanging the dish towel on the oven handle. "It's not about trust, it's about what makes sense. I mean, if he wanted me as *his bride*—which sounds *ridiculous* by the way—he could've kidnapped me a while ago."

"Look, girl, it's not that I think he's a bad guy. In fact, I kinda like him. He actually does seem to care about you. But this whole local legend and that mystery spirit has me really worried about you. I know you've gotta rescue your mom, and I get that, but I wish you'd let me help you somehow."

In that moment, the TV blared with the sound of police sirens. Gran was watching *Dateline* again. I glanced in the direction of the den and crossed my arms, leaning my hip against the counter and thinking back to the way she patted my knee in the truck. "You *are* helping me. You're watching Gran for me, and I need that more than you know."

Izzie shrugged. "You're going through a lot. I want to help wherever I can."

"No, really, you're amazing for doing this." I remembered early this evening when I had wandered through the house looking for things to do while Izzie had already done so much. "Not just any friend would be willing to do what you've done."

Her smile faded slightly, then her gaze moved to stare out the window at the fireflies in the garden. "Don't take this the wrong way, Brye, but as long as I've known you, I've always felt like you were…pretending somehow."

Her statement threw me off guard and unwillingly, my heart stung, enough to make me wince.

"Not like you were lying or deceiving anyone," Izzie said hurriedly, "but more like you were pretending to…be yourself. Like you didn't necessarily know who you were or what you liked. One time it took you ten minutes to decide on a flavor of ice cream, and when other girls complained you took too long, you started making snap decisions. As if to pretend you knew what you wanted all along."

I listened to her every word, hanging on each one. I never knew Izzie had seen through me so easily.

"So when you called me that night to tell me you were going to your gran's, I just…I heard *it* in your voice. I don't know what *it* was exactly. But I knew I wanted to be there for you."

Our conversation came back to me from the phone that night. *"You'll still be you,"* she'd said.

So that's what she'd meant.

I hugged my best friend tightly. "You are getting, like, seven new friendship bracelets."

It was so early in the morning that it was still dark out when I dropped from the trellis into Gran's garden. With one day until the solstice, I was now officially panicking. I just had to pray that this next gate was relatively easy to open.

As I stepped through bluebells and the climbing star-shaped clematis, I scanned the tree line of the forest, looking for any sign of Alder.

The few wisps out in the gardens and woods seemed to wake up when they sensed my mana. I imagined them without their misty glowing aura—as regular fireflies pulsing with soft flashes of yellow light—but the image didn't come to mind easily. These spirits had been a part of my world, and even though I couldn't remember the details, I felt their presence like I felt my toes—there, but not always conscious of them.

One floated by my elbow, and I watched, entranced, as it

landed on a black-eyed Susan and the glow took on a green hint. As the wisp sank into the flower, four more black-eyed Susans sprouted before my very eyes.

It was as if the wisp had taken on the element of the physical matter it touched...and enhanced it. It fed energy through it, and the flowers responded, like my own body had when touching the ethereal poison ivy. I'd been infused with mana, bursting with it.

"Briony!" a whisper called across the garden and through the trees. Alder stepped from between the trees, his silver hair radiant in the light of the wisps that hovered around him.

Making sure to step as lightly as I could, I hurried to the edge of the garden, and Alder fell into step beside me.

We moved through the forest, the crunch of growth under my sneakers echoing in the early morning. Several birds called from the trees, and through the leaves I could just barely make out the hints of sunrise as it crested the mountains. The signature mist of the Smokies was sure to be settling and hanging low on the ridges. I somewhat regretted not being able to see it, since the morning was always the perfect time to see what made the Blue Ridges...blue.

"So," Alder said after a while, reminding me how we really hadn't said all that much since the moment in the abandoned house during the storm, "you're up early."

"I'm antsy," I admitted, thinking about the letter and the very tight deadline. We had so little time to open two more gates before the solstice.

Alder nodded. He seemed a little on edge, too. He was usually tense, but the mana around him felt electric this morning, as if it was taking on Alder's nervous, anxious emotions.

Again, I wondered if I should tell him about the letter, but I didn't think it would change anything. Alder knew there was a spirit that tried to take me to the ethereal plane as a child. What he hadn't mentioned was anything about the local legend of some strange bride sacrifice.

He'd even said multiple times that he knew very little about the spirit world himself. He was a spirit, but with a human body. While Raysh was ancient, Alder was no more than eighteen. How much could you know as an eighteen-year-old about a world as old as time, especially when most of these spirits didn't seem very forthcoming about its history or rules?

So maybe there was another powerful spirit…or god… that actually did mark girls and spirit them away to be their brides. It was worth asking.

"Hey."

"Hm?" Alder glanced over his shoulder, parting branches for me, and I ducked under them. I paused and his brow furrowed, reading the stress on my face. "What is it?"

"Are there…gods in the spirit world, too?"

Alder's hand gripped the spot above my elbow. I glanced up at him in surprise. His gold eyes glowed, and his whole body seemed charged and electric, as if a lightning bolt just hit him. "Why do you ask?"

I hadn't quite been expecting that reaction. "Some of the women Gran plays bridge with mentioned a local legend. Something about a god taking a girl away to be his bride."

Alder paled but said nothing. He dropped my arm.

I hadn't been expecting *that*, either. I thought he would've just brushed it off. With a laugh and a shake of his head and say, *"Are you listening to all that nonsense?"*

"What? Is it actually true?" I said, a nervous chuckle escaping me.

"I…" He took a deep breath, rubbing his hand over his eyes. "No, it's not true."

He hesitated.

Instantly, alarm bells went off in my head. He was lying. How could I trust him if he lied?

But as I studied him, I noticed his expression. He was pained—conflicted, the muscles in his neck tight and his eyes pleading. Something was wrong. He'd been genuine and truthful up to this point. There had to be a good reason.

Closing the distance between us, I tugged his arm lower so I could look him in the eyes. "Alder, please tell me what you know."

I thought about my mother going into the spirit world on *my behalf.* To take *my place.* This wasn't just about me finding out about my past anymore, this was about saving an innocent woman who'd loved me.

Grazing my hand up his arm and around his wrist, I wound my fingers into his. "You can tell me anything."

He looked down at our fingers intertwined, then swallowed and said, "It's probably *me* they're talking about," he confessed, his eyes searching my face, gauging my reaction.

"What do you mean?"

"There were other conduits before me, Brye. It's not like I had parents or anything like that, but there were other human spirits in this valley before me. What if my predecessors *did* kidnap other humans away to the spirit world? Maybe because they were lonely. Just like..."

"No, *not* like you," I said forcefully.

"But there were so many times I just wanted someone to *be* there." Alder's voice was strangled now, yet still quiet, like he couldn't stand to say it too loud. To admit the depth of his longing for companionship.

I took a step closer, pressing my other hand against his chest, right over his heart. "Who cares what your predecessors did? *You* haven't taken anyone away from their friends and family. Alder, you tried to *send* me away when I got here because you were worried for me."

Alder moved his hands to my wrists. His thumbs swept across the back of my hands while his strong fingers rested on the inside of my pulse. I worried he could feel its incessant, wild pounding. I tried to calm it, but that only made it worse, and before I knew what I was doing, I was opening my big fat mouth. "The Firefly Festival."

His brow furrowed in confusion. "The festival in the town?"

My cheeks burned as I kept my gaze locked with his. "Yes, so you know it?"

"Of course, it happens every solstice. It's to celebrate the firefly synchronization in the Smokies—I mean, they *think* it's fireflies."

"Alder—"

"But it's actually the mana of the wisps aligning during the solstice when the barriers weaken—"

"Alder, I'm trying to ask if you want to go with me," I said, louder than I meant to. But I was so flustered that it came out a few decibels too loud.

Alder blinked, staring down at me with raised eyebrows and parted lips.

And so I started to blabber. "I mean, of course, that's if we get Mom back and everything goes smoothly. But if we can't make the festival, then I think that—"

A rustling to our left cut me off, and I was actually grateful to see Raysh jump through the bushes and land gracefully in front of us, his tail flicking irritably.

"Finally found you two. Come now, we haven't a moment to waste."

My gut churned uncomfortably. Raysh was right. What was I *doing* talking to Alder about going to festivals when we had only a day before the solstice?

Argh! Darn him and his puppy-dog eyes.

"Something wrong?" Raysh asked, looking from me to Alder.

I shook my head vigorously. "Nope. Absolutely not. Let's go."

Alder said nothing, but his hand was hot as he held mine, and we stepped into the ethereal plane.

We arrived in a grove of mountain maple and ash trees. I knew them to grow only in the highest elevations of the Smokies, so we had to be farther up in the mountains than we'd been before. Even in the spirit world, my chest was a little tight from the elevation, making it slightly harder to breathe. Through the trees, I could see the valley stretch out before us in emerald slopes and a crystalline blue river running through.

Raysh's red-orange fur glowed bright in the light of the rising sun. The entire grove was illuminated in a rustic gold hue, with the shadows of the trees stretching the length of the clearing.

We'd barely taken two steps before a voice pierced the quiet of the grove. *"I've foounnnd her,"* it sang.

Alder tugged me behind him just as a mountain lion appeared around the bend of the trees.

Terror ran through me as its mouth rippled back into a snarl, showing sharp white fangs. *"The human."* Its voice had a gleeful, creepy note to it.

"Oh, look what the cat dragged in and hacked up," Raysh sneered, his own lips curling back to bare his fangs, too.

The mountain lion, technically an eastern cougar, swung

its head to glare at Raysh. Its yellow eyes gleamed in the faint, early light of the grove. *"Run along, Raysh, if you don't want to see me slice up your little human."*

Raysh took two steps forward, positioning his slender body in front of me. *"She's not to be touched."*

"Who are you to tell me that? I'm actually surprised you're not on my side." The cougar jumped onto a rock that jutted out of the ground in the middle of the grove, its claws scraping over the stone and tearing at my nerves like nails on a chalkboard.

Alder flexed his wrist at his side as if he were preparing to throw a wind-up pitch. "Back off, Ashka."

The cougar called Ashka swung her head toward Alder and let out a hiss. *"Don't tell me what to do. Spirit or not, you smell like a human and you brought her here. Which might make you the worst of them all."* Her eyes flashed and she crouched low, shoulders hunching and claws curling in, preparing to pounce.

"We don't need to fight," Alder said.

"We do." The next second, Ashka lunged, her claws directed right at my very exposed neck. But Alder was too fast—or just fast enough. Throwing out his arm, shots of green mana hit two mountain maple trees and large branches grew at lightning speed, catching the cougar in a web of wood and leaves.

Ashka snarled and snapped, twisting in between the branches, scratching at the wood, large shavings falling to the ground in clean peels. Under hissing and growls, I could just barely make out her threats. *"You'll regret this, boy. I'll have this girl's heart in my jaws before she can do any more damage."*

It might have been all the snarling, but the cougar spirit's words prickled the hair on the back of my neck.

Alder pressed a gentle hand on my lower back and guided me out of the grove, his other hand glowing green while more branches wound themselves into a sort of makeshift cage for the angry cat.

After we got a bit away, I glanced up at Alder. "What did she mean by that? What damage have I done?"

"Nothing. Ashka just doesn't like humans."

I could understand that, given that most of the cougar population in the Smokies had been wiped out, thanks to hunters in the early 1920s—which happened to be the case with most wildlife before the formation of the Great Smoky Mountains National Park.

But something didn't sit right with me. No spirits had sought me out before I started opening the gates, but now that I'd opened two, I had a cougar spirit coming after me? Raysh had made it seem like opening the gates wasn't that big of a deal, but was it a bigger deal to some spirits more than others?

"What are you two doing back there?" Raysh called from way up ahead. I could just make out the fox's silhouette against the backdrop of the sunrise peeking over the uphill path.

"We're coming!" I called.

"For fox sake!" Alder added.

I raised my hand, and he high fived it.

As if we'd done it a thousand times.

Even after our heavy conversation, it was comfortable walking alongside him…or it would've been if the cougar's growls and snarls hadn't kept echoing through my mind. She'd been so angered by my existence in the ethereal plane, which made me wonder, just how mad at me were the guardians for stealing their keys?

And I was about to steal another.

Chapter Twenty

The air gate, naturally, was at the very peak of the mountain.

The pressure in my ears and chest was immense, but nothing compared to the immense beauty of the ethereal plane.

It unfurled below me, a moving patchwork quilt of colored mist. All shades of green, from peridot, to lime, to emerald, to a deep olive. Variations of blue, from sky blue, to periwinkle, to sapphire, to violet. Golds, oranges, pinks, and reds rippled through the valley as the sun's rays touched each layer of mist, illuminating and saturating the mana in a broad spectrum of vibrant hues.

It was like a Van Gogh painting. And for a moment, I admired the painter's unique ability to see beyond the physical and look at the world through the lenses of energy. Of seeing the life in every single color. In the starry sky, he saw a thousand shades and brushstrokes, instead of one dark canvas. And that's how life was—mixing, merging, swirling, beautiful strokes of energy.

"How are you holding up?" Alder asked, shooting me a concerned glance as we got to the top, clearing the copse of mountain ash trees and entering a rocky outcrop of boulders and red spruces and Fraser firs. Dark green mana swirled around the branches and sticky needles of the fir trees, mixing with the silver mana from strong wind gusts that struck the mountain tops.

This time, Alder's concern was warranted. I didn't feel very good—probably didn't look very good, either.

But I couldn't let him think I wasn't able to handle this. We needed that key. "I'm fine," I said quickly, straightening even though the pressure in my spine and chest felt like someone was driving their knuckles into my lower back and collarbone.

"Any idea where the guardian is?" I asked, scanning the skies.

Based off the other two guardians, it wasn't hard to guess that the air gate was an animal connected to its element. In this case, a bird of some sort.

"He's out there. Be careful." In my peripheral, I noticed Raysh curl up under a large spruce, his green eyes flicking about warily from one corner of the sky to the other.

It was the first time I'd seen him look a little nervous.

It made me *more* nervous.

Meanwhile, Alder glowed silver. All around the outline of his body was a fine layer of silver mist, luminous and curling around his arms, legs, and fingers.

"Heads up." Alder nodded toward the sky.

Soft blue-silvery clouds descended upon the mountain, touching the ridges around us. High above, through the clouds of heavy fog, a piercing cry split the air.

My heart thundered in my chest.

This is it.

"Are you ready?" Alder asked, the fingers on his right hand glowing green as his earth mana rose to the surface of his skin.

Nodding, I flattened my back against a big and sturdy spruce fir. Alder reached down and pressed his hand against the earth right at my feet. From the spot he touched, vines broke through the ground, wrapping around the tree and giving me handles to hold during the oncoming gales. He'd warned me that any blast of wind he threw at the guardian could knock me off the mountaintop just as easily, so when he offered a solution of a nature harness of some sort, I was all for it.

I couldn't remember a time when I'd taken someone else's suggestion so easily and readily. But unlike the water gate, I wasn't going into this blind. Yes, Alder had powers, but now that I kinda had them, too, it wasn't *just* about *using* him to help me get the key. It was also because…I wanted him there with me this time.

Alder helped wrap the vines around me and I could tell in the way he moved—short, staccato movements—that he was terrified for me. But he didn't try to push me away. He knew I had to do this, just as I knew I needed him to open this gate with me.

"Remember, if you use your mana," he said, as he tightened the last vine, "you need to hold back. If you try and just let it loose, it can backfire. It'll lose control."

I nodded even though I didn't quite agree. If I had to use my mana, it would be however I needed. As much as I needed.

As Alder stood, his gaze locked with mine. "Please, be careful."

I gave him a tiny, hopefully courageous, smile. "Right back at ya."

As Alder opened his mouth to reply, a blast of wind moved the heavy fog before us, layering itself over our mountaintop in a thick blanket of mist—producing the signature "blue smoke" as the Cherokee had dubbed it so long ago.

My science teacher from ninth grade would have told us that the "smoke" of the Smoky Mountains was actually a fog created by the "volatile organic compounds" released by the millions of trees, bushes, and wildflowers in their photosynthesis stage. The fog's blue hue came from the scattering of light particles from the blue sky.

But the ethereal plane told a different story.

The guardian of the air gate shot through the blanket of mist like a rocket, its great, powerful wings folded close to its body. It was a hawk—a red-tailed hawk with stunning bronze feathers. The tips of the hawk feathers were made of clouds.

I gaped at the creature as it stopped its nose dive, pulling out its wings and gliding through the blue haze. The feathers' tips, instead of being dark and smooth like satin, were wisps of ice particles, water droplets, and dry air—the properties of a cloud. They left a trail of light blue jet stream in their wake...which merged with the fog hanging just above us.

The air guardian created the "smoke" of the Smokies with its wings.

Raysh had told us the key was a feather, but I hadn't been expecting a feather half made of the air itself.

Alder stood below, away from the copse of spruce firs, following the hawk with his gaze. The guardian let out another cry, and I flinched against the shrill sound. It sounded like the wind was screaming in my ears.

Alder wound back his right arm and shoved his fist forward, as if he was punching the air. With his attack, the air around me grew thinner. Alder had summoned a blast of wind against the hawk spirit and I held on to the vines as my clothes beat against my skin and my ponytail whipped my cheeks.

Caught in the force of the gale, the giant bird was thrown back, disappearing into its blue fog canopy and leaving behind a hole within the clouds. Feathers fluttered down and I let go of my nature harnesses, rushing forward to grab one before they fell where I couldn't follow. Breathing hard, Alder flicked his finger and the feather carried itself on a small breeze directed right for me.

I caught it easily, my fingers closing around the soft feather and the moist tuft of cloud at its tip. Cupping the treasure in my hands, I studied the key. The feather was bronze—almost like real metal—with thin stripes in varying shades going down its stem, ending in smoky blue mist.

A shriek echoed over the mountain top—angry and shrill. The blue fog increased in density as the flapping of the guardian's wings could be heard over the winds battling against one another.

Crap, it's pissed. I gripped the feather tight in my fist and sprinted back to the vines.

The hawk broke through the blue smoke. It clipped its hooked beak, letting out another screech, and tipped its head to the side to scan the mountaintop with a vibrant bronze eye.

Spotting me, it dove, pulling up with its silver talons extended like it was about to pick up a rodent or a snake—its prey. Me.

Alder sent another blast at the air guardian, but it met the wind strike with a squall of its own. Blue mist and silver mana gusted toward Alder, knocking him backward and sending him flying.

I swallowed my scream as Alder thrust back his hand, summoning a mound of earth to stop his fall. Backing up against the dirt, he shook his head, eyes dazed and unfocused, and shoulders visibly shaking from his overuse of mana.

But *I* still had mana. It rose up inside me at my call, and my fingers and palms and wrists glowed with the heat of it. As if it begged me to summon it.

If I could just send the hawk above the mist again, then maybe we'd have enough time to get away.

An idea began to form, and I disliked it almost immediately.

So Alder was sure to *despise* it.

Stuffing the key into my jean shorts pocket, I lifted my hand, now glowing silver with the air mana rising and manifesting on my fingertips.

The hawk turned its attention back to me, flapping its wings and sending ripples of blue fog flying from the tips of its feathers. It came for me a second time, talons out and exposed.

Sucking in a breath, I began moving my arm in a circle. The air around me responded immediately, influenced by the astral energy flying off my hand in a corkscrew motion. I moved faster, and the small wind tunnel expanded.

Soon a whole mini tornado grew outward, with my arm at the center of it. My hair and clothes batted around as the air fed this wind vortex. Seeing my trap, the hawk tried to stop its trajectory, but the tempest caught its wings and it got sucked into the tornado, spinning around it like a fish caught in a whirlpool—unable to escape.

I gasped, feeling the mana flow out of me in torrents. Now I couldn't seem to stop it. Alder was right. I'd let out too much and now it was uncontrollable. A dam that I had broken and couldn't close back up.

Staggering, I fell to my knees and watched in horror as the massive wingspan of the hawk got closer and closer and then hit me in the arm.

The force of it knocked me backward, sending me flying and stumbling over the peak and the rocks and boulders. Alder screamed my name over the windstorm, and I scrambled to find purchase—on the rocks, the trees—on anything. But too late, I was going over the edge, down, down into the valley of mist below.

Chapter Twenty-One

My fall was epic. Just like before, but this time I was vertical instead of horizontal. My fingers and the toes of my sneakers raked down the cliff face as I slid down the mountainside. Every part of me groaned in agony. My arm felt like it was broken where the air guardian had smacked against it, and every other body part ached and stung.

I was falling, sliding, and I couldn't stop it. The wind shouted in my ears, and I wanted to call for Alder, but I could barely breathe, let alone yell.

As the cliff jutted out, my sneakers found nothing but air, and my sore, bloody fingers gripped the side of the cliff right before I fell for the third time.

I didn't have the strength to look down into what I was sure was an abyss.

And I didn't have the strength to climb back up.

My shoulders and arms trembled with exertion. Exhaustion, pain, and the depletion of mana threatened to pull me under, and I was inclined to let it.

I couldn't think.

I couldn't breathe.

I couldn't hold on.

As a roar shook the cliff I was gripping, and the vibrations of it rippled through my body, I let go.

And everything went black.

Warmth. Fuzziness. Not just in my head and my limbs, but underneath me. Was it some kind of cloud?

Had I died?

But I was in the ethereal plane, and I knew better. Falling through mist didn't mean you'd end up hitting solid earth. Sometimes, if you were lucky, you ended up in a meadow with a mother you thought had abandoned you.

I groaned, shifting against the soft, warm fur beneath me. *Fur?*

Ignoring my pounding headache and the soreness everywhere, I opened my eyes and blinked. Only colored shapes came to me, nothing concrete and certainly nothing that made sense. I closed them again and reached out with my other senses.

The thick scent in the air was comprised of blackberries and pine, but a little musty. I heard only deep, steady breathing and the pounding of heavy footsteps against the forest floor. The warm fur below me shifted with the movement of powerful muscles.

Clearly, I was on top of some sort of creature. Being carried?

It took everything in me *not* to panic. I opened my eyes again and moved my face against the black fur, the smell of pine and blackberries flooding me.

Black fur.

I pushed myself up onto my elbows and gasped.

I was on the back of a massive black bear. Roughly the size of an elephant if I was to take a guess.

It lumbered along at a slow, easy pace, its light brown snout lifting into the air to sniff occasionally. One long pink tongue darted out and licked its nose and then it yawned, without breaking its huge stride.

"Um," I squeaked, then cleared my throat. "Excuse me, uh, Mr. Bear?"

The bear continued on as if it hadn't heard or understood a thing I'd said.

Frowning, I scanned the black fur and the rest of its enormous body. Around his tail, ears, and paws were some tangled brambles with blackberries literally growing on them.

A very large sprite? Or an actual spirit?

I had no way of knowing, but I guess it couldn't hurt to continue trying to communicate with it.

"Mr. Bear, I'd like to get down now, please."

Nothing, just a pause in its pace to scratch at the earth and pull up some roots with his big teeth. Chomping on the roots like a beef jerky snack, it continued onward.

"Do you know Alder? You know, looks like a human, smells like a bottle of Old Spice?"

The black bear sneezed but didn't even break its strangely graceful but heavy gait.

Scooting closer to the edge of its broad back, I eyed the ground. It wasn't that far down, and even though I felt like crap, I was fairly positive nothing was broken. I should be able to get down, no problem.

Swinging my legs around, I braced myself to jump off, but the black bear swung its head around and snarled at me, snapping at my ankles.

I let out a little squeal and pulled my legs back up,

hugging my knees.

Seemingly satisfied I wasn't going anywhere, the bear moved its head back to face forward, continuing on its leisurely stroll.

"That's cool. Just keep walking. I'm good," I grumbled.

I rode on the bear's back for what had to be at least an hour. Sometimes, I just talked to it, knowing it couldn't talk back, to get things off my chest. I had nothing else to do. Every time I tried to get off, the bear would growl at me in warning.

So, we had a very one-sided conversation.

"I mean, he's cute, sure," I said, lounging in the black fur and threading my fingers through it. "But there are other cute guys, you know? Wes Havers is cute. I mean, really cute. And he asked me out, but it didn't feel right. We could talk okay—we're both on the swim team and we both like fantasy novels, so it wasn't like we didn't get along. But Alder… Geez, I don't know. I'm comfortable *and* nervous around him. Gah! What was I *thinking* asking him out like that? I've *never* done that before. Obviously, I'm attracted to him—but what can happen?"

I scooted over to the black bear's head and leaned over, my own head upside down to look the bear in the eye. "No, I mean, seriously. What can happen? He's a *nature spirit.* Our relationship wouldn't exactly be normal."

The black bear huffed.

I flopped back onto its neck. "No, you're right. I know I'm not talking about marrying the guy. But…"

What if I fell in love with him? Head over heels, high-school sweethearts, romantic comedy, together-forever love? Elizabeth Bennet and Mr. Darcy-type love?

Something told me, if I let myself get too close, I'd never be able to leave.

I wasn't my mom. I doubted I was selfless enough to be able to walk away from someone I loved so much.

The forest stopped moving past me. Blinking, I sat up, eager to see the black bear's final destination.

It was at the mouth of a large cave. Was this its home?

Oh *no*, had it been bringing me back to its den to *eat* me? From what I knew of black bears, they didn't feast on humans. But who knew about gigantic *nature spirit* black bears?

Then it started moving again, lumbering into the shallow cave and dropping itself down on its round belly.

Taking that as a clear sign I was allowed to get down now, I climbed off its back and patted its great side affectionately. "Thanks for the ride, bud. Even though I technically didn't ask for it."

I was about to walk out of the cave to try to find Alder, when something out of the corner of my eye stopped me.

The hint of a yellow blouse.

Breath stalling in my chest, I ran to the corner of the cave, where a beautiful woman lay on her back on a bed of autumn leaves.

The woman had long dark brown hair, parts of it streaked with fine silver, and wore jeans and a yellow sunflower-printed blouse.

Mom.

Choking on my own breath, I dropped down next to her, sweeping my hands across her inert body. Her chest rose and fell, but her eyes were closed.

My hands trembled as I tried to shake her awake, but like Alder had said would happen, she didn't wake up. Didn't even flinch.

I'd found her body, but her spirit was still trapped in the astral plane.

But I was *so close.*

I could touch her face, feel her pulse, brush her hair behind her ear. Kiss her cheek.

The woman before me technically was a stranger, but I still felt this inexplicable connection to her. Maybe it was simply knowing that she had sacrificed everything to save me from a spirit who'd tried to take me away. Or maybe, even if all my memories had been removed, the feelings and longings were still there, buried deep and woven into the person who I was, who I'd always been, before the fire stole everything away.

A slight huff from behind reminded me that I wasn't alone. Glancing over my shoulder, I looked at the bear. Had it been watching over my mother's body this whole time?

And did it bring me here to find her? Or had it simply found another human and thought, *I know where this goes!*

Either way, I felt a rush of gratitude toward the great spirit.

I crossed to the bear and rubbed its caramel-colored snout. "Thank you, Mr. Bear."

It closed its eyes, like it was enjoying my touch. "*Welcome.*"

Reeling back, I stared at the bear. "You can *talk*?"

A rumble started in his belly that I could've sworn was a chuckle.

"The whole time?" My face flushed, thinking of how I'd spilled my guts to him.

More rumbling.

Oh, well. I had a feeling the bear wouldn't exactly tell a lot of people. And hopefully not one nature spirit in particular.

I glanced back at my mom. There was no way I could carry her, and I needed to find Alder and open the air gate, and then the fire gate, too. I wasn't sure how much time had passed, but it had to be at least noon. We were running out of time, and quickly.

With anxiety mounting, I turned to Mr. Bear. "Hey, can you keep watch over my mom?"

"Yup."

"You are a bear of few words." Scratching under his big chin, I asked, "Any chance you know where I can find the spirit that looks like a human? Alder?"

The black bear spirit shook his giant head.

Drat. What had I been expecting? The ethereal plane was massive, and this particular spirit seemed to be a bit of a loner.

"Thanks anyway."

I gave my mother one last look, then hurried out of the cave.

Cupping my hands around my mouth, I called, "Alder!"

The forest remained still and silent. The trees around me gave off large amounts of mana that pulsed with energy, even more than usual. Just how deep into this forest had the bear taken me?

Sourwood, short-leaf pine, and black walnut trees towered above with trunks the width of car tires. Green mana misted over them while light silver mana blew, tickling the branches and breaking off a few leaves that fluttered to the ground.

Maybe I could find a river somewhere and Rikki, Tikki, and Tavi could lead me to Alder, or at least get a message to him about where I was.

"Alder!" I called again, feeling the panic rise in my throat at the empty echo that reverberated back to me.

"I fooouunnnd her."

My heart almost jumped out of my skin as Ashka the eastern cougar came out from behind a tree.

White fangs bared, she hissed, *"The human."*

Chapter Twenty-Two

The mountain cat lunged for me. On instinct, I dove out of the way, rolling to the side, barely escaping its powerful claws. Skidding across the ground, Ashka hissed and lowered herself, ready for another pounce.

I wasn't sure I had it in me to dodge again. My whole body ached from the fall, and using so much mana had me drained and weak. But maybe I still had a little left. Calling upon the astral energy inside me, I directed my attention to the ground.

The image of Alder manipulating a mound of earth against the charging buck came to mind. I knew I'd never be able to pull off something as incredible as that, but maybe I could throw the cougar off her balance. Enough to get away and hide. Maybe back to the black bear spirit.

"Please, Ashka," I said, green mana coating my fingertips as I began collecting the mana, ready to be expelled. "I don't mean any harm."

Whiskers quivered as she snarled. *"So you say, but you will not take my home from me, as your species has done to my kind in your world."*

No sooner had she finished speaking than she leaped forward, but I was ready. The green mana flowed from my hand, crashing into the ground and causing the earth to explode in a shower of dirt and rock. I threw up my arm against the dust and debris, but it caught Ashka in her eyes. She skidded across the grass, hissing and spitting.

Now was my chance.

As I twisted away to run, a bolt of pain arced up and down my arm and side where the air guardian's wing had struck me. Gasping, I stumbled forward, dropping to my knees. Paralyzed with pain, I could do nothing but watch as the mountain lion recovered from the face-full of dirt. It didn't take her long. She lowered her front half while her back legs pushed off the ground, springing for me.

Sharp claws dug into my shoulders. The beast pinned me to the ground, and I let out a cry of pain. Warm liquid blossomed on my shirt—sticky and metallic.

Ashka opened her mouth, and hot, smelly breath blasted me in the face. Her claws pierced my skin farther, and I whimpered and squirmed beneath the cat.

"Hold still. This can be quick."

But before it could end—fast or slow—a gust of wind hit Ashka square in the side, sending the cougar flying into the tree, cracking the bark with a great sound that echoed in the near-silent forest.

My vision bleary with pain, I turned my head to the side.

Alder stalked toward the cat, a miniature windstorm of leaves and forest debris whirling around him. His gold eyes glowed with energy.

White mana extended outward from him like tentacles, lashing against trees and striking the ground like small lightning bolts.

While he appeared chaotic and wild like a hurricane, I noticed how the bolts of energy were careful not to lash out anywhere near me. The control he had over his mana was impressive, especially when I now understood how truly difficult it was to tame. It had so easily overtaken me, but he was masterful in his movements…even as angry as he was.

Ashka dropped to the forest floor and whined in agony and fear.

The cougar might've almost killed me, but I actually felt pity. She was an animal. A wounded one. Not a thing of evil, just wild and hungry and trying to protect her home.

And Alder was trying to protect me.

"Al…der…" I breathed, the pain making my voice crack and hitch.

The gold in Alder's eyes calmed, and immediately his mana fizzled out. He ran to me and dropped to my side, squeezing my hand.

Ashka lifted herself up and limped, as quickly as she could, away into the forest.

"It's gonna be okay," Alder murmured, touching my neck, his fingers coming away with crimson liquid. His hands trembled.

He dropped his forehead to mine while his hands pressed down on the claw wounds. I jolted in pain, twisting under his grasp. Still he held on.

"I'm right here," he breathed against my cheeks. "I've got you."

Before I had time to question it, mana surged out of his hands. Once more, I felt the essence of the mountains seep into me.

The pounding rain of a spring thunderstorm echoing in every tree and hillside. The whisper of autumn wind rustling through the fallen leaves. The crunch of fresh snow underfoot of a young buck.

A part of me.

"Breathe," Alder reminded me, his voice next to my ear.

My lungs expanded, a deep gasp vibrating through me as my back arched and the last tiny spark of mana jumped into my bloodstream. Gripping his forearm tightly, I focused on controlling my breathing.

I could…*feel*…everything. Mana pulsed from my skin, and it was almost too much.

Silence in the earth around us, the steps of sprites—a rabbit through the underbrush, the scamper of a squirrel up a sourwood tree. A woodpecker hammering away.

Alder squeezed my other hand, intertwining our fingers. "It's okay," he murmured, his lips brushing my neck. "You're okay."

And I was. The astral energy flowed through me, consuming my soul in its mystical essence until I was sure that soon I would become a mountain spirit myself.

"You're okay," Alder repeated, and I could feel his heart hammer against his chest, the shakiness of his breath and the tremble of his fingers as they threaded into my hair.

With my hands on his skin, I was encased in the senses of my valley. I smelled juniper, tasted blackberries, felt exhilaration.

It was a wonderful feeling, but that wasn't what was exhilarating. It was the touch of just *him.* I ignored the rain, the scents, the bird calls—it all faded away into the background as I ran my hands over the slight stubble on his jaw and the corded muscles on his neck and shoulders.

I just felt *him.* Just Alder.

The feeling of him was like the thrill of standing at the top of the world and seeing the distant forests and the rivers, and the jagged line where the Blue Ridges merged with the sky.

That moment of beauty and amazement. The moment where you look at something and wonder how anything so astounding and unreal could've been created.

Like watching summer lightning illuminate the heavens. My perfect storm.

Being with Alder, breathing him in, was like *that.*

I wanted to always be like that.

"When you went over the edge—" His words were strangled, like snaking vines had wound around his throat.

I wove my fingers into his silver hair, wanting to calm my storm, who could rip up the trees and shake the skies. Assure him that I was alive and with him, and I wasn't going anywhere.

"I missed you, too," I said softly.

Because it was true. It was what this huge hole in my chest had been telling me every time he got close. Nostalgia, longing, loss, all meaning one thing: I'd missed him.

I turned my head only slightly and brushed my lips against his.

He tasted like autumn, like crisp air and the intoxicatingly sweet scent of woodsmoke.

It was only a brush, and yet his lips chased after mine. Sliding one arm under my lower back, he tugged me closer while his other hand tangled further into my hair, kissing me back with firm purpose. With desire.

With hope.

I felt it not in his lips or his kiss, but in the way he broke it and pressed his forehead against mine a second time. Keeping me close meant he hoped for another. And another. As many as I would allow.

I could still taste the woodsmoke and the fall air on my lips.

He swallowed hard, his eyes closed as he kept me in his arms, muscles taut.

Meanwhile, my skin hummed with energy—mana or

hormones or both—it didn't matter. I'd never felt so alive while feeling so breathless.

I had to breathe. I had to keep breathing.

All it took was a small inch of movement to meet his lips, but I would've crossed the whole world barefoot for another.

In this kiss, I felt the subtle shift in him. The shedding of worries, fears, and boundaries. His grip tightened around me, flattening his palm against my lower back, drawing his fingers into the roots of my hair. I slid my arms around his neck, removing the extra space between us and burning the bridge that I'd just crossed.

I wouldn't go back now.

He sensed the change in *me*, and his kiss deepened, drawing me closer, turning our second kiss into our third, then fourth, and it was only then that I realized…

The mountains were gone. The smell of the woods, the taste of blackberries and autumn air…gone. I was wrapped up in Alder, feeling only his warm skin, callused fingers, smooth lips, and rough jaw.

And he could feel me, too. The heat of my flushed neck and cheeks, the knots in my wild hair, and the rough skin of the scars on my lower back.

He broke our kiss, and I felt him go rigid, while his fingers skimmed across the four long scars.

"Brye." His wide gold eyes captured mine. "What is that?"

Still a little dizzy from our kisses, it took me a moment to catch up with him. "M-my scars?" I asked, utterly bewildered.

"Scars…" He pulled me up into a sitting position. "Can I see?" he asked, his voice soft, but full of repressed tension, almost as if he was trying not to panic.

I nodded, confused.

He moved around me, lifting up my shirt just enough to see the shiny pale skin of my scars.

His fingers traced them lightly, and I shivered at his touch. "You never told me you have scars," he whispered.

"I didn't think it was important—"

"They're scars from the fire that day, aren't they? Scars from the spirit." He gripped my hands, and I could feel him tremble just a little from his tight grasp.

His fear was starting to worry me. "Y-yes, I've had them since that day. I thought they were just old burns."

Alder jumped to his feet, eyes wide, chest rising and falling. "No, no, no, no," he said over and over again.

I pushed myself to my feet and tried to place my hand on his arm, hoping to soothe him. Mana came off him in waves and the astral energy was *intense.*

"Alder? Talk to me. Please…"

He buried his face in his hands, and his words came out muffled. "It's true."

"So the little god figured it out."

I whirled around at the familiar voice.

Raysh. The fox spirit sat on a tree stump, his tail flicking back and forth in rhythm. Like the tail of a cat clock.

Alder stared at Raysh, the irises in his eyes burning like two suns.

"You knew all along."

"Of course I did." Raysh's lips peeled back to reveal white fangs. *"I am as old as this forest, and you are merely an infant—a human with the powers of a god. You know nothing of this world and its secrets. Its legends."*

My skin prickled at his last word.

It's an old local legend about how a god who lives in this valley…

Old settlers told stories about a god that roamed the forests. Every hundred years, the god would come down from these mountains and mark a woman and steal her away to make her his bride.

What if the mark came in the form of scars?

Raysh cocked his head at Alder, vibrant emerald eyes burning against the rustic orange hue of his fur.

"Poor little god thought it was just another spirit who tried to steal away his girlfriend," the fox continued, mockingly. *"Poor little god had no idea that it was the god himself who condemned her to her fate."*

Chapter Twenty-Three

"God?" I asked, my gaze jumping from Raysh to Alder.

Alder stood stock still, the mana radiating from him like the smoke off a bonfire.

Raysh turned his head to me. *"Yes. God. What did you think the guardians were? Merely powerful spirits? What are all-powerful spirits if not gods?"*

My skin grew cold to the point of numbness. I thought of the deer spirit who could make earthquakes, the turtle spirit who kept the rivers and brooks chilled, and the hawk spirit who created the blue smoke of the Blue Ridges.

Of course. If there were nature spirits, why couldn't there be nature gods? Especially ones that were powerful enough to affect the physical world.

If I understood it right, Raysh was calling Alder a god as well. My gaze slid over to him and almost everything about him made sense now. He wasn't just a conduit for the mana to flow into the physical world. He was the human embodiment of the valley.

It was why he could use all the elements, why he could give mana to humans, and why his mana contained the essences of the Smokies.

"You're a god," I whispered, brushing the back of my

hand against my lips—lips he'd just kissed.

Alder closed his eyes, his chest rising and falling in one giant sigh, as if he was resigned to this moment. The moment where I found out the truth and rejected him.

Or hated him.

Or got angry at him for not telling me.

I waited for those emotions to come, but they didn't. I waited to feel rage or even disappointment at his lie by omission, but all I kept seeing was his face as he admitted to me that he'd been lonely.

It made sense now. His reactions and worries to things I hadn't quite understood. He'd thought his god status would drive me away. He'd thought I'd be scared of him.

But I wasn't.

If anything, the only thing I felt was an indescribable sadness as I realized that the barrier between us grew taller and thicker. Dating a spirit had felt impossible enough. But a god? It was unfathomable.

I shoved all the feelings away, locking them up until I had time to take them out and examine them. To truly process the fact that I might, *just might,* be falling for a god.

"So, wait, what did you mean when you said he had condemned me?" I asked, feeling like my brain was trudging through quickly drying cement.

"The fire gate and its god are not like the others," Raysh said. *"It is pure energy and therefore the mana has no physical connection to the physical plane. So it requires an anchor."*

"What kind of anchor?" I asked, the scars on my lower back beginning to throb strangely. Meanwhile, Alder had backed against a tree, his wide eyes staring at the ground.

"All of the other gods can exist in the ethereal plane, a plane that is still bound to the physical world. Think of how they affect the physical world. It means they're connected to

it, but the fire god exists only in the astral plane. Tethered to nothing and no one. So the god takes a human soul tied to the valley—a human who possesses the heart and soul of these mountains." The fox paused and tilted its head, green eyes holding mine. *"In other words, a little girl who befriended a nature god."*

At that, Alder winced. "I can't…I didn't know."

"Of course you didn't. If you had, you would've stayed away from all humans. You would've never shared your mana with one of them. Why do you think we needed you to infuse the keys with your mana? The girl"—Raysh nodded toward me—*"is the fire gate's anchor. Or at least, she was supposed to be."*

My mother. Nausea threatened to overtake me, and I drew a shaking hand to my mouth.

"You couldn't know or else the fire god would've never possessed its anchor," Raysh continued, as if he hadn't just dropped a Titanic's worth of guilt on me. *"And without the fire god tied to the valley, without all four elements, the ethereal plane would cease to exist here."*

I remembered what Alder had said before. *"Do you think if I'd known all this, that I would've let any of this happen to you?"*

Alder hated that it was his relationship with me that had caused a spirit to come after me to begin with, but now he was struggling with the knowledge that the legend he'd so despised had actually come to pass when he'd tried so hard to prevent it.

Raysh jumped from the rock he'd sat upon. *"Well, regardless what spirit, or god for that matter, is after you, we still need to open those gates and get your mother back, and we are running out of time."*

"Hold on," Alder said, coming out of his shock. "If we

get her mother back, the fire god will still want an anchor. They will try to take Briony in her place." Alder looked at me, his jaw tight and his eyes full of worry. "It'll be too easy for them to take you, Brye. Think of all the visions you've had. The nightmares of fire. It's the gate. It was the fire god who marked you, and when they did, they established some kind of spiritual connection. The gate has been calling to you this whole time."

Chills danced over my skin and wound down my spine. He was right. Every fire vision I'd had, every face in the flames I'd seen, it was the fire god calling to me.

They might hold my mother for their anchor, but their mark was still on me.

Raysh made a *tsk* noise. *"And so you would just leave your mother there? After she'd sacrificed years there for you?"*

Ever since I'd found out she'd gone to protect me, to save me from whatever spirit had been after me, I'd tried not to focus too much on what that meant. On what it meant that her spirit was trapped in this astral plane with nothing but a terrifying fire god to slowly consume her…

I shivered, my whole body seizing and shaking. Nausea made my gut churn and my knees wobble. Dropping down to the grass, I buried my fingers into the green blades warmed by sunlight.

Was this the fate I was walking into? An eternity spent in an astral prison?

It's the fate Mom had accepted, and I wouldn't condemn her to it a moment longer. It's not like I wanted to spend one hundred years in some spirit cage, but the idea of leaving her there… I couldn't live with myself if I turned my back now.

"Raysh is right."

"Hell no," Alder growled, taking a step away from the tree, fists clenched.

"Alder, I need you to open the air gate," I said as calmly as I could, standing and pulling out the feather from my pocket.

He shook his head. "No, Briony. I told you I wouldn't let anything take you away—god or spirit."

"Alder, I'm saving my *mom*. Tell me you wouldn't do the exact same."

Alder looked from me to the feather, his gaze hard and concentrated, as if he was thinking through his options.

He seemed to have come to some conclusion, because without a word, he wrapped an arm around my waist and took the feather from my hand. One spirit wind tunnel later, we were back in the physical world in a meadow of wildflowers. It reminded me of the meadow in which I'd seen my mother's projection. Where she'd told me to save her. If she'd known that I would have to take her place, would she have told me to open the gates and free her? Somehow I doubted it very much.

The light evening breeze rustled through the tall meadow grass, blowing the blossoms of the wildflowers in its direction. Alder's arm brushed mine, and I looked down at his hands that cupped the key. They were trembling just slightly. Placing my hands over his, I squeezed them, as if to reassure him.

This was my decision.

He closed his eyes and silver light spread from his fingertips, ending in a vibrant flash.

When he opened his hands, a few dandelion seeds had taken the place of the feather. A simple breeze pulled them into the air, and they were carried away, becoming one with the wind.

It was already late in the evening and the wisps were beginning to come out, which meant we had only this night to find the fire gate and open it. As the dandelion seeds disappeared, the wisps around us changed color, becoming silver. Silver like the mana of air.

"Alder—look!" I pulled at his shirt, pointing to the wisps as they changed color, and then suddenly their lights fell out of sync, no longer illuminating simultaneously, but each breaking apart and exploding into a silver cloud of mana, blowing and swirling into the air.

Moving it. Influencing it.

Turning it into a wind storm that ripped through Firefly Valley.

Alder threw himself over me as gales swept like comets streaking through the valley. With one arm wrapped tightly around my waist, he buried his other into the ground beside me. I imagined him holding onto the tree's roots, gripping them tightly as branches broke off and flew over our heads. Meadow grass flattened, and shredded plants and flowers and splinters of wood soared through the air, caught in the tempest that we'd unleashed.

With the air gate now open, Alder took us back into the ethereal plane. Raysh was already there, waiting on us.

"It's the wisps," I murmured, still in awe of what I'd just seen, how they had taken on the mana of the air gate and created the squalls. Had that been what happened with the landslide and the rain storm? Had the wisps initiated the opening of each gate? I supposed it made the most sense. Alder had explained to me once that the wisps were evidence of spiritual planes in this valley.

In the clearing, after the winds had calmed down, I'd

been able to see that there were fewer wisps around. I had to assume it was because their mana had been used up to open the gate—their glow transforming into silvery mana that dissolved into the air.

It had been strange to not have the wisps there at night. Without the glow of the fireflies, it no longer felt like the same place. The special place where spirits dwelled. I'd grown accustomed to their presence. They were a part of the valley just like its trees.

"Indeed." Raysh was lying on the rock, his head on his paws lazily.

Now that it was dark, I really was panicking now. We had so little time before the solstice began. "Let's get moving, Raysh. One more gate to open, right?"

"Oh, our job is done here."

Alder and I exchanged a confused look.

The fox rolled his eyes. *"Fine. Here is your final lesson. As I've said, the fire gate is not like the others. It might need an anchor to the valley, but it has no key. Rather, the key is not protected by the fire god, because it needs no protection."*

"Raysh, *spit it out*," I snapped.

He finally lifted his head off his paws, showing a row of white teeth. *"Do you still not get it? Humans are so ignorant. I've an idea to help you learn. How about a riddle?"*

Something was off about Raysh. He'd been irritating and snooty since I met him, but this attitude now felt mockingly cruel. My stomach clenched tight as the fox stood on the rock he'd been lying on and swished his tail. *"I open the gate every morning, and every night I lock it."*

Time seemed to slow to a snail's crawl as I put two and two together, like that final clue in a crossword puzzle.

"The *sun*?"

An amused laugh floated up from Raysh. *"Yes, it's what*

makes life in this valley possible, after all. The rising sun will mark the beginning of the solstice, and, incidentally, unlock the fourth and final gate. Convenient, isn't it? Now, if you'll excuse me, I believe my job as your emissary is officially done. Give my regards to your mother."

Before Alder or I could say another word, Raysh hopped off the rock and began to trot away. Just as I was beginning to process this information, the relief that I had knowing I was no longer under any time limit to find a fourth key, a now familiar growl echoed through the grove.

I jerked around to see Ashka emerge from the underbrush and tackle Raysh, claws out and fangs bared.

The two animals rolled across the grass, snarls and yips and growls cutting through the silence of the ethereal forest. My instinct was to save Raysh, but when I started forward, Alder threw out an arm to stop me.

"Look," he whispered.

For a minute, I was confused, but then I saw sparks of mana fly from the fox's body. As the spirits fought, Raysh's mana surged upward in a column of gold astral energy, engulfing the fox in a bright inferno made entirely of mana. His body began to morph, growing even larger, taking on the size and muscles of a raging bull, while his tail swept the ground, brushing the leaves and growth and making green mana scatter into the wind.

The cougar jumped backward, spitting and hissing, away from the monstrous fox that now stood before us.

"You've doomed us, Raysh," Ashka snarled, whiskers quivering while her fangs seemed to grow in size before my eyes. The cougar's body grew, too, not as big or as powerful as Raysh's, but more the size of a tiger.

"Stay out of this, Ashka."

Ashka glared at Alder and me, yellow eyes flashing. *"And*

you two, are you even aware of what you've done? What you've condemned your world to as well?"

In that moment of distraction, Raysh slashed out, drawing his claws down the arm of the cougar, leaving a fresh red gash. Ashka let out a roar and shrank backward, wounded.

Alder dropped to his knee and touched the earth. At once, roots burst from the ground, wrapping themselves around Raysh's arms and legs, and neck and torso, pulling him to the ground. Being in the ethereal plane meant he was no longer just a translucent spirit in the way that he was in the physical plane. He could be caught.

"We need one final lesson," Alder's voice boomed through the trees. "What is Ashka talking about?"

Raysh only snarled and snapped and pulled at the roots that bound him.

Ashka limped back, licking the bleeding wound on her arm. *"The barriers, you fools,"* the cougar said. *"Now that the gates are unlocked, the barriers between worlds on the solstice won't just become thin, they will be nonexistent. All three worlds will become one."*

"No, no, no," I breathed, a terrible, freezing sensation seizing my whole body. "No, Raysh said that the gates were like dams. The energy just evens out."

"And what happens first when dams break?" Ashka snarled. *"It floods."*

Chapter Twenty-Four

An image of sprites, spirits, and mana flooding the valley was almost impossible to comprehend, and yet, I knew the cougar spoke the truth.

The gates didn't just open the barriers for *humans* to pass through. It opened them for *spirits* as well. How had I not realized it before? Why would it be one and not the other? It wouldn't. If all the barriers were taken down, then three worlds became one.

"But my mother… She asked me to open the gates. There's no way she would've asked me to open them if she—"

Raysh's laughter interrupted me. He'd stopped chewing his way through the roots.

"That wasn't your mom," Alder said, gaze fixed on the fox spirit.

Raysh's form flickered—like that of an old strip of film—between the great fox monster before me and a slender woman with long dark hair, and the eyes of a vixen, in a yellow sunflower blouse.

Mom.

Raysh-turned-Mom stared at me, her eyes narrowing into slits, as gold mana expanded around her, and the fox tail disappeared and reappeared, in and out of focus. Alder's roots slipped from her thin wrists and she stepped free of them.

"It's too late. You can't stop it. You can't."

Ashka growled and advanced. *"You are destroying our home."*

Mom tipped her head to the mountain lion spirit, eyes flashing. *"You mean how these humans have destroyed our valley for centuries? Tearing down our trees, paving their roads. All of the Smokies used to be our domain, Ashka. And now we are limited to but a valley. Like you said before, we should be on the same side. They had all but made your kind extinct. It's time to take our valley back."*

Ashka pawed the ground. *"Combining our worlds won't send the humans away. It will just kill us all. Have you forgotten what will happen to the wisps when the sun comes up?"*

"No," Raysh laughed, transforming from my mother to an eagle. *"In fact, I am most excited for it."* Then he flapped his wings and took off into the sky.

"Damnit—" Alder raised his arm, his mana shooting outward like an extension of his fist. The eagle dodged away from the explosion of raw astral energy, and its form flashed up into the dark sky far, far out of reach.

With the disappearance of Raysh, my legs gave way. I stumbled backward, and Alder caught me by the shoulders, his hands gentle despite the wave of wild power he'd just unleashed.

How could we stop this? How could we fix what we'd done?

My head was foggy, and my skin was freezing from the icy dread that ran through my veins. Dimly I was aware of the cougar hobbling away from us, limping from her wounded leg.

"Ashka! Wait!" I called, my heart heavy with fear and the unknown.

She stopped, turning her head over her shoulder to regard us with a cold stare.

"What were you talking about? What about the wisps at sunrise?"

The cougar sneered. *"You dare to ask me for help? After everything you've done? Figure it out for yourself, human."*

I was still in shock, watching the cougar disappear into the trees, when Alder wrapped me in his arms and took us back to the physical world.

The wind tunnel died around us, but I stayed where I was, my arms around his neck and pressing my face into his collarbone.

I wanted to rewind time.

Now that I knew the cost of rescuing my mother, of opening up these gates and taking down these barriers…

And there was something else, too. Something selfish that twisted my heart and burned my eyes with tears. It had never been my mother in that meadow. She'd never held me or told me she missed me or asked me to take her home so we could be together. Finally.

I'd come to this valley fearful, but also desperate for answers. To know who I was, who I'd been, and maybe why my mother had left. Now that I had found those answers, I almost wished I'd never looked for them in the first place. They were so much worse than I could've ever dreamed.

The world and the childhood friend I'd lost were precious and irreplaceable, and it made me *crave* my memories more deeply than ever before. And when I'd found that letter and realized that my mother had left for *me*, the guilt was too much to bear.

Everything…*everything* that I'd wanted for six years had

turned out to be more painful and more destructive than living with this gigantic void in my chest. Or *pretending* my life away, like Izzie had said.

I felt crushed by a landslide, drowned by a storm, beaten and broken by gales. Everything that I'd unleashed on this valley, I felt its calamity.

Alder's hand moved into my hair, threading his fingers through it. His soft gesture brought me back to the present, out of my head. "Brye, are you all right?"

I peeked up from his shoulder to see the world around us, the world that was about to be overrun with spirits. We were in the woods, but not far from Gran's house. I could see the lights of the porch in the distance.

The darkness of the forest itself, though, felt heavier and…sinister.

In my heart I knew it was the same valley, the same forests and mountains and the familiar sounds of the nocturnal creatures, but Raysh's trick stung. It tainted my valley with a poison as thick as fog.

A fog that was hard to see through.

"What do we do?" I asked, pushing down tears that I knew we didn't have time for. "Is there a way to stop this? There has to be a way, right? Can we close the gates somehow?" But even as I asked him this, the despair tried to overtake me again. I struggled to stay in the moment. The sun would be rising soon, and with it, the fire gate would open. If there was some miraculous way to fix all this, I had to think clearly.

Carefully, Alder drew me away by the shoulders, his gaze contemplative. More hopeful, actually, than I thought it would be in the face of so much chaos. "Once they're opened, they can't really be closed. Not until the solstice ends." He noticed the confusion on my face and added, "Think of it like a spiritual calendar. The barriers reset after the end of a solstice—of course I'm not sure what happens if all the barriers disappear entirely. But it may not come to that. The only way to stop all three worlds from merging is by preventing the fire gate from opening."

I stared at him, thinking he might have just lost it. "Alder, we can't stop the *sun* from rising."

"No," he said with the hint of a smile, "but we can remove the fire god's tie to the valley."

An explosion of hope and relief erupted in my chest. "Mom."

Alder nodded. "Forget the sun, *she's* the key."

"So how do we get her out of the astral plane?"

"Briony, absolutely *nothing* physical can enter the astral plane. That includes you. Remember how your mom's body is somewhere in the ethereal plane?" he said.

"Yes—I saw her!" I shook his arm excitedly. "I forgot to tell you—there was a big black bear spirit, and he took me to her."

"Your mom is with Bruley?"

"I think he's been watching over her this whole time."

"He never mentioned it to me," Alder groaned, pinching the space between his brows.

"Well, he doesn't talk much." I folded my arms, scrutinizing him, wondering if this wasn't just another idea to prevent me from walking into danger. "*You're* physical matter. How can *you* walk into the astral plane?"

He raised an eyebrow. "Well, for one, I'm a god."

"Well, that's convenient," I muttered.

"And secondly," he continued as if he hadn't heard me, "I'm able to separate my spirit from my body easily. Attempting to do that to you would be ridiculously difficult. We wouldn't have time to try and manage it. You're just going to have to trust me to get her out myself."

My initial reaction was *absolutely not*. In fact, every fiber of my being hated the idea of it, especially after Raysh's betrayal.

The little voice inside my head kept saying, *see? This is why you don't trust people. This is why you don't work well with others. He tricked you and betrayed you when you relied on him.*

And yet…the very reason I had stopped trusting people had been wrong all along. For six years I'd thought my mother had abandoned me, when instead it was the exact opposite.

Alder had shown me time and again that he could be relied on. That I could trust him and have faith that he would pull through for me. That we could work together and *win*.

But was I ready to entrust my mother's life in his hands? No, not just her life, but the fate of this whole valley?

It seemed like I didn't have a choice.

I stared up at him, his gold eyes glowing in the darkness and his silver hair shining like there were pieces of moonbeams threaded through it. His expression earnest, open…

"Okay," I said softly. "I'll trust you."

A few seconds passed before Alder bowed his head and brushed his knuckles against my cheek. "Brye, even if we didn't need your mother to stop the fire god, I would still go get her."

I opened and closed my mouth. "Why?"

"I want to give her back to you, because you gave something very important to me." Alder took my hands and this time, he let his mana flow through me. And while my senses were overwhelmed with the Smokies, my heart was overwhelmed by the simple feel of his skin.

My breath hitched. "And that is?"

His fingers threaded through mine and squeezed. "A childhood."

And I'd lost mine. The irony was painful, but it was also sweet. I was happy I'd been able to give that to him. I only wished I could remember it, too.

Taking a deep breath, I nodded. "Go get her. Bring her back to me."

He leaned forward and kissed me gently on the cheek. The butterflies in my stomach fluttered, and I wanted to cling to him longer, but there wasn't time.

"I will, I promise," he whispered. "In the meantime, I need you to do something for me."

"Anything," I agreed.

"You have to save Firefly Valley."

Chapter Twenty-Five

"I'm sorry, but I thought that's what we were doing!" I called to Alder as we sprinted through the forest together, dodging bushes and trees and jumping over tiny brooks. I was able to see in the darkness only because a few wisps had located Alder and were following him, as they usually did, lighting up the surroundings like the floating candles at Hogwarts. More seemed to be accumulating after the opening of the air gate, which I supposed made sense. If the other gates had been opened by the wisps causing the landslide or the rainstorm, then there still had to be more left over from the air gate. They were the manifestations of the spirit world after all. As long as the spirit world remained in the planes beyond our own, there would be wisps.

"You saw what happened with the air gate," Alder said with ease as we ran—any normal person would be panting by now—"the wisps took on the mana of the element. As soon as the sun starts to rise, the wisps will—"

We came to a skidding stop just outside of Gran's garden, my chest tightening and constricting with panic. With realization.

"They'll turn into fire," I breathed. "It'll be the worst

wildfire ever in the Appalachians."

Alder took my arms, his gold eyes skimming my face. "The Firefly Festival. People will be coming from all over the Smokies. Forest fires will start to spread anywhere there is a wisp. If I don't get back in time, you need to make sure everyone is safe."

Porch lights blinked on, and Izzie's voice called from the doorway. "Brye? Is that you?"

My heart thudded painfully, but I wouldn't stand here and think that this could be the last time I saw him. It wouldn't be like that. "Go." I started to gently push him away, when he caught my hands.

"Briony…" Alder's hands ghosted over my skin, moving up my neck to cup my cheeks. "The festival."

"Don't worry, I'll get everyone away." I started to pull away from him, but he held on.

"No, not that. Would you go with me? To the festival?"

I blushed, my face so hot I could toast marshmallows on my cheeks. He was bringing this up *now*? I couldn't stop my smile, though. "Just go make sure there still *is* one."

His mouth hooking to one side in a handsome half smirk, he leaned down and kissed me lightly. It was painfully brief, but necessarily brief.

Then he turned and disappeared into the darkness of the forest, while I headed into the light of Gran's porch.

Izzie stood leaning against the rails of the porch, her eyes wide. She pointed in the direction that Alder disappeared. "Um, did I just see him kiss you?"

"Maybe," I said, bounding up the steps.

Her eyes wide, she stared in the direction that Alder had disappeared. "Okay, if this bride-stealing thing is legit, I still get to be your maid of honor, right? Remember, outdoor weddings are better in the spring. Can he wait till March?"

I hooked my arm in hers. "C'mon, Iz, I've got a lot to tell you."

It took approximately too long to catch Izzie and Gran up to speed, but I had no other choice other than to explain what I could.

Given everything, though, I was surprised how well they were both taking it. Gran didn't seem to need proof or confirmation of spirits and gods in her valley, or the fact that Mom was trapped in the prison of an elemental god. She focused on the important things: her daughter was alive.

"And you think this…Alder…can bring her back? Truly?" Gran asked, squeezing the bars of her crutches that leaned against the side of the couch. Her eyes were glassy with unshed tears. It was impressive that she was this calm—worried, desperate, but calm. My grandmother was a strong woman. I couldn't imagine what it would be like to discover that your child was finally coming home.

"Yes, he has to." I knelt in front of her. "Gran, I'm sorry I lied to you."

Gran leaned forward and hugged me. "Oh, sugar pea, I understand. But if there's anyone who believes in fairies and sprites, it's your gran." She drew away and smoothed her wrinkled hands down my cheeks. "Because I knew I had one for a granddaughter."

I grinned, clasping my hands over hers, silently promising to myself that I'd spend every spare moment I could catching up with this amazing woman I'd missed out on for sixteen years.

Meanwhile, Izzie paced the floor in Gran's living room so much that I was surprised she didn't burn a hole into the carpet. "It's like, two o'clock in the morning. Everyone is going to be asleep. How the hell are we going to do this?"

"The town is small—we'd be able to get everyone up and out of there by sunrise, right?"

But even as I said it, I knew why Gran was already shaking her head. "People live *all* over this valley, Brye. Far apart from each other. It would take much longer than that to alert everyone."

"Can't we call them?" I asked, gesturing to the phone.

"The windstorm knocked out the phone lines," Izzie grumbled.

Of course it did.

I paused, thinking hard. What would get everyone out of their beds? What could put the festival to a grinding halt?

I told Alder that I'd get everyone out of the valley before the fires, but now the task seemed impossible. Not in the middle of the night. Not with everyone so far apart with no phones.

"How am I going to do this?" I muttered, biting my thumbnail.

Izzie nudged my toe with hers and I looked up at her. "You mean *we*. How are *we* going to do this? Teammates, remember? Dairy Queen, amiright?" She gave me a big, obnoxious wink.

Teammates. Izzie was right. There was no way I could do this alone. It was why I had gone to them in the first place. I needed Gran and Izzie's help to round up the folk from the town and get everyone as far away from Firefly Valley as possible.

But I wasn't limited to just humans.

"Would an earthquake work?"

Izzie and Gran stared at me. Then Izzie gasped, catching on.

"Briony! You can't be serious!"

"The earth god might help," I said, getting to my feet and running into the back to grab Izzie's car keys. If Ashka had been against the opening of the gates, then I had to imagine other spirits shared her position. *Especially* the guardians of them. "Not all of the spirits are like Raysh. And with the barriers down, the earth god might make big enough tremors to alert the entire valley. It's worth a shot at least."

"But how are you going to get into the spirit world?" Izzie asked as she snatched the keys from my grasp. "Your ticket there kinda peaced-out to go save your mom."

I whirled around to face Gran. "How did Mom get to the spirit world?"

Gran blinked at me behind her large glasses. "Heather?"

"Yes—Mom went to the spirit world herself. I know she did. I saw her leave that night. How? Do you know?"

Gran drummed her fingers on her knees as she stared hard out the window. A few wisps darted about in the gardens, chasing after each other playfully, completely unaware of the damage they could do in just a few short hours.

"There was this place..." Gran started. "Your mother took you there often. It's a nature trail. She used to tell me it was the most spiritual place in the valley. One time she told me where it was and I tried to find it so I could walk the trail, but I couldn't. I called her that night, told her that she had given me the wrong directions. She insisted that it was right. She even tried to take me there once, but the two of us never found it. Then the next day she went out alone and she was able to find it." Gran shrugged. "Eventually I gave up, but your mother was always able to walk it."

It was only then that I remembered Alder saying there was a nature trail into the ethereal plane. *Mom had found it.* I grabbed a notepad and a pencil. "That has to be it. She followed it to the spirit world."

"Is that even possible?" Izzie asked skeptically.

"It's possible. Alder said once that humans have accidentally wandered into the ethereal plane—ones that were deeply connected to the valley." I handed the notepad and pencil to Gran. "Gran, can you remember the directions?"

She didn't write anything. I waited while her pencil was poised, until I couldn't take it any longer.

"Do you not remember?" I asked, trying to keep the panicked edge out of my voice.

"Doing this…would be against your mother's wishes. She wanted you *safe,* Briony. Not running into the ethereal plane and going up against a *god.*" Gran looked up at me; this time tears were trickling down her cheeks. "I love your mother. Around the moon and down the slopes of the valley. She's my baby girl and I want her back, but you are *hers*. If anything were to happen to you…"

"This isn't about me, Gran," I said, gripping her hands. "It's not even about our family. It's about the rest of Firefly Valley and getting them out safely. This is their one chance. You have to let me do this."

Gran bit her lip, then lowered her head and scribbled down the directions that she could remember. I kissed her temple. "I'll be back, I promise."

Izzie jangled the keys by the door. "C'mon then, I'm driving."

That was the best thing about Izzie. I never had to ask her for anything.

"You sure about this, Iz?"

"As sure as I am that Idris Elba is my soul mate."

I laughed and shook my head, relieved to know I wasn't going there alone. Then I stopped right before I reached the door. "What if the path doesn't show itself to you?"

"You said the barriers were coming down, that spirits will be able to cross over soon. It'll be the same for humans. Plus, I've still got a little bit of Alder's mana in me," Izzie said. "I'll be able to make it through. Now let's go charm the antlers off this nature god."

Ten minutes into the drive and I was already worried we were lost, but every direction that Mom had given to Gran was accurate. Each time I thought we'd taken a wrong turn down a country road and gone too far, another street sign would be around the bend.

I was also fiercely proud that Gran had remembered them all. It made me wonder how many times she'd *really* tried to find this place.

Maybe she'd even gone there looking for Mom after she'd left. Maybe she'd wanted to take her daughter's place like Mom had for me.

That thought, the idea that Gran kept searching for her daughter and trying time and time again was almost more devastating than knowing in a matter of hours there could be forest fires the likes of which the Smokies had never seen.

Finally we got to the last turn, finding an old faded sign with ivy growing all over it. It read Firefly Grove.

Izzie maneuvered her CRV as close to the sign as possible, and we both jumped out, slamming the car doors in unison. I consulted Gran's scrawl on the note. "It says the trail is supposed to be a mile up ahead. You ready to run?"

Izzie groaned. "There's a reason I'm a swimmer."

"Hey, you wanted to come."

"Do you think this is even the right place?" Izzie asked, glancing around.

There were so many wisps around I couldn't see how she'd think otherwise. They glowed softly, pulsing through the trees and bushes, each one a different faded color: violet, aqua, light green, blue, periwinkle.

"Definitely. Let's go."

Izzie grumbled under her breath but fell into step beside me. We ran as hard as we could and jogged for the rest of it. After about twelve minutes or so, Izzie's Fitbit blinked at her. We skidded to a stop and raised our hands above our shoulders to let the air pass through our lungs better.

"That's a mile," Izzie wheezed. "I feel like I actually need to borrow your inhaler. How are you doing so well?"

Somehow I knew that, even without Alder's mana coursing through me, I'd still be feeling just fine. Not even winded. The more mana I had, the mountains became more a part of me.

Pointing toward the cluster of wisps near a break in the trees, I said, "There. That's the trail."

"How are you so sure?" Izzie asked.

As our feet crunched over the grass and twigs, I side-eyed her. "Alder's mana ran out, didn't it? You liar."

Izzie snapped her fingers. "Ohh, got it. All the fireflies. Right. Makes sense."

Rolling my eyes, I stepped onto the path.

Immediately, the world seemed to tilt. It was the feeling I'd had when I first got out of Izzie's car at Gran's. It was the feeling of stepping into a place that was special.

Where spirits dwell.

Izzie sucked in a breath beside me, and I knew she felt it, too.

Glancing at each other, we took off running down the trail, into the spirit world.

Chapter Twenty-six

The ethereal plane at night was spooky, but also beautiful. It wasn't totally dark like any other forest. The mana that dripped and swirled around the trees and other parts of nature glowed, illuminating the surrounding woods like bioluminescent jellyfish were all trapped within the bark and hidden in bushes.

"Whoah," Izzie whispered. "This place is trippy."

"I know," I agreed, stepping tentatively along the path. The mana swirling around my ankles seemed more alive. More active and energetic. I had to assume it was because the barriers to the astral world were thinner as well. More and more astral energy was seeping through. I shivered to think what would happen once it went down entirely.

No, *if* it did.

I had to believe in Alder. Trust that he'd bring Mom back.

"So where is this god?" Izzie asked, looking around.

"I'm not sure, this place is huge."

"Oh great. Well, can't you tell where we are, though, or something? Does anything look familiar? Don't you have plant ESP?"

"That's not how that works."

"Oh, as if you know how any of this works."

She had a point.

"Let's just ask for directions." I pointed to an owl sitting on a nearby branch of another yellow poplar. The owl was watching us warily, its big gold eyes unblinking and somewhat haunting. It had leaves in its feathers, and when it ruffled its wings, a few floated down at our feet.

"Oh good, the human girl whooo started all this mess. Hoo."

My gut twisted, and I opened my mouth to reply.

"Yes, yes, she's real sorry," Izzie said gesturing with her wrist. "Can you skip the guilt trip and tell us where to find the earth god? Big buck dude with branches for antlers."

"How could youuuu think they want to see you? Hoo."

"Because they can help us fix it. Will you please take us to them?"

I swore the owl puffed out his chest before he took off from the tree in a flurry of feathers and leaves. *"Try to keep up. Hoo."*

I raised my eyebrows at Izzie.

She gave me a smug smile. "You think you're the only one who has a way with animals?"

The meadow was similar to how I remembered it, but now that it was dark, it seemed emptier. Lonelier.

"Where is the god?" Izzie whispered.

I shushed her and pointed to a cluster of branches protruding from the middle of the field.

Izzie reached down and took my hand. It wasn't much, but I was glad for the show of support. And I was glad she was here. I knew I'd be scared out of my mind if I had to do this alone.

"Excuse me?" I called across the meadow. "Um...lord?"

Slowly, the branches shivered, and the god picked their head up, green eyes glowing along with the mana from their antlers, the energy fluttering away on the night breeze.

"We need your help."

The god began to lower their head back into the grass.

Thinking of Bruley the black bear, I stalked across the meadow with Izzie at my heels. "I know you can talk, dude!"

"Uh, Brye? You don't know for sure," Izzie offered, the meadow grass brushing against our shins.

No, it was a god, and if not a god then a powerful spirit. They could talk. Just like Raysh, Ashka, Bruley, even Rikki, Tikki, and Tavi.

I stopped five feet away and folded my arms. "No, the god is just being a stubborn jerk."

At that, the stag picked their head back up, green eyes narrowing at me. *"What do you want, human?"*

Their voice shook and trembled with power and energy. It seemed to vibrate the very ground at our feet.

"I want to save my valley."

The deer huffed, silver mana blowing from their nostrils in a cloud. *"It's a bit late for that."*

My stomach flipped, but I pushed the anxiety down. "No, it's not. We still have time."

The god returned to ignoring me, laying their head back down into the meadow grass.

"Hey! This is *your* world, too! Aren't you supposed to be its guardian?"

At that, the god lifted their head, blowing another cloud of mana. Every breath seemed to get more and more irritated. *"I* was *its guardian. And I failed."*

"So...what? You're feeling sorry for yourself?" I demanded.

The god stood, green mana surging outward in a force field rivaling the shields of the Starship Enterprise.

"Careful, Brye," Izzie warned out of the corner of her mouth.

"'Sorry for myself?' What a human thing to do. No, I am accepting my fate. Now you and that human god must endure the consequences of your actions. You made the decision to steal my key and open these gates."

Rage welled up inside me. "Because we were tricked by Raysh!"

The god stomped their hooves irritably. *"The conduit should've known to never help a human like you."*

"How should he have known? None of you TOLD him anything!" I exploded, my voice carrying over the meadow almost loud enough to shake the earth, ironically.

"He's been alone for *years*, never belonging anywhere." My fists trembled at my sides. "He barely knew his powers and definitely *not* the rules of these gates. He's just supposed to exist and move mana from one world to another? Humans aren't like that. We need purpose and other people. So I might have torn down these barriers and put this valley in danger, but not watching out for him, even just for the purpose of protecting these gates—that's on you."

"The fire god must have its anchor. It is for that reason that the boy is kept in the dark and forced to make a connection with a human."

"And it is for that reason that our worlds are merging," I said mockingly, folding my arms. "So how has that worked out?"

There was a long silence. The silver mana of the wind blew through the surrounding trees and ruffled the meadow grass. It made the flowering petals and leaves on the god's antlers dance.

"Listen, um, Lord of All that is Green," Izzie said, breaking the silence, taking a step forward and holding out her palms in a sign of peace. "We just need your help. We think we can stop the fire gate from opening. But you have to help us save the valley from all the fires."

The god cocked their head at Izzie. *"The fires will come no matter what, because the sun will rise, and you cannot stop that any more than you can stop that boy from loving you."*

It was like the god had kicked me with their hooves in my stomach and sent me flying. I imagined myself soaring through the starry sky.

"Whoah," Izzie said again.

"He doesn't..." My throat grew tight, unable to finish the sentence.

"Of course he does. They all do. How do you think that connection works so well?"

I hated that Alder's feelings had been orchestrated by these gods, but I refocused. What's done was done, and I would have to sort through my feelings later. "We have another idea to stop the fire gate."

The buck got up and trotted toward me, staring me down, eyes, branches, and the moss growing on their hooves all glowing with astral earth energy. The very air around them sizzled with power, and I knew it would take just one well-placed stomp to kill me.

"I'm listening."

All right, I had to admit—riding on the back of an all-powerful nature god was pretty freaking cool.

At first the earth god had not been enthusiastic. Their

part in saving the valley involved saving the humans, after all. Which, like Alder had said, none of the spirits really cared much about.

In the end, it was actually Izzie that had persuaded them.

"Might I remind you," Izzie had said, holding up a threatening finger to the earth god, "that humans are a part of this valley. Whether you like it or not. And, more importantly, if the three planes become one, humans will be all up in your space. Especially if they get trapped here because of the fires. Now, does that sound like fun to you? Hmm?"

I had to hand it to my friend. She had this way of shutting down arguments.

So now we were riding on the back of the deer spirit as the mana blurred all around us. It hadn't even been our idea to climb aboard, but they complained that our human pace was too slow. Which was how I ended up holding onto antlers as they galloped through the forest, leaping entire rivers in one single bound.

Izzie squeezed my waist, letting out terrified squeaks and muttering, "I am *so* not a horse girl."

When we reached the path back to the physical world, the god slowed down to a trot and stopped under a large chestnut oak that marked its entrance. *"I cannot follow you any farther. Not until the solstice would I be able to fully cross over."*

I slid off their back and helped Izzie down as well. She whimpered as her feet touched solid earth and shot the god a withering glare.

"I get it. Thanks for bringing us here. But you're closer to the physical world so your…quakes should be stronger, right?"

The god huffed again, silver mana twirling out of their

nostrils in smoky tendrils. *"That is the theory. But I will need something from* you *first."*

"Something from me? Like what?"

"You stole my key. I no longer contain the powers of a god. To be able to produce these earthquakes, I will need to take some of your mana."

I blinked. "*My* mana? You mean what I get from Alder."

"No, if I had meant his, I would've said it," the buck replied shortly. *"I need yours."*

"But I don't have any except his."

The god shook their head, leaves and flower petals sprinkling to the ground. *"I'm not referring to his elemental mana. I require your spiritual mana. You were born in this valley. Therefore you are connected to the spirit world just like we all are. You have your own mana. You just don't know how to use it."*

I stared down at my hands, trying to process the god's words. "But then…how can I give it to you?"

"I have no idea."

"Maybe if you tried praying," Izzie interjected.

I glanced over at her, raising my eyebrows.

She shrugged. "Well, that's what you do with gods, right?"

Yes, it was.

Shutting my eyes tight, I started…praying. Talking to them. Not with my mouth, but with my heart. My soul. The void in my chest, usually so cold and empty, seemed to warm.

Please, take my mana. Save this valley. Save our worlds.

A sound from the god made me open my eyes, and I gasped as pearly white mana floated off my skin, white and luminescent and fusing with the green mana of the buck.

Tossing their head, the god pawed the ground, hooves digging into the earth as my mana surrounded them. The stag seemed to grow larger. Stronger. Greater.

I swallowed, taking a step back. "Will that do?" I asked, mouth dry. I didn't feel any different at least. It seemed to be an energy that I had endless amounts of.

Their eyes blazed a fierce emerald. *"It will. There is one more thing you should know."*

Inwardly, I groaned. I didn't think I could take any more obstacles. "What now?"

"When you open the gates, you take part of the god into the physical world."

The branch, the shell, the feather. "Yeah, and?"

"The fire god is made wholly of energy, so there isn't just a piece of him that can be taken into the physical world. When the sun begins to rise, the barriers will begin to lower, but it isn't until the fire god crosses fully out of the astral plane that the worlds truly become one."

"So what if the fire god just doesn't cross?"

"They will."

"How can you be sure?"

"Like us all, they are drawn to this valley."

I waited for more, but I realized that the earth god had said their piece. And while I didn't understand how a god of *literal fire* felt drawn to anything, I had to take their word for it.

With a deep breath, I said, "Okay, give us an hour, all right? We need to get to the town."

As Izzie and I started for the path, the god caught my sleeve between their teeth, nibbling on the cotton. *"Save our valley, Briony Redwrell. Prove to me what that boy clearly sees in you."*

I brushed my hand along their velvety nose, and I felt the earth god's own mana—rich like fertile soil—rush through me as they allowed it.

Smell of wildflowers and pine, and petrichor—the scent of

the dry earth after a hard summer rainfall. The touch of rough rocks and the smooth stone of limestone within caverns far beneath our feet. Whisper of leaves and the creak of crickets.

I smiled, my senses and spirit full of the earth essence of the Smokies. "Thanks for your help, Bambi's dad."

Chapter Twenty-Seven

By the time we got back to Gran's house, picked her up in Izzie's car, and headed toward town, it was nearing five o'clock in the morning.

According to Gran, sunrise in the Smokies today happened at exactly twenty after six.

If the earthquakes occurred now, then the people in Firefly Valley would have only under an hour and a half to get out.

That had to be enough time.

Just as Izzie swung down the turnoff into the downtown area of Firefly Valley, the earthquakes started. At first, it was subtle, hardly able to tell, but the next one created ripples in Izzie's water bottle just like a T-Rex was coming for us.

Izzie went above the speed limit but still moved pretty slow thanks to the streets clogged with festival preparations, much of which had already gone up yesterday.

Many of the residents of the valley had their booths prepped—ready to make money and ready to showcase crafts and baked goods they'd slaved over. I imagined them all going up in flames, and my heart ached.

As we neared the end of the small street, I could see a stage in the meadow that stretched behind Ms. Tilly's café.

It was set up with speakers and wires, awaiting the musical instruments of a local Tennessee bluegrass band. Farther out in the meadow sat the great pile of wood for the bonfire. The whole tower glowed a sheer, yet vibrant, white. It was full of everyone's mana. From all over the valley, they had taken their spare wood, their chopped trees and loaded them and driven them here. Each piece of wood was their connection to the valley.

"*It makes us feel connected.*"

Izzie parked in the same spot as she had before when she and Gran went to play bridge. It already felt like a lifetime ago.

Being not much of help hobbling around in crutches, Gran stayed in the car, while Izzie and I jumped out. As our feet touched the gravel, the biggest earthquake yet shook the valley.

It made Izzie and I stumble, and I had to grab hold of the car door to stay upright.

Another earthquake and then another caused shouts of alarm from nearby houses. Ms. Tilly was actually the first to emerge in a bathrobe, her hair done in curlers and her face white with panic.

"Briony? Izzie?" she called from her porch. Her two cats ran out from behind her and darted down the steps, right under Izzie's car. "What's going on?"

Following Ms. Tilly were the rest of the residents, each of them stumbling, bleary-eyed, as they came out of their homes and wandered into the streets.

Izzie cupped her hands around her mouth and yelled, "Everybody, get yer asses over here!"

It took much, much too long for all the residents to gather at Ms. Tilly's porch. While precious minutes ticked by, I scanned the horizon. It was still dark, but the sun was coming. Very soon.

How was Alder? Had he found Mom in the astral plane, yet? Would he have been able to get her past the fire god and through the boundary? And Mom? Was she still all right?

I prayed to Bruley that he'd kept watch over her body. That she was unharmed and safe, and ready for her spirit to be whole once again.

"Brye? You okay? You're shaking." Izzie rested a hand on my shoulder, her brows furrowed in concern.

It was lighter outside, just a bit, just a small bit, but I could see the outline of the houses better. Something jolted inside me, telling me to look up and look out.

My stomach sinking to my knees, I zoomed in on something in the distance. A dark column of smoke outlined against the dim, but lightening sky.

Fire. The wisps were starting to take on the element.

Izzie followed my gaze and her touch on my shoulder turned into a squeeze.

"We've gotta tell everyone, c'mon."

Just as a car's headlights swung into the town, hopefully a resident from the mountains that had felt the earthquakes, another tendril of smoke curled up into the heavens.

It was starting. *Where was Alder? Where was Mom?* If the wisps were igniting, then didn't that mean the barrier was thin enough for Mom to pass through? Why weren't they here yet?

I started to move with Izzie, up the steps, when I caught sight of a tall silhouette standing out in the meadow, with sharp, growing branches climbing into the sky.

The earth god was in the physical world.

I sucked in a breath. "Something's wrong."

"You mean besides the entire valley about to go up in smoke?" Izzie asked, exasperated, then she, too, caught sight of the god at the edge of the meadow. "Oh, shit."

Before I could say anything else, she hugged me. "Go, girl. Go. I'll make sure they get out okay."

With a quick nod, I raced down the steps, pushing past people in their night clothes and robes, my heart rate accelerating to a dangerous point. Over my shoulder, I called, "Make sure they set up road blocks! No one into the valley!"

Just as I was about to sprint into the meadow, Gran caught my arm. She took my cheeks in her hands and my breath hitched.

"You have to go, I know," she said, her voice tight, but steady. "But listen to me, Briony. This is important. You bring yerself back here. All right? Your momma wanted you to live. But she and I… We both forgot something important. Sending you away, it killed another part of you. This valley *is* you." She took a deep breath. "That boy didn't *give* you that magical energy or whatever it is—he brought it out. That's all."

My frazzled brain tried to make sense of what she was saying, but only some of it seeped through the constant screaming of *fire* in my head. I kissed her cheek. "I love you, Gran." I peeled her hands away from my face. "I'll bring Mom back. I swear."

Then I took off running past Tillywater's Café and through the tall grass, fear making my legs move faster. In one single jump, I leaped onto the back of the earth god and they galloped across the meadow, straight back into the valley where the fire gate was beginning to open.

"What's happening?" I yelled over the hoof beats. "Where's Alder?"

I couldn't lose him again. Not when we were…whatever we were. Labels aside, he was special to me.

He had to be okay. They both had to be.

The stag said nothing, continuing to run at an impossible, breakneck speed.

It felt like I was running alongside them with how hard my heart was pounding. I kept thinking about Alder leading me through Gran's garden and pulling out the silver pail of our adventuring kit, of the bracelet on his wrist he'd never removed, and that precious memory of him pulling back the sheet hanging on the clothesline and finding me, winning our game of hide-and-go seek.

But those were only hints of our past, and while they had influenced my feelings, they had not dictated them. His presence to me now—kind, sincere, protective, with a corny sense of humor. He had wound his way into my heart again.

I was about to yell at the earth god to ask what the *hell* was going on, when I noticed a glittering of gold light through the trees ahead. The mana flew out of the wisp like a trail of shimmering gold thread—being offered up to the illusive god. The wisp pulsed red once…twice…

The wisp exploded into a ball of flames—pure, hot, astral energy burning up into the sky. The sparks leached themselves onto the bark and started the easy, fast climb up into the branches. The trees caught fire, and before I could tell the earth god to stop, the deer dove through the flames, bringing back a horrid memory.

Smoke, heat, ash…a voice calling for me. Calling for my spirit.

I'd wanted to follow it. But it was so hot. Unbearably hot.

I missed crisp autumn wind and cool spring water.

I gasped into the god's fur. They'd never slowed as they cantered deeper into the forest, following the flames into more of the unknown. As we journeyed farther, I began to see a faint hint of mana brushing against the trees and radiating off the early morning dew on the grass.

The two worlds were becoming one.

Alder should be back by now.

He promised me.

Please, please, please be okay. I bowed my head and blinked back tears of panic, hopelessness, and fear, as I prayed to him.

More smoke climbed into the sky, carving dark, twisting pathways of gray into a light purple and pink sky. Dawn was cresting over the mountains and the stars were disappearing behind me, to the west.

Finally, I couldn't take another second. I yanked on the antler-branch, and the deer slowed, driving hooves into the earth, creating large divots. Their legs pranced and they shook their head irritably, leaves and twigs falling to the ground while grass and flowers sprouted where they landed.

"Those are attached, you foolish girl."

"Use your words!" I snapped. "What. Is. Going. On?"

"Your boy is losing."

My blood ran cold. "What are you talking about? What's happening? Is he fighting the fire god?"

"If that were the case, he'd be dead. I've brought you to him. He's just there beyond the trees. Save him, or we're all doomed."

Numb, my mind reeling, I dropped off the stag's back. As soon as my feet touched the ground, the earth god galloped away, and I was left alone in a shadowy forest that looked somewhat familiar.

But I didn't have time to figure out why, because to my right, a wisp whirled and twisted in the air and then burst into flames, its combustion showering sparks and igniting the grass. The flame skipped up, claiming the trees for its own.

I threw up my arms just as the fire roared upward, catching the dry leaves and bark of the surrounding trees. An inferno rose before me faster than I could've ever dreamed. Orange flames licked the trees and crawled across the ground like little fire demons grappling for my soul.

For a moment, I could do nothing but stare. Haunting memories had me rooted in place.

I'd spent the better part of the past six years avoiding anything with fire or extreme heat. No Girl Scout bonfires. No candles or incense. I preferred swimming and electric stove tops.

And now here I was, faced with an entire forest of fire and smoke, and it was *real* this time. Not visions or nightmares. They hadn't been any less scary, but I was distinctly aware of the fact that I could truly be consumed by these flames this time. Flashbacks of that day threatened to pull me back in, while I struggled to stay in the present, to concentrate on *this* fire.

I was going to do this. I *had* to do this.

I forced my feet forward. *Move!*

And I did. I had someone who needed me, someone who relied on me and trusted me. I wouldn't let Mom or Alder down. I ran through the fire because I had to.

As I neared the lakeshore, I caught sight of a wisp flying high above the top of a tall mountain ash tree. Just as the other one had, it sparked once, twice, and then erupted into a ball of flames.

It caught in the tree and the fire surged downward, eating up the bark.

A crack came from above and the trunk splintered, falling toward the road, blocking it.

I was out of its range, but I still felt the wave of heat wash over me. It made my throat dry and singed the air on my arms. Turning away from the burning tree, I focused on the forest. It wasn't yet fully consumed, but it was only a matter of time.

A matter of very short, short time.

Whirling around, I looked for a place to maneuver around the fire—to keep going. There was no way I was turning back. To my right there was a clear gap between two big trees, so I charged through. Branches and brambles clawed at my clothes and legs and arms as I charged through the growth of the forest. Mana whirled around me like I was caught in a tornado of soft colors and translucent fog. As the fire spread, it sucked the life out of the mountains, turning everything into ash—matter devoid of life and spirit energy.

Still I ran.

My lungs burned with the hot air and the distinct lack of oxygen from all the smoke wafting through the forest. Ash clung to my hair and arms, and my muscles screamed in protest from pushing them to the limit. Brambles and thorns nicking my skin as I crashed through the forest and emerged past the tree line to the edge of a lake.

Of course it was familiar. This was the place I'd first seen Alder transform.

Ironically, it might be the last place I'd ever see him.

Because there he was, in the middle of the lake, swarms of wisps dotting the sky, with streaks of fire climbing up and down the mountainsides, battling a monster fox.

Chapter Twenty-Eight

The earth god was right. Alder was losing.

He was losing *bad*.

From the look of his injuries, they must've been going at it for a long time. Maybe since he'd left me. Raysh might have been lying in wait for him. Knowing that we'd try to somehow stop the fire gate from opening.

Blood trickled down the side of Alder's face, while long scratches decorated his arms, and teeth marks were visible on his left leg. His mana was weak, flickering around him like the dying flame of a candle.

My first reaction was terror—terror and panic. Alder hadn't even been into the astral world to find my mom yet. And the sun was rising.

But what was more… Alder was losing. Dying.

I *wouldn't* lose him. Not again.

Rage rushed through me as hot and fast as the fire that ate away at the mountains. *My* mountains.

Raysh had said he'd known what would happen to this valley when the wisps started to ignite. He had known what he'd been about to unleash, and he hadn't cared. He seemed to hate humans for what we'd done to these mountains and wanted to watch our houses burn.

We weren't perfect. We'd caused species to be almost extinct and tore down sides of these mountains.

But we'd begun to learn. Wildlife protection, park preservations. We were *trying*.

I couldn't let Raysh have his way, and not just because of the three worlds becoming one. Homes and precious keepsakes inside them that were lost in wildfires, or floods for that matter, were *devastating*. It was a tragedy no family should endure.

I had to stop it.

But first I had to get out there.

Redirecting my focus to the lake, I wondered if I could use my mana to manipulate the water. I'd never attempted it in the physical plane, but now that the physical world and the ethereal world were merging into one, it might be possible.

Blue mist swirled within the water. I imagined the mana forming a solid surface that could hold my weight. Kicking off my shoes and socks, I reached down and placed one bare foot on top of the water, flexing my spirit muscles and pressuring the mana to remain strong beneath me.

Carefully, I lowered my other foot and when I didn't immediately sink, I threw caution out the window and pushed my mana toward the center of the lake where Alder and Raysh fought. Droplets of water kicked up around me as I splashed across the lake, running as fast as I dared toward the two dueling spirits.

Billows of smoke, ash, and sparks rolled across the lake, and as a powerful explosion took place at its far edge, Alder spun toward it. The spirit fox took advantage of the distraction and pounced on him, pinning him into the water and sinking fangs into his skin. For a horrid moment, I worried that was it—that Alder had used all he had left.

With a yell, he aimed a kick at Raysh's broad, furry chest.

The kick was only strong enough to send Raysh back a few feet, but the damage had been done. Alder was practically bleeding mana. Silver mist poured out of his arms and legs, blending into the blue energy swirling below the surface of the lake.

The fox stalked toward his prey, giant paws causing ripples, the tip of his tail brushing the water. Alder rolled over, his arms shaking, to push himself onto his elbows.

Even though I was only a few yards away, neither of the spirits had noticed me, and I could hear Raysh's voice carry on the wind.

"Weak. Weak. Weak. You don't deserve to be a god of this valley, little boy."

As Raysh came upon him, Alder shuddered and collapsed, his body slowly sinking below the surface.

"RAYSH!" I bellowed.

The fox swung his head toward me, and his green eyes glowed bright with rage. *"You."*

"Back off. Now." I took slow, measured steps toward Alder. Half his body was already submerged, but I couldn't risk moving any faster in case Raysh suddenly went for me. The last thing I needed was for him to bite me. Alder was in no state to heal me.

But I could heal him.

Raysh seemed to guess my intentions, because the fox dipped his head low, shifting his powerful shoulders and back paws. A column of mana shimmered around him like he was drawing mana from the air itself and pulling it into his own spiritual gravity.

Facing him there, on the lake, all alone—I took a step back. How had Alder fought him for so long by himself? If *a god* had failed, there was no way I had any kind of chance against Raysh.

But I wasn't giving up yet. I had to save this valley.

No. *We* had to save this valley.

I wasn't alone in this. In Firefly Valley, I'd never been alone.

It was in that split second where I had one last memory. It was a memory so faint and from so long ago, that it almost felt like a distant dream.

I was small and walking through the woods, sniffling and calling for Mom. As I wandered in the forest, a few fireflies blinked on and off along the darkening path. Entranced, I followed them to the shade of a poplar tree where a blond boy emerged from blackberry bushes only a few minutes later.

Alder hadn't found me, at least not entirely. I'd found him. The wisps—their glow had led me to him.

The wisps were everywhere in this valley. Even now, they were with me. They might be tiny slivers of real nature spirits, but I was connected to them.

And they could help me.

Raysh growled and advanced one paw on the lake at a time, bringing me back to the present as I came up with my plan. He watched my movements carefully, green eyes narrowed in smoldering fury. *"You're too late. The barriers are fading. I am winning."*

"This isn't a *game*, Raysh."

He took another step toward me, his pink tongue licking his jowls. *"Everything is a game."*

"Okay. Then let's play a game now."

Raysh blinked, his ears perking up and his large head cocking to the side.

I glanced down at Alder. Most of his body was almost entirely submerged. Blood and silver mana mixing into the lake as he floated, motionless. I swallowed back a thousand emotions and lifted my gaze back to the fox spirit. In that brief moment, Raysh had already taken two steps toward me. Wisps still floated above, swarming, full of mana.

"You like riddles, don't you?" I asked, echoing his words from before.

Finally, I was only two feet away from Alder. His eyes were closed, and he looked terribly human. No mana anywhere. He didn't have much time left.

If any.

Raysh watched me, his eyes narrowed and wary, as if he knew I was up to something, but couldn't figure out what.

"So how about a riddle? Are you good at them?"

"Of course I am."

"Then riddle me this," I said, my gaze pinned to a spot right behind Raysh, as I sank down next to Alder and grabbed his cold wrist.

Kneeling down into the water, I closed my eyes and prayed to the wisps of Firefly Valley. I called to them from the depths of my soul, reaching out with my spiritual mana that the earth god showed me I possessed.

I opened my eyes. Raysh was only five steps away.

"I am made of two elements. I am a creature with two names. I am stronger when there are two of me. What am I?"

Hundreds of wisps dropped down from the sky, swarming behind Raysh, coming, flying, answering my call.

Raysh's lips curled in triumph. *"A firefly."*

The explosion was epic. At least two of the hundred wisps reacted to the fire gate opening and took on its element. The eruption of fire went off right above Raysh while I let go of the mana in the water, to drop Alder and I through the lake. Beyond the rippling water above, I could see fire and sparks latching onto Raysh's fur, the pure astral energy of the fire eating him up, consuming him.

The fox spirit howled, and he crashed into the lake as

well, sinking deeper, much deeper into the dark depths. He seemed to shrink, becoming smaller and smaller. Still holding Alder's wrist as I treaded water, I waved my hand, and the mana responded at once, carrying the small fox to me. With my other arm, I cradled the troublesome nature spirit, then I kicked and, like I had at the water gate, I shot forward to the lake's edge. This time I was ready as the shore came upon me fast. Remembering how Alder summoned a wave, I urged the water to rise up and set us down upon the pebbled shore.

We crashed upon it in a rain of water and astral energy. Alder and I rolled across the pebbles, their hard surfaces sticking to my damp, cold skin. Setting aside the fox that was limp, but breathing, I turned my attention back to Alder.

I was losing him.

Dried blood had been more or less washed away, but fresh crimson liquid trickled out his wounds. And I could not find a single speck of mana to speak of.

"Don't you dare die!" I cried. I raked my hands down his face, fanned my fingers across his lips, and felt only the slightest hint of breath.

How had he healed me? The poison ivy didn't count, since he had been drawing out the harmful mana, but with Ashka's scratches, Alder had pushed the mana *into* me. How had he done it?

I had to imagine it was like manipulating the mana inside me to do what I wanted, only I had to look at it beyond elements—from a purely energy state. Life itself.

When I had given some of my *spiritual* mana to the god, had that been the same thing? Or close to it at least? In both scenarios, I was offering up my mana to a god.

Moving my hands from his face to his chest, I passed them over his heart, feeling it beat ever so slowly underneath my fingertips.

I imagined the mana inside me—the energy of this valley and this ethereal plane that was quickly bleeding into my world—rise out of me and back into him.

And, like I'd done to the earth god and to the wisps, I prayed. To Alder.

Please, please please. Come back to me. Find me. Please. I need you. I've always needed you.

The fires raged at the edge of the lake and began brushing its surface as if they were growing braver. Their light illuminated the valley like the sun itself had fallen to earth. But I ignored it, concentrating only on the boy in front of me, and only on bringing him back to me.

The spot where my hands were over his heart began to glow. Soft and subtle at first, then it grew brighter and brighter like I was holding a star in the palm of my hands and praying that Alder would take it.

He did.

Alder gasped, his back arching as the mana I'd been feeding into his chest rippled out over the rest of his body. It didn't heal all his scratches or wounds left over from his fight, but it brought him back to me.

His eyes honed in on my face and he winced, probably feeling every bit of his injuries.

"Briony..."

As much as I wanted to hug him, to stare into his eyes and tell myself over and over again that I wasn't going to lose him in any way, ever again, I knew I couldn't.

The fire gate was opening, if it wasn't already. And since Alder was in no shape to go anywhere, I had to rescue Mom.

"Good to have you back," I said, swiping my thumb across his wet cheek. "Are you ready to send me off into the astral plane?"

Chapter Twenty-Nine

Alder stared in horror, taking in the lit sunrise sky above me and the hint of the star itself just beginning to peek over the ridges.

He tried to sit up but flinched with a gasp and held his side. "I failed you."

No. Leaning into him, I wound my arms around his neck and tucked my cheek under his jaw. "You never have."

His fingers wove into my hair. His chest rose and fell under me, and I was so happy that he was breathing again.

"Send me into the astral plane."

He pulled me back to stare in my eyes, fear in every part of his features. "Briony…I'll…"

"You're too weak. You can barely lift your head. But I can go. The barriers are lowering—I won't need to leave my body behind."

He was shaking his head. "It's too dangerous."

"We don't have any other choice. Besides, you said yourself that this fire gate has been calling to me this whole time. I'll find it."

His brow furrowed and he tilted his chin at the raging inferno at the other side of the lake. "You'd literally be walking through fire."

"Nothing I haven't done before. And I've got a friend who can help with that. I just need you to guide me back."

"Briony..."

Although the very concept of walking around in a world where physical matter was not supposed to exist was scary as hell, I believed that I would make it out okay. As long as Alder was there to pull me back. I'd come to rely on him, and in more ways than one, I needed him. It wasn't just to win something as unimportant as a relay race at a swim meet. It was to save a whole valley—a mountain range and the homes and lives of everyone in it. In the face of all that danger, I would've never been able to trust that we could make it out *alive*.

But I did now. And it wasn't just because I had to. It was because of something you had to possess when dealing with gods.

Faith.

I cupped his face, staring into his brilliant gold eyes, his silver hair and copper skin—all beautiful, precious metals. "I'll come back home. With your help."

"What if I can't find you?"

"You will."

After all, it was how we'd met.

That night in the garden, I'd ask about our past and he'd told me that he'd found me lost in the woods.

But there were other times, too. That brief memory of us playing hide-and-go seek. When he'd found me at that old, burned house when I'd been so lost and looking for answers. He'd also found me and saved me just before Ashka had been about to claw me to pieces.

He was always finding me. He would be able to again.

My thumb stroked his cheek and I gave him another

smile, stronger and brighter this time. "You've always been able to."

In answer, Alder drew me into a firm embrace. And then I felt his spirit envelop me. It was the mountains and the forests and the rivers. The rage and wildness of a thunderstorm, the calming current of a brook, the scents of the wildflowers like honeysuckle and monk's hood. And finally a human boy. Scared, lonely, but brave. Happy, despite everything.

He drew back and stared into my eyes. "Once you find your mom, you need to get out—as fast as you can. If we're able to get your mother out far enough from the astral plane, the fire god can't follow you and it will lose its anchor."

"How will I know where *out* is? If the worlds are merging, it might be hard to tell where one ends and another begins."

"The lake. Get to the lake." Then he lifted his arm, using his teeth to tear at the worn threads keeping his bracelet tied to his wrist. With nimble fingers, he took the bracelet and looped it, tying it around my wrist. I watched in fascination as I felt a strange sensation of an energy current flowing over my skin. There was a translucence to my body that hadn't been there before. Mana wasn't just inside me. It was all around me like a second skin.

"This bracelet has been absorbing my mana for ten years," he said. "It has much of my spirit inside and I should be able to lead you home as long as you have that bracelet."

"It won't leave my wrist," I promised, then I leaned in and pressed my lips to his. Once again, I was able to ignore the mana that came with his touch and enjoy the sensation of a simple kiss. His fingers tightened around my wrist that he still held after tying my bracelet, and I could taste his fear for me among the passion.

Before I lost my nerve, I pulled away and rose to my feet.

Starting my trek over the water, leaving wet footprints in my wake as the mana supported each one of my steps, I reached out to a spirit a fourth time. Prayed. Offered up my spiritual mana and felt it rise into the heavens. *Help me, please.*

In my short six years, I don't think I'd ever asked for help as many times as I'd done in the past few hours. There was always a part of me that flinched at the idea of being let down, of having the pain of rejection followed by the snap of a back door. But it was a risk I had to take. A risk that everyone had to.

I got closer to the flames on the side of the lake, and that familiar anxiety started to creep up. Maybe they wouldn't come—maybe they thought like Ashka. *You've dug your grave, now lie in it*. My mind was already racing through other ideas, when the shrill call of a hawk split the air. I craned my neck back to see the air god swoop down over the slopes of the mountain, bronze feathers reflecting the orange and red glow of the fires while their tips trailed blue mist across sections of raging forest fires. I ducked on instinct as the great hawk spirit soared overhead and flapped its massive wings once.

A blue mist tempest gusted toward the raging inferno, clearing a distinct path through the flames and into the encroaching mist of the astral plane.

The astral plane was a world of fog. I walked upon solid ground, but the ground was only possible because the barriers were almost completely gone and the physical matter of our world and the ethereal were blending together.

Like three stories of a building falling into one another. And, like a building, they would crash into one another, sending debris and rubble flying everywhere, causing destruction in the wake of the collision.

I had maybe *minutes* left before the barriers completely disappeared.

Alder's bracelet glowed on my wrist and his mana rippled across my skin like a protective shell. More than anything, though, it felt like I had his spirit inside that hole in my chest. Almost like I had him here, walking beside me.

I traveled into the mist for a long time, and the anxiety frothed and turned in my stomach like a living demon. Whispering in my ear that I shouldn't have come here, that there was no way I was going to make it back, and that Alder wouldn't be able to find me.

I told the whisper to shut the hell up.

Eventually, I realized the white mist was growing darker, thicker, pulsing with agonizing energy. It was like the poison ivy, except it was in the air and I was breathing it in. I wanted to cough, to expel it out of my lungs, because it burned like fire inside me.

My scars throbbed on my lower back—burned, actually. It was like playing a game of hot-cold. I moved in the direction when my scars became more and more painful, knowing that I had to be getting closer.

The smoke and mist blew into my hair. It spun around me, thrashing against me like the gales created by the air god at the top of the mountain. Like they would send me flying over the edge.

She's close. Call her.

For a moment, I wasn't sure if that was my own instinct or Alder's spirit speaking to me.

"Mom!" I screamed into the mist. "Mom!"

At first, I heard nothing, just the wind and the mist that turned gold and orange and red with hot, fiery energy.

It singed my skin—or would have if not for the layer of thick mana that protected me and repelled the poisonous, wild, chaotic energy that wanted to consume me.

"Mom!"

My throat was raw from calling for her.

Hurry, Briony. Hurry.

That one was definitely Alder. His spirit calling to me. Urging me forward.

I started to run.

But before I could stop it, a memory rose to the surface of my own dark depths.

Fire and flames thick all around me, smoke billowing out the windows and an animal-like claw drawing four long slashes across my lower back as it began to pull me, and I was helpless to follow, bound by its gravity like a moon to a planet.

A woman's voice calling on the other side of the door, a pounding like she was trying to break it down.

A boy crashing through the window, sending a wave of silver and blue mist that dispersed and displaced the flames so close to me. He tugged me to his side, but still the fire licked the roof and ate at the wood.

The door burst open, and the woman with dark hair ran to me. The boy disappeared, and she picked me up, cradling me to her as she ran back through the house, back through flames and smoke, her body trembling.

A voice called me from the memory, soft and weak.

I ran faster, deeper into the red mist and the raging storm around me. "Mom! Mo—"

I almost collided with her.

A woman, slender and beautiful, with dark hair and hazel, vixen-like eyes, wearing jeans and a sunflower top. Her body was translucent. I grabbed her arms and she breathed my name.

"Briony?"

Somehow I was able to touch her, even though she was a spirit without a body. The barriers lowering seemed to be making me into a spirit, too…

When the lines between what's real and what's not become blurred…

I coughed through the smoke and fog and reached for her hand. "Mom. Come with me."

Her white, ghost-like hands skimmed over my face. "You got so big," she whispered.

A roar shook the mist around us. A tree materialized next to me. Soon there would be more. The whole forest. The whole valley.

At my lower back, I felt a tugging. My scars ached and itched, and I could feel it. The whisper of the fire god's call.

I tugged Mom forward, and she stumbled with me, but she could walk. I turned inward to Alder's spirit, and he was loud. Yelling at me inside my chest.

Briony! Hurry!

I ran with my mother, pulling her and supporting her as much as I could. The mists chased after us like a tsunami, impossible to outrun.

More trees materialized around us, bushes, wild flowers, all columns of smoke and vibrant, mystical, ethereal energy. Leaves and thorns whacked against us, but it was difficult to feel anything but the poisonous wild energy in my lungs.

I only focused on Mom's spirit and Alder's. They were the only living things to me.

Closer. Closer, Brye.

But I couldn't move much more. My legs were sluggish, even though they'd never felt lighter.

Mom twisted around in my grasp, and the mist blew at our backs, knocking us forward. We both tumbled to the ground, the very earth feeling like a hot stove. It was so energetic and magnetic that it was like lying in a bed of poison ivy. I started to try to heave myself up, my forearms shaking, but it felt like a cord was attached to my lower back. My scars burned and scorched, and my strength gave way. I was unable to get up, unable to continue.

I writhed on the ground, rolling over and looking up into the astral world. It was like being caught in a storm on Mars. Red, crackling energy, no oxygen, poisonous atmosphere. I gasped, inhaling it.

Maybe energy-infused air should have given me strength. But it was too much. My human body couldn't take it. My vision blurred, so I closed my eyes and gritted my teeth, trying to summon strength.

"Briony!" Mom yelled beside me.

The fire god was close.

I could feel them calling my spirit just like Alder's was calling. I was trapped in an angry tug-of-war.

But why did I have to choose? Why did I have to feel separated by both?

I already knew these mountains were a part of me. Along with Alder's voice, Gran's echoed inside.

This valley is you. That boy didn't give you that magical energy or whatever it is…he brought it out. That's all.

I wrenched my eyes open and saw the astral figure looming above me, a sight that should never be seen by human eyes. The shape of a humanoid creature. They didn't have a real body—just energy that looked like a shadow amid their own storm—a living embodiment of the sun. Two bright white wisps stood out where their eyes were supposed to be, and their outline kept shifting and breaking apart and reforming. Tendrils of their "skin" curled upward like smoke, disappearing into their astral domain.

They opened what looked like might be a mouth and moaned, their arm reaching toward me. Looking at their clawed-shaped hand, I felt their…longing. I knew that deep ache all too well. Of wanting an anchor to this valley.

As I pulled myself up to sit on the burning ground, wind and energy blew through me, tossing back my hair and batting my clothes. Looking up into this god, desperate and reaching, I couldn't help but see my own god—Alder. He stood between the planes of existence. A foot in one world, a foot in another. Not truly belonging in either.

It was…the same.

This god didn't necessarily want me *or* my mother. They just wanted to be connected.

To this special place where spirits dwelled.

What must it be like to have an astral body? To exist in an entire world all alone. This god wasn't just an all-powerful entity. Like the others, they were a sentient being.

And maybe they were lonely.

It was such a human thing to feel. Maybe that's why they felt like they needed a human spirit to feel connected to the valley. And maybe that was true. But they didn't need to *take* my spirit…

I'd give it to them freely.

I began praying to the fire god. I don't remember any words I used, but the message was conveyed. The sentiment.

Plumes of mana rose out of me, off my skin and into the wild chaotic storm of the energy of the astral plane. My mana, and also Alder's, seeped out of me. I was bleeding it.

I offered my spirit and felt the valley's spirit rise to meet my own.

The cry of a hawk flying over mountains. The taste of

sweet wild strawberries. Night winds sweeping through the sky and shaking the stars. Storms echoing as every individual rain drop hit every surface. Flashes of heat lightning in the far distance. Raging white water rapids, and the scampering paws of raccoons, the thump of rabbits, and the pounding hooves of deer.

The fire god drew back, the shadowy outline momentarily encased in pearly white mana. I wondered then if they were feeling what I could feel every time I touched Alder. The senses of the valley racing through like lifeblood.

Now's my chance.

Standing, still pouring mana out into the raging storm, I helped Mom to her feet, and we continued to run.

Glancing behind my shoulder, I saw the god in the same place, not crossing anywhere…just staying there, ensnared by my mana. I understood the feeling strangely. It had been the same when I'd first touched Alder. While the Smokies ran through me, I hadn't been able to even move.

I hadn't needed to. I was home.

Pulling myself to face forward, I ran faster with Mom right beside me. Alder's call was faint now, as more and more of my mana flowed out behind me in a jet stream. I didn't know if I was going the right way, didn't know if I was running out into the ethereal plane, or deeper into the astral one.

But I had faith that he would find me.

Wherever I was.

I'm not alone.

Water sloshed around my ankles, and the juxtaposition between the fiery wrath above me and the cool serenity at my feet grounded me. The lake. *I must be close.*

As soon as I thought that, as soon as I hoped, crisp autumn wind blew against my hot skin, tossing back the wisps of my hair, rippling my singed top, and rolling the mists across the surface of the lake, driving back the astral energy that encompassed us.

And Alder was at the center of it.

Still gingerly holding his side, he held out his other hand, controlling the energy around us and calming the storm. He stood on a small island in the middle of the lake, a big silhouette behind him. About the size of an elephant.

Bruley.

Mom's body. The bear spirit had brought her to me.

Just as I turned to tell my mother's spirit that she needed to go back to her body, she disappeared in a shimmer of white mana. For the briefest second, I panicked, thinking I'd failed. After all that, I hadn't brought her back. I hadn't stopped the three worlds from colliding.

But it was just for a moment, because in the next, the mist receded. The smoke and the fire storm pulled backward, retreating like all of the astral energy was being sucked into a black hole. It converged against the backdrop of the distant blue mountains, outlined by the rising sun, and for just a breath, it was quiet. Still.

Then the worlds separated, and the barriers went back up. At least, that was my guess, because waves of white mana rolled across the lake and up the mountainside throughout the valley.

The fires were gone. The smoke that had been climbing toward the stars was gone. And now, all around us, the trees that were once charred to the point of ash were now alive and growing rapidly. Grass sprouted at the lake's edges. Buds of flowers peeked through and their petals unfolded, fully blooming all in the span of seconds. Grass grew higher and higher, and trees broke through the ground, twisting and transforming into full-grown behemoths. Leaves uncurled on branches. The mountains burst with color and *life.*

In fact, I could see the mana glowing in an aura around each plant and tree, see the silver mist ripple in the breeze and feel the water mana brush against my shins.

We were in the ethereal plane. It made sense for us to end up between the two. I only hoped the physical plane was just as healthy. The wisps would have stopped taking on the fire element, but would the fires already burning have stopped?

Any other worries briefly flew out of my mind, though, when I saw Alder climb off the island and run toward me, a smile stretching across his face, his bare feet kicking up splashes around his ankles.

Throwing my arms around his neck, I let him pick me up and spin me once. As he held me tightly, his arms wrapped around my lower back, I asked, "Is Mom okay?"

He pulled his head back, just far enough to brush a wild strand of hair away from my face. "She's fine. The minute she got close to her body, her spirit returned. You did it, Brye."

Looking over his shoulder, I saw Mom lift her head next to Bruley's big paws.

"No, *we* did it."

In a minute, I wanted to go and meet my mother. The woman who had been a stranger to me, and then a disappointment, and then a mystery, and then a hero.

But for just a few more seconds, I wanted to hold on to the nature god I had been in love with back before I even knew what love was.

Back when we were just little kids, playing from dusk until dawn, catching fireflies in the foothills of the Smokies.

Chapter Thirty

With much difficulty, I pulled away from Alder and stepped up onto the island, my bare foot scraping against the side of…

I paused, kneeling down and peering into the water, thinking maybe…

Sure enough, the head of the water god was below the surface. He'd been willing, apparently, to provide transportation across the vast lake.

Accepting Alder's hand, I stepped up and walked through the grass of the island, which just so happened to be the shell of a giant turtle god.

Mom sat, leaning against a tree, looking tired but otherwise healthy and very much alive. "There's my girl," she said weakly.

I bent down next to her, and she lifted a hand to caress my cheek. "Look how big you've grown," she murmured again, her eyes beginning to slowly close.

"Mom? Are you okay?" I asked, squeezing her hand as she lowered it from my cheek.

"I'm fine," she whispered, her voice thick with exhaustion. "This is just a mother being in awe of her daughter." Her eyes closed all the way and her breathing turned steady with sleep.

"Will she be all right?" I asked Alder, brushing a piece of hair away from her cheek.

"She'll be fine," Alder echoed. "The ethereal plane has preserved her body well. She just needs to return to the physical world. Back where she belongs."

"Well, then, let's get her there." I stood, turning back to Alder, all the worries that had vanished upon seeing him and my mother safe rushing back to me like rapids. "Do you think the fires are still going?"

Alder sighed. "I'm not sure. When the barriers came back up, the worlds separated, and I wound up on this plane."

He had barely finished his sentence before three dark shapes shot toward the water god within the lake, and as they got nearer, I grinned. The otter spirits had come to see us. Climbing up onto the island, the otters began to prance around our shins, tittering excitedly.

"Lord, lord, wet, wet, wet, Lord!"

"Slow down, Tavi—"

"Alder," I said, grabbing his shirt sleeve. "She has something."

In the otter's mouth was a shell fragment, a little smaller than the one we had taken from the water gate as its key. As the otter dropped the shell into Alder's outstretched hand, I gasped, realizing the intentions of the river spirits.

"You can use the shell again. Make it rain like it had when we opened the gate."

Alder ruffled Tavi's head affectionately. "Well done, my friend." Turning to me, he kissed me on the cheek and scooped Mom up in his arms. "I'll be right back."

"Yes, go," I said with a smile. Mom was finally going back home, and the fires were about to be fully put out with the help of the water god and three mischievous otter spirits.

I felt like I could finally breathe.

And yet...

I stared down at the bracelet tied around my wrist, thinking of what now lay before me. The question that had been uncertain and terrifying and unimaginable since I found out what might happen if I removed Mom from the astral plane.

If I removed the fire god's anchor.

I was so lost in my thoughts that I hadn't even noticed the island—the water god—swimming back to shore, and as we got closer, I could make out the shape of a large buck with branches for antlers standing on the pebbled shore, water lapping against their powerful hooves.

"I see you succeeded."

I jumped down from the back of the water god and hit the lake water with a splash. "With your help, thank you."

"Perhaps it is I who should be thanking you. You have saved our worlds."

"I had never meant to put them in danger in the first place." I hesitated, dreading the answer to my next question but needing to hear it anyway. "What will happen when the sun goes down and the fire gate no longer has an anchor? Will I need to go and take Mom's place?"

We'd prevented the worlds from fully merging by stopping the fire god from crossing over, and the only reason the barriers went back up was because we'd removed the anchor—Mom—who had bound the fire god to the valley. But now that Mom's spirit was gone from the astral plane, the fire gate had only a day before it was locked with the sunset, and without an anchor, would it no longer be tied to the valley? What would happen then? Would the ethereal plane cease to exist?

A rumbling began in the chest of the earth god, and it took me a moment to realize the deer was *laughing* at me.

"What's so funny?" I seethed. "Does the prospect of my century-long imprisonment within the astral plane amuse you?"

"No, merely the idea that you think that boy will be content to have you to stay in there. I'm quite sure he had plans to take your place instead."

I thought about the look on Alder's face when he unlocked the air gate. The determination. The earth god was probably right.

I swallowed. "There's no way that's happening."

"How did you drive the fire god back?"

"What?" I asked, surprised at the sudden change in topic.

"He almost had you. I can smell his mana on you. You reek of woodsmoke. How did you escape?"

I thought back to the moment where I had offered up my mana. "I gave the god some of my mana, like I'd done for you."

"Why would you do that?"

"I guess I just thought that he wanted to feel connected to the valley." For so long I had wanted the same thing. To know my past, to feel like I belonged somewhere, and to fill this aching void deep inside me.

"Then perhaps that is all the god needs."

As I was thinking on those words, Alder appeared, coming out of the mist a bit down the lakeshore. He was dripping wet—evidence of his success in using the shell fragment to cause a rainstorm.

We'd saved the valley. Everyone would be safe, thank the gods—even all the people coming to the festival.

The festival.

I latched onto it, an idea beginning to form…

The earth god turned to me and fixed me with an eerie, glowing stare. *"I trust that you will do what is best for this valley. I leave you now, Briony Redwrell. But before I do…"* The great stag dropped their head, giving me perfect access to the antlers full of leaves and small white and purple blossoms. *"Take what you need to heal your world. As thanks."*

The damage done in the fires across the valley was widespread, but luckily no lives were lost. A few houses were burned, along with some old dilapidated sheds and barns that had long since been abandoned, but it wasn't as bad as it could have been.

The Firefly Festival had turned into a response and recovery center where locals joined together to help the firefighters and the police assess the damage and coordinate relief efforts.

They all agreed that had it not been for a freak rainstorm that happened shortly after dawn, much of the valley and possibly half the Smokies would've been lost to the wildfires.

I'd spent most of the morning at the Maryville hospital with Gran, Izzie, and Mom.

Alder had been right. The ethereal plane had preserved her body well. The doctors had basically run a few tests, checked her vitals, and kept repeatedly asking, *Why are you here again?*

We couldn't tell them that she'd spent the last six years in a spiritual plane without food or water and simply surviving on astral energy.

So she was discharged, and we took Mom back to Gran's. Gran kept crying randomly, hugging her daughter and kissing her temple, while Mom didn't seem to mind one bit. She would, occasionally, reach over and take my hand and squeeze it, but other than that, she seemed to respect this area of unknown between us.

I was confident that in time Mom would *feel* like a mom to me, but she was still mostly a stranger. What I remembered of her was little, tainted by the trauma of the fire and dealing with the aftermath of amnesia. But what I knew of her now was that she was a remarkable woman, and what I wanted, more than anything, was to get to know her.

Halfway through the day, Izzie and I agreed that we should both return to the town to check on the recovery efforts. Mrs. Farrafield had called twenty minutes ago to tell us that Ms. Tilly had opened her café to the families who'd lost their belongings in the fire, and we had decided to bring a carload of supplies, such as fresh towels, blankets, clothes, and some extra toiletries.

Before I walked out the door, I noticed Mom curled up on the couch, staring at the slip of paper I'd given to her with Dad's cell phone number on it.

He was still on his business trip in Chicago, but I'd told her that if she called him, he'd come.

"Mom?"

She looked up, her eyes a little red from crying with Gran. "I don't know if I can call him," she confessed before I even had time to ask her what was wrong. "He'll hate me. I left him with hardly any explanation. I thought I knew what was best and what I was doing. But I should've...I should've trusted him that we could've figured this out together."

Huh. Like mother, like daughter, I guess.

I took a seat next to her, setting aside the bag full of towels I'd been hauling to the car. "He won't hate you. He's *never* hated you. And while he didn't believe the legend then,

I think we can get him to believe it now."

Mom swept her finger across the number written on the paper, and her jaw clenched. As she got up to move toward the kitchen to call her husband, Izzie barreled into the living room, ripping open the screen door and letting it catch and close slowly behind her.

"Brye, your not-boyfriend is here," Izzie said, jerking her thumb over her shoulder. "Hurry up, or I'm leaving you behind with your not-fiancé."

I patted her on the shoulder with a laugh. "Thanks, Iz, I'll just be a minute."

Alder sat on the porch steps, his elbows resting on his knees and his fingers loosely threaded together. They were covered in both soot and dirt, and as I sat down next to him, my heart sped up a little.

We had so much to talk about, and yet all I wanted to do was wrap my arms around his neck and kiss him.

"How did it go?" I asked, clearing my throat.

"All of the earth god's twigs have been planted in the worst spots of the fire. You can barely tell there even *were* fires anymore. It was amazing. Flowers and trees, and everything just sprang up. It would've taken me *months* to be able to heal the valley like that."

"That's good. I can't wait to see it all."

We fell into somewhat of an awkward silence and then we both began with…

"Alder, look —"

"Briony, listen—"

It might've been funny if the subject matter wasn't so terrifying. We had until sundown to decide how we were going to create an anchor for the fire god.

Alder was shaking his head. "We have to find another way. I don't want to lose you for a second time. I can't do it again."

"About that, I've been thinking..." I said, tugging Alder's bracelet on my wrist and twisting it, "and I might have an idea."

By late evening, most of the firefighters, police cars, ambulances, film crews, and disaster relief teams from hospitals were gone and the locals were trying to salvage the last bit of their beloved festival they could.

The bluegrass band was playing "Tennessee River and a Mountain Man" on the stage across the meadow, and tangy, smoky barbeque was being served on paper plates with large wedges of sweet corn and scalloped potatoes.

Alder and I stood at the edge of the lake near the tower of wood for the bonfire that folks had brought in from all over the Smokies. I'd heard it was bigger this year than it had ever been. Apparently, the wildfires had not driven people away but brought them closer, wanting to show how much they loved the valley and how not even an act of god—a nature god, specifically—could crush their spirit.

And their bonfire was evidence of that. It glowed bright white with their mana. All their spirits together in one offering.

It wasn't yet time to light the bonfire, but the sun was going down, and in order for my idea to work, it had to be now.

"Are you ready?" Alder asked.

"Let's do it."

Kneeling to reach the bottom of the firewood pile, I threaded my hand through the grates to touch the dry wood. Mana flared under my fingertips, and I offered up my own mana like I'd done to the other gods. I wanted to touch every piece that had been hauled across the Smokies.

This valley was ours, and we cherished it as much as these gods did. If we could give this same connection back to the fire god, then we could always anchor him here.

White plumes of mana rose high on the pile of wood, almost like it was already burning with white fire instead of red. As I took a step back, Alder flicked his finger. A spark of flame skipped into the pile of wood and the fire took hold.

And grew.

The smoke of the bonfire was not thick and gray, but white and silvery, full of mana. Full of my own spirit and the spirit of everyone from these mountains.

Shouts of surprise came from some of the festival goers, asking questions like, *Was the bonfire supposed to have been started? Who lighted it?*

Alder and I just took a step back and watched the flames climb higher into the darkening sky. I held my breath as we waited for evidence my idea had worked to keep the ethereal plane tied to this valley.

There were only a few at first, but soon the whole meadow was alight with wisps.

Alder sighed with relief next to me, while his hand wrapped around mine.

"So we ended up going to the festival after all," Alder said quietly, just barely heard over the crackle of flames.

I couldn't help but laugh. It was a nervous, happy laugh. "Yes, we sure did."

"Will you come next year?" he asked.

I nodded to the bonfire. "Looks like I'll have to."

Alder tugged my hand, enough to pull me around to face him. With the sun going down, his spirit form was beginning to show.

"Alder, your hair—"

"I'm not talking about for the valley. I mean for *us.* I need to know *now*, Brye. Watching you leave was the hardest thing I'd ever done. You weren't just my best friend. You were a part of me." He lowered his gaze then lifted it back up to hold mine. "But I understand if you *want* to leave, then—"

Cutting him off, I wound my arms around his neck, lifting myself up on my tippy toes to match his height. "Are you kidding? For once, *I* found *you*. I'm not going anywhere."

From across the meadow I heard a few gleeful shouts of some local kids, calling in delight as they saw the first fireflies of the evening.

Acknowledgments

First, thank you to Aunt May whose enchanting garden inspired this story. I miss you and Grandpa every day. Love to my brother and cousins with whom I caught fireflies on summer evenings in the mountains of West Virginia.

Lydia, my stellar editor, you saw this book for what it could be, and I'm eternally grateful for it. Judi Lauren and the rest of the publishing team at Entangled Teen—Heather, Stacy, Curtis, and everyone else working behind the scenes—you're all so wonderful in making these books come to life. And thank you to my agent, Frances Black of Literary Counsel.

To my BR writers' group who had to suffer through all the versions of this book, and to Melissa who read it first—y'all push me to be a better writer.

Then, to my associate in Phandalin, thanks for all the matcha soy lattes.

Thank you to Kourtney and Christa for friendships that last lifetimes.

Finally, thank you to a family who gave me a childhood I'll never forget and always treasure.

Turn the page to start reading the book Sarah Beth Durst calls "thrilling, hilarious, addictive, and awesome."

BY SARA WOLF

1

THE STARVING WOLF AND THE BLACK ROSE

KING SREF OF CAVANOS WATCHES me with the deadened eyes of a raven circling a corpse—patient, waiting to devour me the second I let my guard down. I briefly debate telling him humans don't taste all that good, until I remember normal girls don't eat people. Or fake their way into royal courts.

Normal, I think to myself. *Completely and utterly normal. Bat your eyelashes. Laugh like you've got nothing in your head. Old God's teeth, what in the flaming afterlife do normal girls do again?*

The other girls would know. There are three of us, three girls in cake-pink dresses, kneeling before King Sref's throne. We wear veils to hide our faces. I'd ask them, but we're currently busy drowning in expensive lace and the silent stares of every gilded noble in the room. Well, the other two girls are. I'm doing more of a *laughing internally at the way they carefully tilt their gorgeous heads and purse their pouts* thing. Look More Attractive Than the Girl Next to You is the name of the game their mothers have been teaching them from birth.

Mine taught me how to die, and not much else.

"You are all as lovely as rose blooms," the king says finally. His face is weathered with a handsome age. Dignity carves lines around his steel-colored eyes. The smile in them doesn't reach those eyes, though, a sure sign it's only half sincere. He is old, he is powerful, and he is bored—the most dangerous combination I can think of.

"Thank you, Your Majesty," the two girls echo, and I quickly mimic them. I've nicknamed them in my head—Charm and Grace. Charm and Grace don't dare look at anything but the marble floor, while my eyes dart about, thirsty for the rich silks of the nobles' clothes and the gold serpents carved into the majestic stone columns. Three years stuck in the woods serving a witch makes your eyes hungry for anything that isn't a tree or deer droppings. I can't raise my head for fear I'll be singled out, but I can look just high enough to see the feet of Queen Kolissa and her son. Crown Prince Lucien d'Malvane, Archduke of Tollmount-Kilstead, Fireborn, the Black Eagle—he has a dozen names, all of them eye-roll worthy. If there's one thing I've learned from my single day at the royal court, it's that the more names someone has, the less he actually does.

I haven't seen more than the prince's booted toes, and I already know he's useless.

And soon, if I have my way, he'll be heartless.

"I welcome you, the newest additions to our illustrious court," King Sref says. His voice booms, but out of decorum, not of passion.

"Thank you, Your Majesty," Charm and Grace say, and I echo. I'm starting to get the hang of this—thank everyone a lot and look pretty. Infiltrating the palace might not be so hard after all.

Queen Kolissa's saccharine voice rings out after the

king's. "I hope you will bring honor to your families and uphold the ideals of this great nation," she says.

"Thank you, Your Majesty," we respond.

I hear the queen murmur something. A deep voice softly says something back, and then her voice gets an inch louder—but still so quiet only the three of us, kneeling at the foot of the throne, can hear it.

"Say something, please, Lucien."

"That would be pointless, Mother, and I tend to avoid doing pointless things."

"Lucien—"

"You know I hate this outdated ceremony. Look at them—they're here only for their families. No girl in her right mind would subject herself to this humiliating display." The prince's voice is laced with dark venom, and I flinch. It's nothing like his father's carefully emotionless tone or his mother's sickly sweet one. Unlike the rest of these restrained nobles, his emotions burn hot just beneath the surface. He hasn't learned how to hide them completely, not yet.

"It's a tradition," the queen insists. "Now say something to them, or so help me—"

The screech of a chair across marble resounds, and the prince demands of us: "Rise."

The two girls, graceful as swans, lift their skirts and stand. I bite back a swear as I do the same and nearly trip over my ornate shoes. Note to past self: four days of training isn't nearly enough time to teach someone to walk in a pair of ribboned death traps. How Charm and Grace do it so effortlessly is beyond me, but the blushes on their faces aren't.

I look up to the prince now standing on the top step before us. Even without the advantage of elevation, I can see he's tall—a warrior's height, his silver-vested torso lean and his velvet-caped shoulders broad. A year? No, he's maybe two years or so older than my ageless teenage form of sixteen; the corded muscles tell me that much. Why they call him the Black Eagle is obvious now: his hair is blacker than a raven's, windswept about his face and long in the back, kept in a single braid that traces his spine. His face is his father's in its prime: a proud, hawkish nose, cheekbones so high and dignified they border arrogance. His skin is his father's, too, sun-kissed oakwood, and yet his eyes are his mother's—piercing dark iron sharpened to a fine, angry blade point. He is all pride and sable darkness, and every part of me hates it—hates the fact that someone who's to inherit so much power and wealth is striking as well. I want him hunched and covered in warts. I want him weak-chinned and watery-eyed. But the world is unfair, always. I learned that the day my parents were killed.

The day I was made into a monster.

The girls beside me all but salivate, and I do my best to look bored. On my way here I saw much better-looking boys. Dozens. Hundreds. All right, fine—there was only the one, and he was a painter's model in the streets of the artists' district, but none of that matters, because the way Prince Lucien sneers his next question wipes every ounce of attraction from my mind.

"A lady isn't merely a decoration," he says, words rumbling like thunder. "She is the mother of our future, the teacher of our progeny. A lady must have a brain between her ears, as must we all. For what is beauty without purpose? Nothing more than a vase of flowers, to wither and be thrown away."

Books written by the smartest polymaths have told me the planet is round, that it rotates about the sun, and that there are magnetic poles to our east and west at the coldest parts, and I believe them, yet in no way can I believe there's someone who exists who's *this* arrogant.

The nobles titter among themselves, but it quickly dies down when King Sref holds up a hand. "These are the Spring Brides, my prince," the king says patiently. "They're of noble lineage. They've studied and practiced much to be here. They deserve more respect than this."

Someone's getting scolded, I think with a singsong tone. Prince Lucien throws his sharp gaze to the king.

"Of course, Your Majesty." His disdain at calling his father "Your Majesty" is obvious. *Consider yourself lucky, Prince,* I think. *That you have a father at all in this cruel world.*

"But"—the prince turns to the noble audience—"all too often do we equate nobleness of blood for soundness of mind and goodness of judgment."

His eyes sweep the room, and this time, the nobles are dead silent. The shuffling of feet and cough-clearing of throats is deafeningly uncomfortable. I haven't been here long, but I recognize his stance. It's the same one young forest wolves take with their elders; he's challenging the nobles, and by the looks of the king's white knuckles and the queen's terrified face, I'd guess it's a dangerous game he's playing.

"Let us welcome the Spring Brides as the kings of the Old God did." The prince sweeps his hands out. "With a question of character."

The nobles murmur, perturbed. The silver half circles with three spokes through them dripping from every building in the city weren't exactly subtle; the New God, Kavar, rules here in Vetris. The Sunless War was fought for Kavar thirty years ago, and the Old God's followers were slaughtered and driven out of Vetris. His statues were torn down, his temples demolished. Now, carrying on an Old God tradition is a death sentence. The king knows this—and covers for his son quickly.

"The kings of the Old God were misguided, but they built the foundation upon which this country thrives. The roads, the walls, the dams—all of them were built by the Old Kings. To erase them from existence would be a crime to history, to truth. Let us have one last Old tradition here, today, and shed such outdated formalities with grace."

It's a good save. You don't have to be a noble to see that. Prince Lucien looks miffed at his father's attempts to assuage the nobles, but he hides it and turns back to the three of us.

"Answer this question to the best of your abilities as you raise your veils. What is the king's worth?"

There's a long moment of quiet. I can practically hear the brain-cogs of the girls churning madly beside me. The nobles murmur to one another, laughing and giggling and raising eyebrows in our direction. The king is immeasurable in his worth. To say anything less would be madness. A swamp-thick layer of scorn and amusement makes the air reek and my skin crawl.

Finally, Charm lifts her veil and clears her throat to speak.

"The king is worth…a million—no! A trillion gold coins. No—seven trillion!" The nobles' laughter gets louder. Charm blushes beet-red. "I'm sorry, Your Majesty. My father never taught me numbers. Just sewing and things."

King Sref smiles good-naturedly. "It's quite all right. That was a lovely answer."

The prince says nothing, face unimpressed, and points to Grace. She curtsies and lifts her veil.

"The king's worth cannot be measured," she says clearly. "It is as high as the highest peak of the Tollmount-Kilstead Mountains, as wide as the Endless Bog in the south. His worth is deeper than the darkest depths of the Twisted Ocean."

This time, the nobles don't laugh. Someone starts a quiet applause, and it spreads.

"A very eloquent answer," the king says. The girl looks pleased with herself, curtsying again and glancing hopefully at Prince Lucien. His grimace only deepens.

"You, the ungainly one." The prince finally points to me. "What say you?"

His insult stings, but for only a moment. Of course I'm ungainly compared to him. Anyone would be. I'm sure the only one he doesn't think ungainly is the mirror in his room.

I hold his gaze, though it burns like sunfire on my skin. His distaste for me, for the girls beside me, for every noble in this room, is palpable. He expects nothing from me, from anyone—I can see that in the way his eyes prematurely cloud with disdain the moment I open my mouth.

He expects nothing new. I must be everything new.

I lift my veil slowly as I say, "The king's worth is exactly one potato."

There's a silence, and then a shock wave ripples through the room, carrying gasps and frenzied whispers with it. The celeon guards grip their halberds and narrow their catlike eyes, their tails swishing madly. Any one of them could rip me in half as easily as paper, though it wouldn't kill me. It'd just betray me as a Heartless—a witch's servant—to the entire noble court, which is considerably worse than having your insides spilled on the marble. Witches are Old God worshippers and fought against humans in the Sunless War. We are the enemy.

I'm the enemy, wearing the mask of a noble girl who's just said something very insulting about her king in the foolish hopes of catching the prince's attention.

The queen clutches her handkerchief to her chest, clearly offended at my words. The king raises one eyebrow. The prince, on the other hand, smiles. It's so slow and luxurious I barely see it form, and then all at once his face is practically gleeful. *He's handsome*, I think to myself—*handsome enough when he isn't being a hateful dog turd*. He tames his expression and clears his throat.

"Are you going to elaborate, or should I have you thrown in the dungeons for slandering the king right here and now?"

The celeon advance, and my unheart quivers. The prince is enjoying the idea of throwing me in the dungeon a little too much for my taste. I raise my chin, carefully keeping my shoulders wide and my face passive. Strong. I will make an impression here, or I will die for my loose tongue. It's that simple.

Except it isn't that simple.

Because I can't die.

Because unlike the girls next to me, I'm not here to impress the king and win a royal's hand in marriage or a court position for my father.

I'm here for Prince Lucien's heart.

Literally, not figuratively. Although figuratively would be easier, wouldn't it? Making boys fall in love is easy, from what little I remember of my human life before—all it takes are compliments and batting eyelashes and a low-cut dress or five and they're clay putty in your hands. But I'm here for the organ beating in his chest, and it will be mine, by gambit or by force. In order to get that close, I must earn his trust. The prince expects idiots and sycophants. I must give him the opposite. I must be brilliance itself, a diamond dagger between the flesh of his stagnant noble life.

"To the common people of this country," I press on, "one

potato can mean the difference between starving in winter and making it through to spring. A single potato means life. A single potato is a saving grace. To the king's people living in his villages, in his kingdom, nothing is more precious than one potato."

The murmur that goes around the room is hushed, confusion written on the nobles' faces. They have no idea, I'm sure, of what it's like to starve. But it's all I've ever known.

I lock eyes with the prince once more. His face, too, is confused, but in a different way from the crowd's. He looks at me like he's never seen a person before, as if I'm some odd specimen kept in a cool cellar for later study by a polymath. The boredom in his gaze is gone, replaced with a strange, stiff sort of shock. I should look away, act modest or shy, but I don't. I make my eyes sing the determined words my mouth can't say.

I am no flower to be ravaged at your whim, angry wolf—I am your hunter, bow cocked and ready. I am a Heartless, one of the creatures your people fled from in terror thirty years ago.

I let the smallest, hungriest smirk of mine loose on him.

If you were smart, you'd start running, too.

The queen smiles, squeezing the king's arm, and the king laughs. Nothing about it is bland or subdued; it leaks with the hoarse edges of unbridled amusement. For the briefest moment as he smiles at me, he looks ten years younger.

"What is your name, clever little Bride?"

My mind says, *Zera, no last name, daughter of a merchant couple whose faces I'm starting to forget: Orphan, Thief, Lover of bad novels and good cake, and indentured servant of the witch Nightsinger, who sent me here to rip your son's heart from his chest.*

I dip into a wobbly curtsy instead and spill my lie with a smile. “Zera Y’shennria, Your Majesty; niece of Quin Y’shennria, Lady of the House of Y’shennria and Ravenshaunt. Thank you for having me here today.”

Thank you, and I’m sorry.

As sorry as a monster can be.

The Witchling Academy series delves into themes of forbidden romance, betrayal, and the cost of power.

MIRROR BOUND

by Monica Sanz

Conspirator. Failure. Murderer.

Seraphina Dovetail is used to being called all these things. As the seventh-born daughter to a witch, and the cause of her mother losing both her powers and her life, Sera has always felt isolated. Until Nikolai Barrington.

The young professor not only took an interest in Sera—he took her into his home, hired her for his moonlighting detective agency, and gave her the one thing she'd always dreamed of: a chance. Under Barrington's tutelage, Sera can finally take the School of Continuing Magic entrance exam to become an inspector and find her family. Now if only she could stop her growing attraction to her maddening boss—which is about as easy as this fiery elementalist quitting setting things on fire.

But when ghosts start dragging Sera into possessions so deep she can barely escape, and then the souls of lost witches and wizards appear trapped in mirrors, these two opposites will have to work together to uncover a much deeper secret that could destroy the Witchling world...

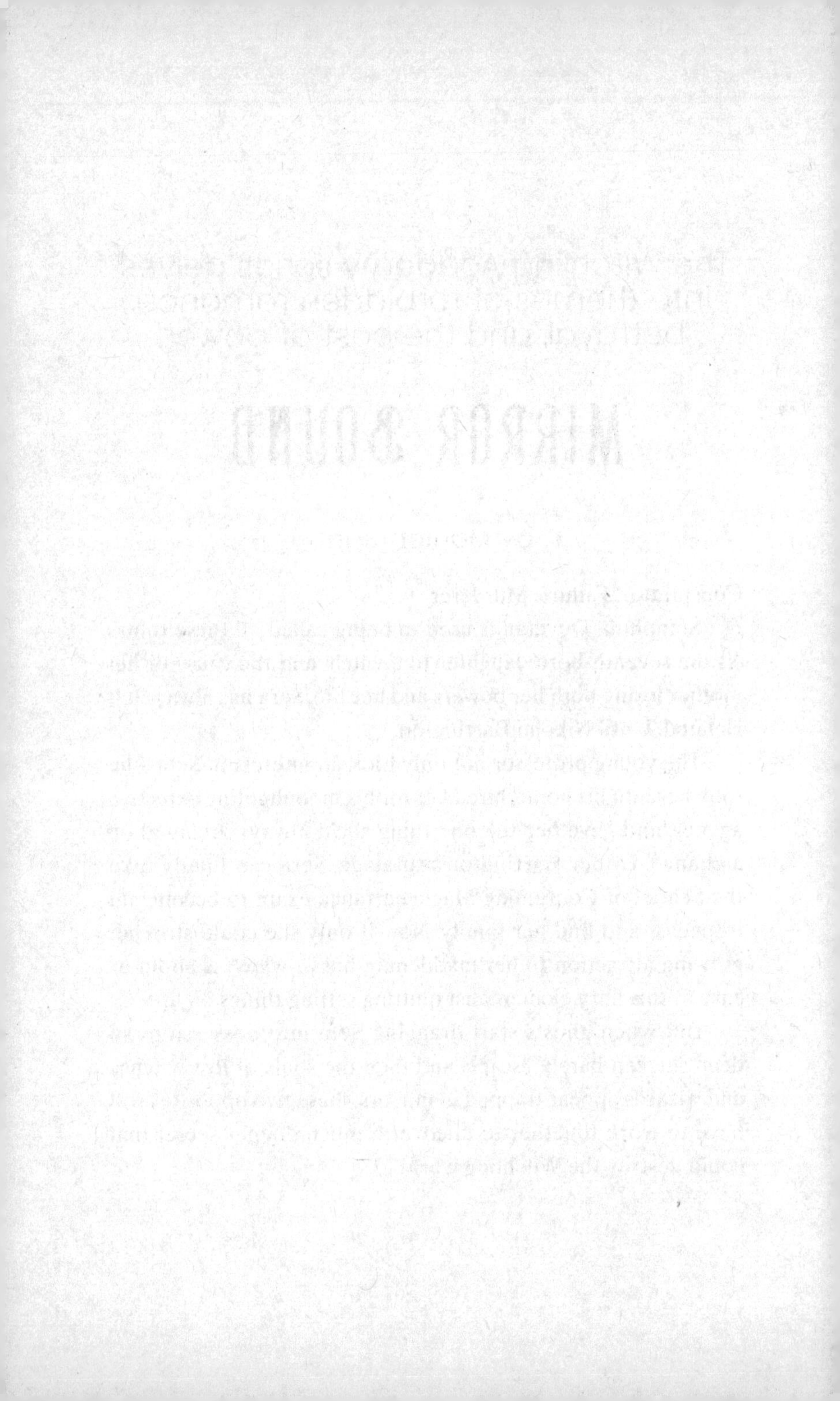

A thrilling sci-fi romance perfect for fans of Beth Revis and Amie Kaufman

toxic

by Linda Kang

Hana isn't supposed to exist. She's grown up hidden by her mother in a secret room of the bioship *Cyclo* until the day her mother is simply gone—along with the entire crew. *Cyclo* tells her she was abandoned, but she's certain her mother wouldn't leave her there to die. And Hana isn't ready to die yet. She's never really had a chance to live.

Fenn is supposed to die. He and a crew of hired mercenaries are there to monitor *Cyclo* as she expires, and the payment for the suicide mission will mean Fenn's sister is able to live. But when he meets Hana, he's not sure how to save them both.

As *Cyclo* grows sicker by the day, they unearth more secrets about the ship and the crew. But the more time they spend together, the more Hana and Fenn realize that falling for each other is what could ultimately kill them both.

A dark psychological romance
perfect for fans of Holly Black
and Maggie Stiefvater

by Meg Kassel

A simple but forgotten truth: Where harbingers of death appear, the morgues will soon be full.

Angie Dovage can tell there's more to Reece Fernandez than just the tall, brooding athlete who has her classmates swooning, but she can't imagine his presence signals a tragedy that will devastate her small town. When something supernatural tries to attack her, Angie is thrown into a battle between good and evil she never saw coming. Right in the center of it is Reece—and he's not human.

What's more, she knows something most don't. That the secrets her town holds could kill them all. But that's only half as dangerous as falling in love with a harbinger of death.

Let’s be friends!

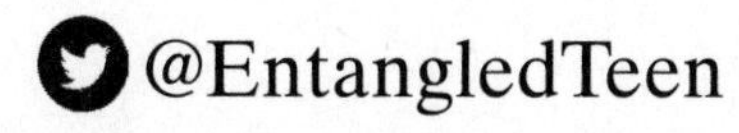
@EntangledTeen

@EntangledTeen

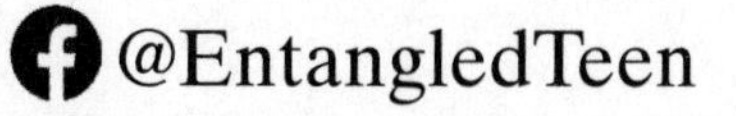
@EntangledTeen

bit.ly/TeenNewsletter

entangled teen
an imprint of Entangled Publishing LLC